it's a Wonderful DEATH

it's a Wonderful DEATH

SARAH J. SCHMITT

Sky Pony Press
NEW YORK

Sky Pony Press books may be purchased in bulk at special discounts for sales promotion, corporate gifts, fund-raising, or educational purposes. Special editions can also be created to specifications. For details, contact the Special Sales Department, Sky Pony Press, 307 West 36th Street, 11th Floor, New York, NY 10018 or info@skyhorsepublishing.com

This is a work of fiction. Names, characters, places, and incidents are either the products of the author's imagination or used fictitiously.

Sky Pony® is a registered trademark of Skyhorse Publishing, Inc.®, a Delaware corporation.

Visit our website at www.skyponypress.com.

10 9 8 7 6 5 4 3 2 1

Library of Congress Cataloging-in-Publication Data is available on file.

Print ISBN: 978-1-63450-173-6
Ebook ISBN: 978-1-63450-921-3

Cover design by Georgia Morrissey
Cover photograph credit Thinkstock

Printed in the United States of America

To Grams and Becca, who got it right the first time.

it's a Wonderful DEATH

Chapter 1

The gypsy fortune-teller at the Halloween carnival predicts I'll have a long life full of possibilities. Of course, that's right before she uses me as a human shield to avoid the out-stretched hand of a black-cloak-clad, sickle-wielding Grim Reaper and then flees hysterically from the tent. Really, if you think about it, that makes her a liar and a murderer. I better get a refund.

And no matter what the Grim Reaper says about not meaning to collect my soul, it doesn't change the fact that I'm looking down at my lifeless body while my friends stare at each other. Hello? Call 911. Or maybe someone could start doing CPR. Idiots.

"Come with me," the Reaper insists, tugging on my arm. "There isn't much time."

I shake him off and shoot my best withering glare in his direction. "I don't think so. You saw what she did. You were coming for her, not me. She's the one you should be hauling out of here."

And then he shrugs his shoulders. Is he kidding? He rips my soul from my body and the next minute acts like I'm asking to change the station on the car radio.

He smiles a saccharin sweet smile. Yeah, like I'm going to fall for that.

"My job is to transport the souls. Nothing more. Nothing less." He's talking to me like I'm a four-year-old.

I don't know if it's the smile or the tone of his voice, but I've gone from being confused to really ticked off. My hands curl into fists. "Well, it's my senior year and *my* job is to win homecoming queen next week. And to do that, I need to be alive. You have to send me back."

"I can't do it."

"And why not?"

He whips around to face me, his hood falling down around his neck. He's actually kind of cute with his chiseled face and coal black eyes. Of course he's unnaturally pale, which is a total turn-off. And let's not forget he's a big part of the reason my body and soul no longer appear to be connected.

"I don't have that kind of clearance," he says. "Even if it was an accidental collection, it's out of my hands."

I find his words ironic. After all, it was his hand that got me into this mess in the first place.

"Like you said, it was an accident," I fume, refusing to admit my argument might be pointless. "If you can't, can someone else?"

He continues watching me with a blank gaze. When I can't take his silent treatment for one more second, I look back toward my body.

"Wait a minute!" I shriek. "Is that blood coming out of my ear?" I look closer and notice my blue eyes are staring at the ceiling with a vacant expression. Other than the eyes and blood, I look normal. Okay, sure, maybe my skin is a little on the gray side, but the lighting in the tent is horrible. Why do fortune-tellers always use so many flickering candles? When I get back into my body, I am definitely calling the fire marshal. There has to be a violation here somewhere. She may not die, but that gypsy woman is still going to pay for what she did.

I scan the rest of my body and notice the way my neck is tilting at a weird angle. Of course that could be because my jet black hair is pulled up in a messy bun. No one can lay comfortably with a bun. It's physically impossible.

Other than all that, I look like I always do: perfect. Well, except for the bruise on my cheek. I must have slammed it into the cash register when I fell. It's going to take some serious cover-up to camouflage that bad boy.

A flash of movement captures my attention. Finally someone starts doing chest compressions. Fat lot of good it'll do me if the Reaper doesn't figure something out and fast.

With nothing left to lose, I try a different approach. "Hey, you never told me your name."

"What?" he asks in genuine surprise.

"What am I supposed to call you?"

"Gideon." He's looking at me like he thinks I'm up to something but can't quite figure it out. I get that a lot.

"Well, Gideon," I say as nicely as I can, "there has to be something you can do. Maybe snap a finger, wish on a star, or whatever. No one ever has to know about this silly misunderstanding. Then, once I'm back among the living, you can track down that stupid gypsy, have a piano fall on her head, and everything works out the way it was supposed to." I glance at the group of girls who have been at my beck and call for the last three years. They're all sobbing and looking around in disbelief. Except for Felicity, who's taking a picture with her phone. Why couldn't the gypsy have picked her?

"No," the Grim Reaper says.

"Okay, fine. Maybe a piano is a bit of a cliché. How about a meteorite?"

"No," he says again.

"You're right. It should be a small one that drills into her brain without damaging the planet. I don't want you to be responsible for destroying the entire Earth."

Instead of answering, the Grim Reaper turns around, the edge of his cloak hanging unnaturally in the air before finally settling around his ankles.

"Wait," I call after him, running to catch up. "What about sending me back?"

"We're leaving," he says, shifting his scythe to his other hand. "And I already told you. I can't send you back."

"But somebody can, right?" He keeps walking, and I have no choice but to follow. The air around us grows misty and I squint to see what's up ahead. "Where are you taking me, anyway?"

"Do you always talk this much? Most people are at least a little shocked when they die."

I scoff at him. Obviously the nice-girl act isn't working. "You screwed up. Maybe if you'd been a little better at your job, I wouldn't be dead in the first place."

"But you are dead."

"Not really."

This time he laughs and the sound startles me. I was beginning to think the guy was a black hole of emotion. "Did you not see your body back there? You know, the one on the ground?" he asks. "You are really dead."

I look down and fight to keep from losing my balance. Below me is a vast nothingness. "Can't you at least tell me where we're going?" I ask, sucking in my breath, which is pointless since I don't actually need to breathe anymore. Still, there's something comforting in doing it.

"To the Soul Movers."

"The what?" I ask, but my words are swallowed by a whirling gust of wind that precedes a train of railcars pulling up in front of us.

"Get in," the Reaper says, pushing me forward. It's more of a shove, actually.

As I stagger over the threshold, I see another Reaper ushering a crowd of people into the next car.

"What's going on over there?" I ask.

The Reaper looks over, his eyebrow rising slightly. "Fifteen-car pile-up on the 405." He looks envious. What a sick jerk. The doors slam shut and I'm surrounded by Reapers and the newly departed. Everyone looks so sad. Not sad, exactly. Empty. Like shells of actual people.

My Reaper leans in and says, "Told you most of the dead are shocked when they die." He's got a cocky tone to his voice that makes me want to slap him. I manage to stop myself. He's lucky. I've got a well-deserved reputation for not taking crap from people.

Glancing around, I see elderly people and young kids and everyone in between on the train. Most of them have that deer-in-headlights look on their face. Except for one old woman who is smiling at me with pity in her eyes. "So young and beautiful," she says, like I'm not standing right in front of her. "Such a waste."

I look behind me, and then back at her. "Are you talking to me?"

"No, dear, I'm talking about you."

Who knew old people could speak fluent sarcasm?

"What happened?" she asks, her voice ringing with grandmotherly compassion.

"What do you mean, what happened?" Her kindness is starting to get on my nerves.

"How did you die?" she asks.

"I didn't," I try to explain, pointing to the Reaper. "He made a mistake."

"Denial," she says and pats my hand. "It's the first step. Don't worry, dearie. It will pass."

I yank my arm away. "I am not in denial. He screwed up and got the wrong person."

"I'm sure he did, child." It's pretty clear by the look of amusement on her face that she doesn't believe me.

Wanting to take the attention off me, I ask, "So, what happened to you? What's your story?"

She places her hands gently in her lap and smiles serenely. "It was a dreadful case of old age. I'm afraid I'll never see one hundred and one."

What do you say to someone who just tells you they lived a whole century? "That's, uh, too bad?" I mutter before turning back to the Reaper.

"You have to fix this," I say, no longer able to hide my desperation and clutching onto his arm. "I've gotta go back. There is no way I am going to let Felicity steal my crown. That backstabber is probably on her way to get her fat head measured."

"Would you just relax?" he hisses before yanking his cloak out of my grasp and turning away from me.

I sink into a seat. Relax? Is he insane? How can I relax when I'm . . . when I'm dead? And then it hits me like a ton of bricks. I'm really freaking dead. My head drops to my waiting hands and I feel my last breath leave my body as cold overtakes me. I struggle to keep my brain from accepting what's happening. If I deny it, it's not real. And this can't be real. My life was, no, is just starting. This isn't right. It isn't fair. I just can't be . . . dead.

Chapter 2

The doors open again and the Reapers hustle everyone into an empty terminal. Everyone but me, that is. I refuse to move. What if I get off this train and can never go back? Nope. I'll stay here until the train makes the return trip, get off, and stay.

"Get up," Gideon commands.

I ignore him. Why should I make this easy?

"I'm not kidding," he says. "I have a schedule to keep."

This gets me to look at him. "Yeah? Well, so did I. How does it feel to have things not work out the way you plan?"

He leans on his scythe. "Listen, kid, I don't know how many different ways I can tell you that there's nothing I can do to fix your situation."

"That's fine," I answer. "I'll just take the return trip and you can get back to me once you've figured things out."

"It doesn't work that way. There is no return passage. One way. This can only be sorted out if you stand up, shuffle through the doors, and head to processing like everyone else. That's the way it works."

I love how he's still acting like he's completely innocent in my predicament. But if he's telling the truth, sitting on the train isn't going to change anything. I might be passive aggressive, but I'm not stupid. "So is there someone in processing who can help me?"

"They'll know what to do better than I would. I'm sure this has happened before."

"Just not to you," I say with a smirk.

He nods. "Right."

I stand up, reluctantly, and follow him out of the car and down the short terminal that connects to a long hallway. From the ceiling to the floor, the passage is white marble. It's like walking into a really bright mausoleum. Which is creepy enough, but adding to the shiver-up-my-spine factor is that I can't hear anything. Not the echo of my footsteps, not even the sound of the train as it hurries off to its next destination. It is complete and utter silence. I can't even hear the sound of my heartbeat. Like my lungs, it probably doesn't work anymore.

I clear my throat just to make sure my ears still work. The Reaper's head snaps toward me.

"Sorry," I say. Wait a minute. Did I just apologize to him? What is wrong with me? RJ Jones does not apologize to anyone. Not ever. And why do I owe Grim Boy anything? This is his fault. On the plus side, I can still talk. "What happens in processing?" I ask.

He looks at me with contempt. "You get processed," he answers, very slowly, like he's convinced I don't understand the words I'm saying.

I glare at him with as much hatred as I can muster, which, given the circumstance, is pretty substantial. "That much I figured out on my own, thank you. I mean, what does processing entail?"

He sighs. "It's where they check you in and give you the recording of your life."

"You mean like a DVD?"

"Actually, they use laser discs up here."

"Laser what?"

The Reaper gives me a look of exasperation. "You never stop asking questions, do you? Think of it like this: if an album and DVD had a baby, it would look like a laser disc. It's a failed technology experiment from the nineteen eighties and nineties."

"Album?" I ask.

"You don't know what an album is?"

In spite of everything, I'm having a good time watching him get flustered by my random questions. It's one of many weapons in my verbal arsenal. "Relax, I know what it is. I saw one in a museum once."

"Yeah, well, when the laser disc turned out to be a major bust, we had some local scientists fix the flaws and started using them for the new arrivals."

"Good to know Heaven upcycles."

He shakes his head. "This isn't Heaven."

"It's not? Then where are we?"

"Can't you just wait and see?"

"No," I answer, stealing his line. What do you know? It irritates him, too.

"RJ," he says shortly. "I promise, all of your questions will be answered in time. Where we are, what happens, which way you're going—"

I stop dead in my tracks. "Which way?"

He keeps moving. "Well, yeah. No one has a guarantee. Except for Gandhi and Mother Teresa. They were pretty much shoo-ins."

"Wait a minute. By 'way,' you mean like Heaven or . . ." I can't say the word.

Unfortunately, Gideon has no such qualms. "Hell."

"Thanks."

"You're welcome."

Apparently Reapers are *not* fluent in sarcasm.

We catch up with the crowd from the train and amble along in silence. I want to ask more questions, but can't think of any. It's as if my brain is switching off. I shake my head slightly, trying to rattle something into place.

"You'll get used to it," the Reaper says, looking at me sideways.

I try to play it off like I don't know what he's talking about. "What do you mean?"

"The head thing. Your brain is finally accepting that your body is dead."

"How do I make it stop?" I snap. "This is not happening to me. Remember, I'm going to find someone in processing to help me and then I'm going to get my life back."

"If you say so."

"You don't believe me?" I don't know why, but his lack of faith stings a little. Maybe because he's the one who gave me hope in the first place.

He leans closer to me. "Look," he whispers, "in the thousand years I've been doing this, no one has ever gotten a do-over. It just doesn't happen. If we make an exception for you, how long do you think it will take before everyone is trying to appeal their death?"

"But you said—"

"I said processing would figure it out," he says, cutting me off. "And they will. I just wouldn't get too excited if I were you."

Much to my surprise, tears begin to fall down my cheek. How is it that, with all the parts of me that are now useless, the tear ducts still work? Whatever the reason, the salty drops have a transformable effect on the Reaper.

"Hey," he says softly. "Tell you what. If it will help, I'll vouch for you and what happened this afternoon."

"You will?" I say, brightening slightly.

"Why not?" he says with a shrug. "Miracles happen all the time, don't they?"

Chapter 3

Because of every movie made about what happens when you die, I prepare to shield my eyes from the blinding glare of white clouds. What I see is nothing like that. In fact, the movies have it all wrong. The Afterlife doesn't have white clouds or angels with harps, at least not when you first arrive. It looks like a hotel lobby. A really big hotel lobby. For the most part, people are milling around with blank stares and there are small clusters of families huddling together in silence. It's like being on the set of a zombie movie.

The liveliest crowd is made up of the old people. Like the woman on the train, they actually seem happy to be here. There's no shock or confusion. In fact, they greet each other like long-lost friends. Who knows, maybe they did know each other before they got here. From time to time a voice booms over an invisible intercom, startling everyone as it lists off a series of names and directs the chosen few to line up by the front desk at the far end of the room. I find an empty seat and watch people stumble toward the waiting line.

Out of the corner of my eye I see a Grim Reaper herding several people through a door that reads VIP.

"Suicides," someone says next to me.

I turn to see a girl a few years older than me. "Excuse me?" The fact that she's not catatonic like everyone else makes me suspicious and intrigued at the same time.

She nods in the direction of the door. "That's where they take the suicides. I guess they need extra counseling or something."

I look her up and down, sea-green eyes and raven hair that's swept up in a high ponytail. If not for the scar that jags from her hairline to the opposite cheek, she'd be stunning. "How do you know?" I ask, glancing back to the door.

"I've been around for a while," she says, plopping down next to me before changing the subject. "So, what brings you here?"

I think back to the reaction of the old woman on the train and my Reaper's warning to keep a low profile. "Um, car accident."

Her one unmarred and perfectly shaped eyebrow arches up sharply. "You're lying."

"I am not," I answer, a little too defensively.

She gives me a look of amusement. "Oh, please. If you were in a wreck you would be moping around like the rest of these poor suckers."

"What, are you an expert on dead people?" I ask, wishing she would go away.

She shrugs. "When you have nothing to do but sit around and watch the new arrivals, you can pick up a thing or two. I'm Sandy, by the way."

"RJ," I say automatically. "Like what kind of things?" I ask, hoping to turn her attention away from my end-of-life experience.

She scans the room until she finds what she's looking for. "See that guy over there?" she whispers, pointing toward the line at the front desk. "The one with a dazed look who keeps touching his head?"

I look around the room until I spot him. "Yeah."

"Well, he has a biker jacket on, right? And not one of those expensive, flashy ones that college guys buy to wear when they show off their crotch rockets. We're talking old-school biker gang jacket."

"Okay, he rides a motorcycle. Big deal." I wish this chick would get to the point. I mean, I know we have eternity, but come on.

"Yeah, but he doesn't have a helmet with him."

"So."

"When you come here, whatever you have on when you die comes with you. Hats, gloves, jewelry, all of it comes along for the ride." She gives me a mischievous grin. "Even dirty underwear."

"Gross."

She laughs and several nearby souls twitch but no one turns toward us. "Oh lighten up. But seriously, there was this guy who had a heart attack while playing video games. He showed up here with the controller still tethered to his wrist."

"You're kidding," I say, still trying to get the dirty underwear comment out of my head.

"Nope. It just hung limp at his side until someone from processing took it from him."

"Why'd they do that?" I ask, leaning closer to her.

Sandy shakes her head. "I'm not sure. I think it's because they don't want you taking anything with you that will tie you to your old life. You know, like if that guy was playing with his kids when he died, the remote might make it harder for him to move on."

"So maybe someone took the helmet from biker guy?"

"Maybe, but I doubt it."

I look back at the guy who's examining his head. "Well, what do you think happened?"

"It's obvious, isn't it?"

"Apparently not or I wouldn't be asking," I snap.

She puts her hands up in surrender. "Chill. Fine, what I think happened is he died in a bike wreck. He's got that stunned look most people have when they die suddenly. And he keeps checking out his head. Classic sign that he sustained a head injury. He's probably trying to figure out why his skull feels so mushy. That makes me think he was riding without a helmet."

"Huh," I say, no longer looking at the biker.

Sandy turns to follow my gaze. "What?"

I nod toward a woman in a wedding gown. The middle of the dress is stained with blood. On the floor next to her sits a dented helmet. "Do you think they were together?"

"Maybe," Sandy says, standing and walking swiftly across the room to the line.

I race after her. "Where are you going?"

"Don't you want to find out if you're right?" she asks over her shoulder. I catch up with her just as she lays a hand on the biker. "Excuse me," she says gently.

He looks at her and almost recoils from her touch. "Yes?" His voice lacks surprise or confusion or any emotion at all.

Sandy is looking him in the eye, unwilling to let him look away. "Were you in a motorcycle accident?"

He nods and then shakes his head like it hurts to remember.

"Maybe we should leave him alone," I say, pulling on Sandy's arm.

She shakes me off and continues talking to the man. "Do you know where your helmet is?"

"I don't know."

"Were you wearing one when you crashed?"

The man is still for a moment before finally saying, "I can't remember. I don't think so."

Sandy gives me a triumphant look before asking him, "Was someone else wearing it?"

Slowly, he begins to nod. "She was."

"A woman in a pretty dress, maybe?" Sandy prompts, giving me a victory smile.

The man's head snaps up, his eyes growing clearer by the second.

"How did you know?" he demands, the dazed look gone.

Sandy takes a step back just as I answer, "I, uh, I saw a woman with a helmet. She was wearing a fancy white—"

"Where?" he bellows, stepping over the rope line. The person behind him moves up to fill the void, oblivious to the confrontation taking place right in front of him.

He looks wildly around the room until he sees the woman. His eyes grow wide and a guttural howl echoes throughout the hall. I look around, expecting everyone to be watching us, but like the man who took his place in line, no one seems to be aware of anything. The biker rushes past, knocking me and everyone in his path out of the way until he reaches the dead bride. Dropping to his knees, he lays his head down in her lap and begins to weep.

It's the first expression of emotion I've seen since my arrival, unless I count the old people with their geriatric posse. At first, the woman just looks blankly over the biker's trembling body. Then, almost automatically, she lays one hand on the back of his head and absently strokes his hair. When her eyes drift down, she watches as his body shakes with sobs until, finally, she lifts his chin up. Their eyes meet and her blank stare vanishes as tears begin to stream down her face.

"What's happening?" I whisper to Sandy, who looks as freaked out as I feel.

"No idea," she admits, not able to take her eyes off the scene. Her body is stiff as a board. "This has never happened before. Maybe it's you."

Oh no. She is *not* blaming this on me. Gideon's warning to keep a low profile echoes in my mind. So much for that plan.

"I'm so sorry," the biker says over and over. "I didn't mean . . ."

She shushes him, leaning down to kiss him lightly on the lips. The moment they connect, a squadron of figures in white jumpsuits surrounds them, gently pulling the man to his feet and hustling both him and the woman through the unmarked door. One of them remains behind and turns to scan the room. Sandy shrinks behind me.

"Don't let her see me," she hisses, but it's too late. The angelic-looking being makes a beeline toward us. By the time she reaches us, her face is no longer beautiful. Instead, it's a canvas of fury.

"Sandra Donaldson," her voice rings out and the sweetness is a direct contrast to the anger on her face. "What have you done now?"

Sandy slinks out from my shadow. "Hey, Lillith."

"Don't 'hey' me, Sandra. You know you aren't supposed to interact with the new arrivals. Just because you're pining for your happy-never-after doesn't give you the right to jeopardize the fate of others."

I look between Sandy and Lillith. What does she mean by happy-never-after and who hit this chick with the rude stick?

As if hearing my thoughts, Lillith turns and looks pointedly at me. "And you aren't supposed to corrupt them, either."

"I didn't mean to cause a problem," Sandy argues. "I just asked what happened."

"What did you think was going to happen?" Lillith snaps. "And why would you reconnect him with the woman? You know the emotional trauma that could cause. Even for you this is a new low."

"Actually," I say slowly, "that was me."

"But she didn't know what could happen," Sandy says, jumping in before Lillith can admonish me.

I give her a sharp look. "I don't need you to defend me."

"Both of you, quiet," Lillith commands.

I turn to argue, but I can't. I mean, I literally cannot open my mouth or utter a sound. I look at Sandy. She isn't even trying to speak. Who is this woman and why is Sandy afraid of her?

Finally, our silence is met with a look of satisfaction and Lillith continues. "Until souls have gone through processing, we try to keep them unaware of certain events in their life that might prohibit their progress through the Afterlife. You two have managed to mess that up." She turns to Sandy. "From you, I'm not surprised, but you," she says, turning her steely eyes toward me. "Didn't I just see you come off the train? This is indeed unexpected."

She cocks her head as if hearing a sound from somewhere far away and sighs. "Everything has been taken care of, but from now on, until you go through processing, talk to no one." She turns to Sandy and repeats, "No one."

We both nod and watch as she strides away, fading into the crowd. Once she's out of sight, I feel the tension on my lips ease. "What was that all about?" I gasp, grateful for the sound of my own voice. "Or should I ask, who was that?"

Sandy looks shaken. Another round of names echoes over the loudspeaker and this time I hear Sandy's name. "Hey, I think they're calling you," I say, expecting her to show some sign of relief about getting out of here.

"They always call my name," she replies with a sigh. "I just never go."

"Are you kidding me? What in the world would make you want to wait around here when you could go to the light or whatever it is?"

She reaches into her pocket and pulls out a huge ring. "Because I can't let go of this."

Chapter 4

I stare at the ring, not sure what to say next. It's a piece of art. Two leaping dolphins encircle the diamond solitaire and the eyes are set with the most brilliant sapphires I have ever seen. I would kill for a ring like that.

"He had it made," Sandy says, holding her hand up to admire it. "My favorite book when I was a kid was *Island of the Blue Dolphins*. A friend of his, an art student, created the sketch based off the book as a project for an art class and a jeweler turned the drawing into a one-of-a-kind original."

"Who had it made for you?" I ask, studying the ring closer. It really is amazing.

"My boyfriend, well, I guess it's fiancé." She pauses and her expression becomes soft and almost vacant. "Fiancé. Even after all this time, it still feels makes me want to giggle."

"So when you say you've been around a while . . ."

"Nine months, sixteen days, and ten hours Earth time, give or take." There are tears in her eyes and I wonder again why souls can cry. "For this place, that's an eternity."

"Why don't you go through processing and be done with it?"

She motions for me to follow her and I do, mostly because I'm curious but also because the thought of being alone in this crowd of emotionally comatose people freaks me out. We find two chairs not far from the geriatrics and I wait for her to begin.

"He came up to see me a few days after spring term started. I was a senior at Notre Dame, studying business. James and I wanted to open a bookstore when we graduated. You know, one of those cool, independent places that eventually becomes a must-stop on book tours?"

I shake my head. I don't exactly spend a lot of time in bookstores. Or I didn't, I should say. My head starts going fuzzy just trying to think about my life.

She gives a sad laugh and I force myself to pay attention. "Well, I thought it was a dream life. We were going to raise our kids on great literature and live happily ever after. Sure, we probably wouldn't make much money, but we couldn't imagine a better job than being surrounded by books and people who love them." Another deep breath. "Anyway, that night, he was supposed to be at Northwestern, not in the lobby of my dorm. I'll never forget the look on his face." Her sad look slips away as happiness takes its place. "He was so excited. And when I say excited, I mean he was almost giggling. It was so cute. He had dinner reservations for seven o'clock but it was snowing like crazy and there was no way we were going to make it, so we stopped at a little sandwich shop and then headed for St. Joseph Lake." She laughs and her face lights up, almost erasing the scar on her face.

I'm not sure if Sandy is still in this conversation with me or lost in a memory, but I'm enchanted by her real-life fairy-tale love. "Did you know he was going to give you that rock when you saw him?" I ask.

"No," she answers in a dreamy voice. "I thought he was going to ask me while we were home for Christmas, but he didn't. Then I figured it would be over spring break. We were supposed to go to Hawaii as one last hurrah before graduation."

"Wow," is all I can say. Sandy's life seems like a dream.

"All through dinner I kept trying to get him to spill his secret, but he didn't crack. Not even a little. I thought he might have heard back from our realtor on a couple storefronts we were interested in. When we finished eating, James really wanted to walk along the trail that runs next to the water. It was freezing but I would go anywhere with him. It was just one more adventure. I don't think we were more than a few feet away from the parking lot when he dropped down on one knee. The snowflakes made his hair almost completely white and I thought 'this is what he'll look like when he's seventy.' That's when I got it. My heart leapt into my throat."

"Wow. It's so romantic."

She smiles but it doesn't quite reach her eyes, which are now filling with sadness. "The moon was shining overhead and the sparkle of the diamond and the stars blended together. I don't even know if I gave him the chance to actually ask me to marry him. All I remember is saying yes over and over. And then he jumped up and pulled me close. His kisses melted on my lips. I had never been so happy. That's when I saw them."

Her voice trickles off and she seems to be at a loss for words. Finally, in a whisper, she says, "The headlights. The car must have hit a patch of black ice or something. All I knew is it was coming straight for us. I watched it jump the curb and crash through the bushes. I tried to push James out of the way but I wasn't fast enough. The car knocked him down before it ran over him on its way toward the lake."

I'm unable to keep from staring at her scar. "What happened to you?"

Sensing my gaze, her hand raises self-consciously to her face. "I flew over the hood and through the windshield. Believe it or not, it wasn't the head injury that killed me. When the car went into the lake, I was pinned under it."

I expect her to cry again but Sandy chuckles a low, sad laugh. "It was like being in a movie. I still remember flying through the air. I felt weightless and couldn't stop looking at the moon. But then the glass shattered and the pain was unbearable. It was like a thousand fire ants biting every inch of me. And then it stopped. Just like that. The last thing I remember was the muffled sound of the ambulance and the shimmer of the lights dancing across the surface of the water."

My hand flies to my mouth to hold back a gasp. I fail miserably. "I'm so sorry," I finally say.

She flashes me a sad smile. "You want to know the funny part. I was a swimmer. I held three freestyle records on my college team. I could hold my breath longer than anyone else. And in the end, it was death by drowning. Personally, I blame the collapsed lung."

"That's not funny," I say. "It's tragic."

She ignores me. "They pronounced me dead at the hospital, but I was gone long before that. The Grim Reaper met me on the shore of the lake. He tried to rush me away from the scene but I had to see if James was okay."

"What happened to him?" I ask in a whisper. "Did he die?"

"Do you think I would be hanging around this place if he did?" she snaps.

I sit back in surprise. "No. Probably not."

"Sorry," she says. "To answer your question, no. He's not dead. But he's not alive either."

I give her a questioning look. "How is that possible?"

She slumps down in her chair. "His stupid parents have him hooked up to all kinds of machines, but the only thing they're doing is keeping him from coming here to be with me." There's a wildness in her eyes, like her mind is bordering on insanity and now I can see why souls shut off their emotions when they die. "What they need to do is let him go."

Again, the front desk calls her name. "How often does that happen?" I say to her.

"What?" she asks, and I can tell by the blank stare she has no idea what I'm talking about.

"They keep calling for you. How often do they do that?"

"Every few minutes for the last nine months, sixteen days, and ten hours," she ticks off.

My mouth drops open. "They call your name every single time a new group goes up, and they've been doing it since you got here?"

She nods and pulls the engagement ring out, twisting it around her finger. "At first it was annoying, but I don't hear it anymore."

I can't imagine not responding to my own name. I stare at the ring. It's huge. Even with help from his friend, how could a college student afford something like that? I bet he was loaded.

"It really is pretty, isn't it?" Sandy says when she catches me looking. Her face is bright and for an instant, I can imagine her on a college campus, vibrant and alive.

"It's amazing," I admit.

She smiles, one of those memory smiles of hers. "I know. You should have seen it in the moonlight."

Again with the moon. "When you said people who hold on to things from their life have a hard time moving on . . ."

She lets out a throaty laugh. The clatter of the old people stops and I can feel them looking at us with disapproval. Sure enough, when I turn around, several of the blue-haired crew are shaking their heads.

"Ignore them," Sandy says, sticking out her tongue in their direction. "As to your question, you should see how often the processors try to get me to hand this thing over to them."

"But you don't want to move on?"

She looks at the ceiling. "I do. It's exhausting watching trainload after trainload of souls move through here. I feel the pull to move on all the time."

"So hand the ring over and go."

Sandy sighs. "I can't."

I slap my thighs in frustration. I really don't get this girl. "Why the heck not?"

When she speaks, there's a quiver in her voice. "I can't give up on him. When they finally turn off the machines and he dies, I can't let him sit here like them," she says, gesturing to everyone around us. "I can't stand the idea of him being shell-shocked and closed off. He deserves better. We deserve our happy ending. Together. Even if it isn't exactly the way we planned."

"Is that what Lillith meant about you pining away?" I ask, and Sandy nods. "But can't you wait for him on the other side?"

"I don't know what's going to happen once I leave the Lobby. What if I can't find him? What if I forget I want to find him?"

"But—" I start to say.

Sandy's hand slices through the air in resolve. "No. I'm not going. When he gets off the train, I will be right here. Until then, I'll wait."

I don't have time to argue. A moment later I hear my name over the loudspeaker and I know what Sandy means about the pull to move on. Every part of me wants to move toward the line. I look at the front desk. I sense, rather than feel, Sandy's hand on my arm.

"Wait," she says softly. "Don't go yet. I told you my story. Tell me yours."

I shake my head. "I told you, car accident."

"And I called you a liar, remember? Please, give me something else to think about. What makes you different from all the other brain-deads that come through here?"

I look into her pleading eyes. Maybe she knows something that will help me. "Okay, fine. The Reaper was supposed to collect this gypsy at our school carnival. She saw him coming and at the last second threw me in front of her. He caught my soul instead."

Sandy looks at me for a long while before bursting out laughing. "You're kidding, right?" she gasps.

I just look at her.

"You're not joking."

"Nope."

The look of shock is unmistakable. "That's unreal. Did he get the gypsy?"

I toss my hair over my shoulder and get ready to stand. "Not that I know of, though I hope this time they take her out action-movie style."

"So you weren't supposed to die?"

"Not today. But I'm going to find a way back."

"I bet if anyone can do it, you can. You don't strike me as the kind of person who takes no for an answer." She studies me and I can see the wheels turning in her head. And I'm afraid of what she's thinking. She's spent too much time in limbo pining for the not-yet-dead boyfriend. When she opens her mouth, I brace myself. "If you do, could you do me a favor?"

"What?" I say, regretting not heading for the line sooner.

"Find him," she pleads. "He's at a medical center in Indianapolis. Convince his parents to let him go."

"And just how am I supposed to do that? Even if I can find someone who will send me back, I doubt they'll want me to remember all this. My story wouldn't exactly be good public relations for this place."

She beams a smile of hope and I already know I'm going to do it. It's not like it takes that long to get to Indianapolis from my house.

"Take this," she says, tugging the ring off her finger and pressing it into the palm of my hand.

"I can't," I argue, pushing her hand away. "You need it. If I take it, won't you start to forget?"

I can tell by the look on her face that she hasn't thought this plan through. She shakes her head. "It's a calculated risk. If you keep it on you, maybe it'll make it out of the Afterlife when you go back."

I look down at the ring. "What am I supposed to do with it?"

"You'll figure it out," she says, standing up. "Now come on. We need to get you in line. Don't want Lillith thinking you've joined my rebellion."

"For someone who doesn't want to leave, you sure are in a hurry to send me into the great unknown," I say, letting her pull me up and drag me toward the front desk.

Once we're there, she turns and pulls me into a tight hug. "Thank you."

"I haven't done anything yet," I argue.

"Oh, but you have. You've given me hope."

I shake her off. "Don't get too excited. There's still that little detail about getting back to the land of the living."

"Failure is not an option," she says, perkier than a dead person has any right to be.

I take my place at the end of the line. Sandy follows me as I inch forward. Just as I turn the corner, she reaches out and grabs my arm. "Thank you."

I smile at her. What else can I do?

"Good luck," she calls out as I step up to the counter, but the words already sound so far away.

When I finally reach the front of the line, a woman with blond hair and an airbrushed complexion greets me. "Name?"

I shift my weight, taking one last look over my shoulder before turning back. "Um, RJ Jones."

She types in a few swift keystrokes and I hear a buzzing sound from her machine.

"What's that?" I ask, standing on my tiptoes. But all she does is smile. "Is this like check in? Because I need to talk to a manager or someone in charge. There's been a mistake. I'm not supposed to be here."

She looks up at me with a dazzling smile. "We don't make mistakes," she says with a sweetness so heavy my teeth hurt.

"But you did, or at least the Grim Reaper did. He even admitted it to me."

She looks at me in amusement. "Well, if there was some error, I'm sure Azrael will look into it."

Azrael? Why does that name fill me with dread? A loud beep distracts me. "What *is* that?" I ask again.

She slides a thin brown package about the size of a dinner plate across the desk. "Rowena Joy Jones, this is your life."

Crap.

Chapter 5

I stare at the disc and then back up at the woman behind the counter. "What am I supposed to do with this?"

She points to a long hallway. "Pick any open room and watch it."

That's it? She hands me a highlight reel of my life and then tells me to pick a room? People get more counseling before they adopt a dog. When I don't move right away, she clears her throat and tells me with her eyes that I am dismissed. Looking at the line of souls behind me, I decide not to argue. Besides, if anyone is going to be able to help me find a way back, it's not going to be a paper pusher.

Following the red carpet, I slip into the first open room I see. The walls are a sunny yellow, except for the space above a machine that looks like an oversized DVD player. In front of the machine is a high-backed chair upholstered in a deep shade of purple—my favorite color. Other than that, the room is empty.

I slide the disc out from the cover and slip it into the machine before sinking into the soft cushions. It's like snuggling up in a cloud. Too bad there's no popcorn. If I remember correctly, my life is pretty interesting. Ski trips with friends, shopping in Chicago, sneaking backstage at more than a few concerts. Maybe it'll be fun to remember the good old days.

The opening scene of my birth lights up the space just above the laser disc player. I watch my mom's face when they place me in her outstretched arms. She's glowing with joy, which is how I got my middle name. Although it's about as cliché as you can get, it's also pretty cool. After all, I wasn't exactly aware of what was going on during the actual event and my dad didn't have the foresight to record any of it.

Even through the exhaustion of a forty-two-hour labor, my mom looks amazing. Then again, maybe the HD in the Afterlife is better than the projector in our movie room back home. I dip my head to dab a tear from the corner of my eye just in time to see Dad singing softly to a bundle of cloth. It takes me a second to realize he's holding me. A moment later, a petite woman with a huge smile walks in, plucks me from my father's arms, and immediately begins kissing every inch of my face.

"Gladys," my mother says, "you didn't wash your hands."

"Oh pish," Grams says. "I've raised five children, you being one of them, and all my kids turned out pretty healthy. Besides, this is my first grandbaby." She looks sheepishly at my dad, who's grinning ear to ear. "But of course, she's your firstborn." She starts to hand me back but he just laughs.

"You keep her, Grams. But she is going home with us, understand?"

She grins and begins cooing at me.

As the scene fades away, it hits me that I haven't thought about my parents since I got here. What are they going to do when they see their only child lying on a slab in some morgue? Mom will cry hysterically. She'll be inconsolable. I can't even imagine how Dad will react.

Okay. That's it. I have to find a way back. I cover my ears as the humming sound starts up again. This time, I put two and two together and realize that anytime I try to think about returning to my old life, my head threatens to explode.

Another scene flashes, recapturing my attention, and the pain slowly eases. This time I'm on the playground near my house. There are tons of kids, but even now, the only person I see is Abby Richards. She doesn't know it yet, but it won't be long until we are inseparable. Her mom travels for work all the time and Abby's dad stays home.

Abby takes one look at me and bounds over. I've always wondered why, with all the kids at the playground, she picked me. It's like she sensed a connection between us.

"Hi," she says.

"Hi," I respond cautiously.

"You wanna race me down the slide?"

I'm still painfully shy at this point in my life and I remember the debate taking place in my mind. Do I run, full steam, back to my house and lose the chance to make my first friend or do I say yes? Finally, after what seems like eternity, I answer her.

"Sure." Without another word, we race toward the double slide and the picture fades away. A split second later, another takes its place. It's the same park, but this time I'm walking away from Abby, who is cowering on the snow-covered ground in front of several older girls. It's the day of her mother's death, though I won't find that out until later because I'm too afraid to stand up for her.

The images last only a couple seconds before vanishing.

My stomach tightens. If there was one thing in my life I could do over, it would be this moment. Abby had called me to tell me about her mother. But I left her behind. Not only did I lose my best friend, but Abby got a pretty nasty beating from those girls. I wipe my eyes with the back of my hand. I'm not proud of what I did, but what's done is done. I focus intently on the next scene.

In sixth grade, I transferred to a private middle school with a bunch of people I didn't know. Most of my old friends were attending the public school across town. I feel bad for the me back then, especially during lunch time. My younger self walks into the cafeteria, scanning the crowd for any familiar faces, but there aren't any. On the verge of tears, I watch myself stare straight ahead and move toward the door that leads to the quad. My destination is the back stall in the girl's bathroom.

"You can't take that out of the cafeteria," someone says behind me. I turn around and see Marcy Hampton. She's a seventh grader. She's also a cheerleader.

"I was just going . . ."

"To eat lunch in a stairwell?"

The stairs. Why didn't I think of that? Much more hygienic.

"Come sit with us," she says, gesturing to a table full of girls dressed just like her.

My eyes widen in terror. I remember thinking, *Is she joking? This has to be a trick. I can't just sit down with all the popular kids. They'll know I don't belong there and will probably eat me alive.*

"Hey, everyone. This is . . ." she turns to me and whispers, "What's your name?"

"Rowena," I answer.

She shakes her head, a look of disapproval in her eyes. "Okay, what's your middle name?"

"Joy," I say, wishing the floor would open up under my feet and swallow me whole.

To my surprise, her face lights up and she turns back to her friends. "Sorry. This is RJ. I told her she could eat with us." It isn't a question. With that one simple statement, Marcy deems me cool enough to be seen with and gives me a new name. Talk about power.

I watch as the girls pepper me with questions about which teachers I like and the ones I don't. Apparently I give them the right answers because no one laughs at me. By the time the bell rings, I'm in, and insecure Rowena is a ghost. I get the irony.

On the way out of the cafeteria, Marcy says, "You know, they're having tryouts for the sixth grade cheerleading squad next week. You should show."

"Really?" I ask in surprise. "But I've never cheered before." What I don't tell her is I think cheerleaders are a bunch of stuck-up snobs.

She beams a blazing white smile at me. "Well then it's a good thing you know me. I can teach you all the routines. Maybe you can get your parents to hire my gymnastic coach. She can give you a crash course in tumbling so you're ready for tryouts." When I hesitate, she adds, "Come on. It'll be fun."

And then the fuzzy screen fades once more before flickering back to life at my eighth grade graduation. After the principal reads off the names of all the recipients of a ton of worthless awards and the fake diplomas are safe in the hands of our doting parents, everyone rushes back to the quad to pick up the yearbooks. All around me, classmates are passing their books around in a frenzy to make it seem like they have more friends than they really do.

"Just a minute," I say to someone waving their picture in front of me. Before I sign anything, I have to see the superlative page. During the last round of voting I'm on the ballot for three titles: most outgoing, most popular, and most likely to take high school by storm. To win all three is next to impossible, but I want it so badly.

I lean forward, a silly grin spreading across my face. In about three seconds, I'm going to shriek and all heads will turn in my directions, but I won't care. It's the trifecta. All three honors are mine. They even put the photos on the same page. I'm an instant legend.

I pull out a metallic gold marker. Now I'm ready to sign yearbooks, but only on my page. No way am I using the signature sheets in the back where everyone signs. I snap the lid of my pen and jot down so many DON'T EVER CHANGE! and SEE YOU NEXT YEAR! that my hand is cramping by the time I climb into my mom's BMW.

Looking back, I have to admit, this was a pretty cool day.

The disc fast-forwards a few months. It's a week into my freshman year of high school and I'm trying out for the Junior Varsity cheerleading squad. After three years cheering in middle school, I'm actually pretty good. Of course, it doesn't hurt that Marcy is captain of the JV squad. She's spent the summer putting me through brutal practices so I can sail through tryouts. A bonus of Marcy taking me under her wing is that I've been hanging out with a lot of the high school cheerleaders. After a particularly grueling pre-tryout workout, just after school starts, we're all at the Smoothie Shack sucking down protein shakes when someone mentions Whitney, another freshman who's trying out for the squad.

"She's so fat," one of the girls says, making pig noises.

Everyone laughs. "I know. And her upper body strength is horrible. I mean, if you're going to be big, at least be strong. We always need girls for the bottom of the pyramid," someone else adds.

Now, for the record, Whitney is not fat. She just doesn't look like the other girls do. And, she's really nice. We're in geometry together and she's hilarious. I don't really want to make fun of her, so instead of joining in, I concentrate on my drink.

But Bella, the Varsity captain, isn't about to let me off the hook. "What do you think of her, RJ? I could have sworn I saw you talking to her earlier."

I sink a little in my seat, looking around at the expectant faces. I know they want me to join in on the bashing. I decide to try playing it off like I don't know her well. "Yeah, um, we have math together. I couldn't remember the homework assignment."

Bella doesn't look like she's buying it. "Really? Because you looked awfully chummy after practice yesterday. Didn't I hear you tell her you'd go shopping with her this weekend?"

"Well, it's not like she's going to give her the assignment if RJ is mean to her," Marcy says, coming to my defense.

I watch Bella roll her eyes and I see myself squirm under her gaze. If only I knew then what I know now. In a few months, the Varsity captain is going to find herself staring down at two pink lines on a pregnancy test. She'll be so embarrassed she'll transfer to another school and her reign of terror will be over.

But for now, I'm at the mercy of a vindictive and vengeful queen bee who also happens to hold my popularity in her hands.

"So," Bella continues, "what do you really think of her? Do you really want a cow like that on your squad? She can barely pull off a back tuck."

I know this is a test. If I say I like her, my cool factor plummets. If I throw her under the bus, I score points with Bella, but who knows what will happen after that.

Actually, I do know, at least the dead me does. I shake my head and will the buzzing to stop as I watch freshman me take the safe route. "You're right. She's a total pig. Who in the world would want to toss her? And the weak arms aren't the worst part. She sweats so bad. It's gross."

The words make me cringe because I know they are going to come back to haunt me. And much sooner than I can imagine. Later in the day, Bella is going to run into Whitney. She'll tell her everything I said. Unfortunately, I won't know this when I try to talk to her in class and she gives me the cold shoulder. In fact, it won't be until tryouts that I learn the truth behind the hurt look on her face. When Whitney doesn't show for practice, Bella gives me a very public high five and praises me for helping to weed out the undesirables.

There's a long pause between clips and I pull my knees up to my chest to contemplate everything I've seen so far.

Where are the fun times? What about the sleepovers where my friends and I give each other makeovers and prank call boys we like? What about the Thursday night bonfires before Friday night games? The older I get the more hateful this video is making me look. There's no way I was that mean. Is there?

Before I can decide if this is really me or typecast editing, the screen blinks back to life. It's my junior year of high school. I can tell because now I'm wearing my Varsity cheerleading uniform, which means my coach doesn't know about my grades yet and I'm still on the team. The other clue that it's junior year is that I'm flirting with Dave, Felicity's stepbrother.

I know it makes her crazy that we're hanging out all the time, but that's part of the fun. As much as I call Felicity my bestie, the truth is, we're only friends because we know too much about each other to be enemies. It's a relationship of tactical means.

My mind turns to what my friends must be thinking about my death. I'm sure they're all in shock, but are they doing anything? At the very least they should be organizing a candlelight vigil or some other form of group mourning. I bet Felicity is getting plenty of face time in front of the camera. After all, the news has got to be all over this. When a pretty, popular girls drops dead for no reason, everyone makes a big deal about it. I really hope no one thinks it's an overdose.

Hey, wait a minute. How *did* I die? Obviously I know the truth, and when that gypsy does arrive in the Afterlife, I will be more than happy to give her a piece of my mind. But what did the doctors say was my cause of death? Maybe, when I'm done with this replay of my life, someone can tell me.

Oh man, I'm missing an entire scene that's playing on the disc now. All I see is the end and my friends laughing. Of course I miss a happy memory. Apparently a short attention span carries over into the Afterlife.

The next scene has to be the last. It takes place a few months before I see the gypsy. It's a party at my house with the whole gang. We're talking about this scholarship kid at school who's got a rare form of cancer. Her parents don't have much money and the local news had some story on how the family's medical bills are so big the bank is about to foreclose on their house. I'm pretty sure it was a wine cooler–induced moment of compassion, but I come up with the idea to do a charity auction to help them out. Before the night is over, I fire off an email to my high school principal telling him about our plans.

On Monday, he comes up to me smiling and going on and on about how great he thinks it is that we're going to do something to help out a classmate. At first, I have no idea what he's talking about. Then it starts to come back to me. I smile and tell him we can't wait to start.

Fast-forward several weeks and we're back at my house. This time, there are no wine coolers to be seen. The auction has been more successful than any of us thought it would be. After expenses, we're three thousand dollars above our goal.

"You know," Dave says, "I think we should have a party to celebrate. Maybe hire a band and get my older brother to buy a couple kegs."

"And where are we going to get the money for a party like that?" I ask, running my fingers through his thick curls.

"From there," he says, gesturing to the checking account my mom insisted we set up. "We write it off as expenses and then party our butts off."

Several people around the table nod in agreement.

"Yeah, but Madeline's family needs this money," I argue. "And besides, what if someone finds out? We could get in a lot of trouble."

"We made enough for them to keep their house," Felicity chimes in. "I bet they'll be so grateful they won't even notice. Besides, like Dave says, we write it off as expenses and no one's going to question us."

I watch myself thinking it over and I remember the dilemma. On one hand, if I say yes, I'm the hero in their eyes but I'm a thief and a liar in mine. Or I go against them and look like a chicken. Felicity has been trying to knock me off my throne every chance she gets, and, looking at everything from the outside, I can practically see her licking her chops for me to say no.

I know exactly when I make the decision. It's like the light goes out in my eyes and I'm a puppet to popularity. "Fine," I say, throwing up my hands. "Just don't go crazy. We at least have to show that we reached our goal."

"Sweet, we can do a lot with a three-grand surplus," Dave says, throwing his arms around me and planting a kiss on my cheek. "This is going to be epic."

"Yeah," I say. "Why do I get the feeling I'm going to live to regret it?"

"Ah, the careless words of the young," a voice bellows from the doorway. "Did you ever think that statement would come back to bite you?"

Chapter 6

I jump out of the chair and turn to face an angel. Clad entirely in white with an honest to goodness pair of wings, he blocks out any light from the hallway, and I'm pretty sure his smile could melt what's left of the Arctic Circle.

"Well, look here," he says, his thick Caribbean Island accent rolling off his tongue, and I can almost feel a tropical breeze blow gently through the room. "They told me I had a live one."

His voice is hypnotic. An overwhelming sense of calm settles over me, and as hard as I try to shake it off, it's impossible. "Who are you?"

He laughs again and I cover my ears to block the sound. It doesn't work. My ears are still ringing when he speaks. "I'm Yeats, one of your Guardian Angels. But for now, think of me as your personal activity director during your time in limbo. I'm here to answer your questions and help you find peace before you sit in Judgment."

"Judgment?" I ask. "You mean like if I'm going to . . ."

"Heaven or Hell?" he finishes. "Yes, that's exactly what I mean."

He steps into the room, taking up what little space there is. If he's working the intimidation angle, he's doing an impressive job. Leaning against what passes for a wall, I clear my throat and say, "Then I might be your easiest job ever. I'm not going to Judgment."

The only reaction I get is a slight pinching together of his eyebrows. Other than that, he's unreadable. "You're not going?" The laughter is still present in his voice and I flinch under the weight of his amused stare.

I shake my head. "No. In fact, if you could just tell me who I need to talk to about getting back to my life, I'll be out of your hair."

I expect him to laugh again but he doesn't. What he does do is frown and the air around me rushes from the room. "And here I thought you were a sane one. Are you sure you aren't a suicide?" he asks.

"What?" I ask in surprise.

He studies me before answering. "They tend to be in denial more than other souls."

I can feel anger surging through me. Why would he think that? I have, or had, a great life. "I didn't kill myself. If you had to call it anything, I was murdered—"

"Ah," he says like he's having some big revelation. "That was my second guess."

"If you would let me finish, you would know that my soul was collected by accident."

He blinks. Once. Twice. Three times. I see his mouth start twitching and know what's coming next. I barely have time to cover my ears before he erupts in a belly laugh. It's like a bomb going off in my head and I crouch down, turning my back to him. When the eardrum-busting sound stops, I look up from my semi-fetal position. He's still chuckling to himself. "Accidental collection. Now that's one I've never heard before. You're funny."

"I'm not joking," I say, pushing off the ground. "If you're really my Guardian Angel, shouldn't you know that?"

"Well, technically, everyone has two Guardians. I oversee your mental and emotional state, regardless of the condition of your physical self."

"So you don't care if I'm supposed to be alive or dead?"

He shakes his head. "Not really. That's Hazel's job. I've got my own physical charges to worry about."

"Hasn't anyone around here heard of streamlining? If I had only one angel watching out for me, maybe I wouldn't be here in the first place. And if you really are supposed to watch over my mental and emotional state, I would think you would know that all I want to do is get back to the life that was stolen from me."

He shakes his head and steps out of the room. "That's not how it works. Once you're here, you stay. Now are you coming?"

"We'll see," I mutter, but follow him anyway. The sooner I find someone with decision-making authority, the sooner I'll be rocketing back to my old life. Yeats is looking at me expectantly. "What?"

"This is the part where you ask why you had to die so young and what God looks like," he says, leading me down the red carpet that doesn't seem to end.

"I know why I died. An incompetent Reaper couldn't stop his target from throwing me under the bus."

"You don't look like you were hit by a bus," he says.

"I was speaking metaphorically. Hey, wait," I say, stopping short. "I do have a question. Did a Reaper finally get her?"

"I have no idea who you're talking about," he answers, waiting for me to start moving again.

"The gypsy. The woman who started this train wreck in the first place."

Yeats's face no longer holds any hint of amusement. In fact, he looks bored. "Look, I don't know what your problem is, but you really need to take this seriously. Judgment isn't a joke. I saw your life and, for a kid, you sure have a lot of things to answer for."

He's giving me the same look my principal gives when I'm pushing his patience too far. The one that tells me detention is one comeback away. "Okay, fine, what happens now?" I ask.

"You talk to me, we work through all the issues you had during your life, which could take a while, and then we meet up with Hazel."

"Who's that?" I ask.

"She's my partner," he answers, like that's supposed to answer my question. "And she's the Guardian who's been with you the most while you were on Earth. She likes to see her charges when they arrive."

"Wish she could have prevented me from being here in the first place," I mutter.

"What was that?" Yeats asks.

"Nothing. What happens after we meet with Hazel?"

"I walk you through the process of atonement. Once you're done, you'll sit with the Gatekeeper."

"Gatekeeper?"

"The Gatekeeper of Judgment."

"What does he do?"

"It's a she, actually, or she presents herself as a she."

I roll my eyes. "Fine. What does *she* do?"

"She delivers God's verdict."

"What if I don't believe in God?"

He looks at me like he can't believe what I'm asking. "Do you think all this is happening in your imagination?"

"No, I mean, what if I'm Buddhist or Hindu or something else?"

Understanding dawns on his face. "Do you think God cares what name you use? That's something you humans get caught up in."

He has a point and I realize I'm about to ask another question that will continue our philosophical conversation. Why is it so hard to keep my focus on getting back to the land of the living? I'm not here to debate the existence of a divine deity. I'm here to find someone who can get me back to my life. "Look, I just want to find someone who can help me. So whatever hoops I have to jump through, let's do it. What's next?"

"I don't understand. You should have accepted your death by now. You've been through the Lobby, you've seen your life, and you've seen your funeral —"

"I didn't see my funeral," I say quickly.

This gets his attention. "Of course you did."

I shake my head. "No, I didn't. There was no funeral on my disc."

"That's odd. The funeral is part of the closure." His face is now completely transparent as confusion ripples over it.

From somewhere in the distance, a woman's voice is calling his name.

"Yeats."

At first he doesn't hear it. In fact, I have to nudge him to get his attention.

"What?" he asks with a start.

"Someone's looking for you."

Again, the voice calls out: "Yeats." This time, there's panic dripping from the word.

He jumps up. "That's Hazel. Something's wrong." He answers her call with some weird angel language and the next thing I know, a ginger-haired beauty is standing before us, the whites of her eyes match the color of my eyelet sheets and there is undeniable terror in her face.

"Thank goodness you answered," she says. "Yeats, we have a problem."

"Relax," he says, putting his arm around her shoulder to comfort her. "There's never been a problem we couldn't solve. What's happened?"

Hazel is trembling like the last leaf left on a tree in November. This is my physical Guardian? No wonder I died.

"We've lost one of our charges," she cries, burying her head in his robe. "I can't find her anywhere. I just came back from Earth to check the Akashic Records and she's not due to be here for decades."

Yeats answers in a tight voice. "Who is it?" Hazel murmurs into his chest and he pushes her away, forcing her to look at him. "What did you say?"

"She calls herself RJ. She's a self-absorbed princess who doesn't seem to have any remorse about putting herself first and others last, but she's redeemable, I know she is. But she's gone. What do we do?"

I clear my throat. Hazel turns around and looks at me for a moment before her eyes grow wide as saucers.

"Hi," I say, the words sounding as angry as I feel. "You can stop looking. I'm your self-absorbed princess."

Chapter 7

Hazel's face instantaneously switches from fear to jubilation. She rushes over and wraps me into a warm hug. I don't return the embrace. In fact, I don't think I can be more resistant to her, but she doesn't seem to notice.

She pulls back, her hands hanging onto my arms, and gives me a quick once over. "What are you doing here?" she demands. "I was worried sick."

Her scolding only flames the anger I feel toward her. "I didn't know you would be so concerned about a spoiled princess," I say, giving her my best drop-dead look.

"I also said you're redeemable." She pauses, her face dropping as she whispers, "Were redeemable." Turning to Yeats she adds, "This is all wrong."

"Tell me what you know," he says, not even bothering to acknowledge the fact that maybe I wasn't making everything up after all.

She motions toward the sky and says, "Well, as I said, when I couldn't find her, I went to look at the Akashic Records."

"What are the Akashic Records?" I interject.

"It's the compiled knowledge of all human experiences that have ever or will ever occur. It is the history, present, and future of every man, woman, and child," Yeats answers without looking at me.

"Oh," is all I can say.

Hazel continues to ignore me. "That doesn't answer the question of why she's here. According to the Records she still has—"

"Don't say it," he says, giving her a sharp look. "She can't know anything from the Records. Not until after Judgment."

"*She's* right here," I grumble before turning to Hazel. "Do you want to hear what happened to me?"

"No," she says, flicking her hand toward me like I'm a fly buzzing around her perfect head. "You're dead. That's all the information I need to know."

"But I'm not supposed to be dead. It was a mistake." Even I'm aware that I'm starting to sound like a broken record.

Yeats interjects. "Are you telling me RJ disappeared from your radar? Without any warning or explanation?"

Hazel nods. "I felt a stabbing pain followed by hollow emptiness. And then her light was gone."

"When was the last time you checked on her?"

"The party," is all she says.

Yeats nods. "Right, the car accident."

"Wait a minute," I say, inching closer to them. "I wasn't in an accident."

Hazel glances at me. "No, you weren't. And a thank you isn't completely out of the question, you know."

"For what?" I ask, but now they're talking in that creepy angel language. All I can do is sit down and watch their verbal tennis match. From the way Hazel flails her arms, I can tell they're arguing.

"Come on," Yeats says, pulling me up.

"Where are we going?" I ask.

Hazel takes my hand and places it on her robe. I start to pull it away until she says, "If you let go, you'll fall." Of course the thought doesn't hit me until later that it doesn't matter if I fall. It's not like I can die again.

But that's later. Now I find myself lifting off the ground and flying. At first I clutch so tightly onto Hazel that Sandy's ring digs into my skin. But after a little while, it's actually relaxing. Her fluttering wings create a gentle swooshing sound. When it's really my time to go, I have got to get a pair of these! Too bad they don't take credit cards here. I would make a hot angel for Halloween.

We reach our destination and Hazel lands gently on a grassy area. It's a welcome break from the white fluffy cloud decor.

"Where are we?" I ask as her wings fold up neatly behind her.

"Judgment Hall."

I stop suddenly. "Why?"

"You want answers," she says, not bothering to turn around, "this is where they are, but don't tell anyone we brought you through the back entrance."

Yeats pushes open a set of doors so tall I can't see the tops. When Hazel said we were going to Judgment Hall, I thought it would be a depressing place with organ music and quiet whispers, but this place is rockin'. Unlike the Lobby, it's full of activity. Souls cluster together, laughing and hugging. It's like a hundred—no, a thousand—family reunions happening in the same place at the same time.

"Who are these people?" I ask Yeats.

"Souls," he answers, glancing around. "We call them souls. These are the newly departed. They're meeting loved ones who have gone on before them. It's the last step in the transition to the Afterlife."

So it *is* a family reunion. "Like a personalized welcoming committee," I say. "Nice." I look around to see if I know anyone. I don't, and even though it's a good sign I'm not supposed to be dead, it still would have been nice to see a familiar face.

"Well, we have been doing it a while," Hazel quips, her quick retort taking me by surprise. She leads us down a dark hallway to the very end.

I could be mistaken, but I think she takes a quick breath, like she needs a minute to muster up some courage, before knocking on a door.

"Enter," a voice bellows. It could be my imagination, but I think I see Yeats cringe and I wonder what's behind the wall that could make an angel nervous.

"Hello, Azrael," Hazel says, bowing her head as she leads us in.

"Don't look directly at him," Yeats hisses before following her.

"Hazel, why is one of your charges standing before me?" the voice asks and I give in to my temptation to peek.

Big mistake. Instead of a beautiful winged creature with perfect hair and perfect skin, I find myself looking at a figure with four faces and the most enormous pair of gold-tipped wings I can imagine. His body is covered in eyes of various shapes and sizes. One looks directly at me and then blinks out, disappearing completely. I have to bite my cheek to keep from shrieking.

"Begging your pardon, Azrael, but something unusual has occurred," Hazel says.

Azrael's quartet of heads turns in our direction and I snap my gaze away. "Well, what is it?" I hear him ask.

This time, Yeats answers. "RJ, the charge, showed up in the Lobby today. She watched her life disc and then I met up with her to counsel her on the transition."

"Nothing about that sounds remarkable or worthy of my time," Azrael answers, turning all but one of his faces away.

"On our way to the Hall, I found Hazel looking for me. She was hysterical because RJ had disappeared from radar."

"I wasn't hysterical," Hazel says defensively. I hide my smirk. She totally was.

"Get to the point," Azrael roars, and the ground shakes below my feet.

"Her arrival date in the Akashic Records is different than her actual arrival date," Hazel blurts out.

I can feel the heat of all four faces zeroing in on me. I tuck my chin tighter to my chest. "What did you say?" Azrael bellows.

Hazel clears her throat and I glance at her out of the corner of my eye. "When her light went out, I scanned the Earth but couldn't find her. My next stop was the Hall of Records. I didn't think it was possible for me to miss notification about a charge's arrival, but I didn't know what else it could be. When I located her file, the dates were different."

I gather up my courage, praying this Azrael doesn't turn me into a pile of smoldering ash for what I'm about to do. With as much bravado as I can muster, I say, "Can I please say something?"

The room is completely silent. Hazel and Yeats are frozen in place. Out of the corner of my eye I notice the room illuminates in a red glow. I hear the sound of Azrael's footsteps as he comes closer to me. When his hand lifts my chin up, I clamp my eyelids shut, not wanting to see the myriad of eyes looking back at me.

"Look up, child," Azrael says. There's tenderness in his voice that I don't expect and I slowly open one eyelid and then the other. Gone is his grotesque form. Instead, I am looking at a tall tan man with broad shoulders and a serene look on his single face. "Now, you know why they told you not to look at me," he says, the laugh dancing on his words tells me he knows I saw his true self.

"RJ," Hazel says, and if not for Azrael signaling her to be quiet, I'm pretty sure she's about to launch into a lecture.

Turning back to me, he says, "Why don't you tell me what happened. Start at the beginning."

So I do. I tell him about the fortune-teller at the school carnival, Gideon's accidental collection of my soul, and meeting Sandy, Yeats, and Hazel. Except for a few questions to clarify my story, he remains quiet, listening to each detail. It's the first time since my arrival that I feel like someone actually cares what I have to say. When I finish, he nods thoughtfully.

"This is interesting, indeed," he says.

Yeats clears his throat. "How would you like us to proceed? The Akashic Records are never wrong."

Azrael motions for him to be silent. "I'm well aware of the infallibility of the Akashic Records, seeing as how they, like myself, follow each soul's life from birth to death." He crosses his arms in front of him as his long fingers drum on his well-defined biceps. Finally he stops and turns to face my Guardians. "Check with the Record Keepers in Judgment Hall. If there is an appointment for RJ, we know she's where she's supposed to be."

"And if there isn't?" Yeats asks.

Azrael pauses. "Then we have a serious but delicate problem that must be handled with great care. If this is the case, advise the Keeper to summon Gideon, convene the Tribunal, and for everything that's holy, try to get Death Himself to show up for the review."

"Under your authority, I assume," Yeats says.

"Of course."

Yeats and Hazel bow their heads.

"Until then," Azrael continues, "perhaps she would be more comfortable in the Receiving Hall."

Another hall? How big is the Afterlife, anyway?

I see my Guardians look at each other, this time their eyes are filled with concern.

"Is there a problem?" Azrael asks.

Hazel starts to shake her head no, but Yeats speaks up. "While the Receiving Hall might be a good place for her to wait, it is beyond the Gates of Heaven. Since her fate has not been determined, we would be breaking procedure."

"We can't have that, can we?" Azrael asks with a sneer. "It seems to me this entire situation is in violation of all sorts of protocols."

"What I mean," Hazel adds quickly, "is that it would be cruel to expose her to paradise only to send her below, if that is her future."

"Hello," I say, waving my arms over my head. "I can hear everything you say. You know that, right? I might be dead, but I'm not deaf."

"Do you have another idea?" Azrael asks, ignoring me.

Yeats looks at me, probably trying to decide if I'm worth sticking his neck out for, especially with his boss. "Perhaps a better location would be at the entrance to the Gates. Peter can keep an eye on her until everything has been arranged."

Azrael nods thoughtfully. "Perhaps you're right. Yes, I think this plan will cause the least disruption."

As soon as the decision is made, Yeats rushes me out of the room with Hazel following behind. When the door latches shut, they both let out a sigh of relief.

"I can't believe you looked at him when we told you not to," Hazel says briskly.

I almost remind her that she's not my mother but I decide not to. Hazel is someone I need on my side, even if she's only doing it to save her own butt.

"Who's Peter?" I ask, trying to change the subject.

They both stare at me like I'm a child. I'm really starting to hate that look. Finally, Hazel answers, "Peter. The Apostle.

You know, from the New Testament? He hung out with Christ a lot."

I stop in my tracks. "You mean *Saint* Peter? As in the guy who meets people before they enter Heaven?" Great. My babysitter is one of the most famous men in the Bible. There is no way this ends well.

Chapter 8

"So, Saint Peter," I say as Yeats and Hazel hurry me through the maze of passages that lead away from Azrael. "What's he like?"

I see them exchange a look of amusement. "He's hard to describe," Hazel says as she tries to hold back a laugh.

Are all Guardians vague or just mine?

"Is he nice?" I probe. "I mean, I assume he's pretty serious. He was besties with the Son of God, so he's pretty pious, right?"

Yeats chuckles.

"What?" I demand. "What is so funny?"

Instead of answering, he opens a door. I expect to walk into a solemn processional, but what I see is anything but.

Though mild compared to the Receiving Hall, the Gates is a place of revelry. Well, most of it is. There are fireworks sparkling in the sky and cherubs floating lazily in the air, throwing confetti on the new arrivals. If they'd taught us about this in Sunday school, I might have kept going.

For once, something looks like I expect. The gold fence of the Gates of Heaven is as tall as a giraffe. On regular intervals, the entrance opens and trumpets can be heard blaring as the souls enter.

"They're announcing the new arrivals," Hazel explains.

"They blow the horn every single time?" I ask.

She nods. "This is a place of celebration. Unless . . ." she casts a quick glance in the opposite direction.

I follow her eyes. Looming opposite the Pearly Gates is an opening that looks like a cave. "What is that?" I ask.

She rolls her eyes. "It's the Gates of Hell," she says.

"You're kidding? The Gates of Hell are located directly across from the Gates of Heaven?"

"Actually," Yeats interjects, "it's very efficient. Aren't you the one who said we should streamline?"

"Yeah, but doesn't it seem cruel to the poor schmucks heading downstairs? I mean, how would you like to have it thrown in your face that you're facing eternal damnation while the majority of the souls are partying it up before entering Heaven?" I cock my head to one side. "Is that him?"

"Is that who?" Yeats asks.

"Over there. Next to gate. Is that Saint Peter?"

Yeats glances up toward the line waiting to get into Heaven. "That would be him."

I stretch my neck to get a better look. "Who's that guy sitting next to him?"

"Don't tell me you've never heard of the Buddha," Yeats scoffs.

I try to cover up my surprise with indignation. "Yeah, I know who he is, but why is he here?"

"I thought we covered this already," Hazel says with a sigh. "It's not God who has problems with other religions. That's a mankind thing. Buddhists have as much right to the eternal grace as anyone else."

A smirk spreads over my face. "What about Scientologists?"

Hazel's face turns bright red as she starts to answer, but Yeats steps in front of her. "Why don't we go see Peter?" He takes my elbow and leads me through the crowd, leaving Hazel to simmer.

"What was that about?" I ask, craning my neck to see if she's following us. She is, but slowly.

"Oh, Hazel just has a strong opinion about some of the beliefs that have popped up over the years." I can tell by the look on his face that this isn't an issue I should push. Behind me, I hear a dog barking.

"Wait, there are dogs up here?" I ask, thinking about the beagle we had when I was in elementary school.

"Do you see any dogs?" Yeats asks.

I shake my head. "But I heard one."

"No, you heard Cerberus."

"Who?"

"Cerberus. He's the Guardian of Hell."

I shake my head again. "I have no clue who you're talking about."

"Don't they teach the classics anymore?"

"You mean like Shakespeare?"

Yeats slaps his forehead with the palm of his hand and groans. "I'm talking about Greek and Roman mythology."

"No one cares about myths anymore," I say. "It's all math and science now. Blame it on the global economy, but literature plays second fiddle at my school."

"That's another thing I wouldn't mention to Hazel," he says before changing directions and leading me toward the Gates of Hell.

I pull back. "You are not taking me in there."

"Relax," he says, giving me a slight tug. "Let me add a little culture to your pathetic education." He stops short and looks up. "This is Cerberus."

Before me are four paws at the base of tree trunk legs. As I follow them up, I see a broad chest as wide as my mom's SUV. On top of that are not one but three heads, each with huge jowls. Saliva drips onto the floor in front of me and I take a step back to avoid it soaking my shoes. The three sets of teeth look razor sharp and I shudder at the sight.

"Oh, he won't bite," a heavyset woman with curly brown hair says with a laugh.

"How do you know?" I ask, stepping behind Yeats just to be safe.

She laughs again, one of those sounds that rise from the pit of the belly. Like Santa Claus, but without the "ho ho ho" business. "Because you aren't trying to escape," she looks at me a little closer. "You aren't, are you?"

Cerberus lets out a growl and my eyes widen with fear that that thing is going to eat me. Yeats is shaking his head and I realize I have a tight grip on the sleeve of his robe. The woman is doubling over, laughing and slapping her thighs with her hands.

What is wrong with her? And then Cerberus begins to howl and I swear the beast is *laughing* at me too.

"I'm sorry," the woman says, wiping tears from her eyes. "It was too easy."

Yeats pulls himself together. "RJ, this is Alexandra, Cerberus's handler. Al, RJ."

She sticks out her hand. "Pleased to meet you."

I look up at the dog, but it's not paying any attention to me at the moment. Slowly, I take her hand and give it a quick shake before pulling my arm back.

"So, Yeats, why are you slummin' it here in the trenches? I thought you winged types were afraid to get your whites dirty."

I can't believe she's talking to Yeats like that. Even more unbelievable is the grin on his face. "Now, Al, you know if it weren't for my kind, your job would be a whole lot harder."

"If you say so." She looks me up and down. "What's with your plus one? Why is she here? I can tell she hasn't been through Judgment yet."

How does she know that? Do I have a stamp on my forehead or something?

"We're trying to figure that out," Yeats answers candidly.

As if hearing an inaudible warning bell, Al and Cerberus turn at the same time. "Hey," she yells at a soul trying to sneak out of line. "You kill eight people and fail to show any remorse, you go in there. Try getting away again and Fluffy will be picking his teeth with your bones."

She doesn't wait to see if he gets back in line before turning back.

"Wait," I say. "How do souls have bones?"

Al lets out another cackle. "It's a figure of speech. Obviously Cerberus won't eat them."

"Oh," I say with relief.

"They'll spend eternity in his bowels."

"That's just gross."

Al laughs again. "So, Yeats, is she the soul everyone's talking about?" she asks as she wipes a tear from the corner of her eye.

"Yes," Yeats answers just as Hazel arrives.

After casting a curt nod in Al's direction, she asks, "What are you doing here? We're supposed to drop her off with Peter and talk to the Gatekeeper."

"She didn't know who Cerberus was," Yeats answers.

Hazel stares at him in disbelief. "How is that our problem?"

"Hey, Halo, relax," Al says. "We were just making small talk."

Hazel looks at her, not bothering to hide her disgust. "Make sure the mutt doesn't get his paw prints on my robe."

From deep in his throat, Cerberus issues a low warning growl, but Hazel ignores it. "We need to get her to Peter," she says to Yeats.

"Okay. We'll be right there," he answers.

As Hazel stalks off, Al gives a hiss. My Guardian pauses for an instant, her hands clenching into fists at her side, and then continues on.

"You shouldn't goad her like that," Yeats says with a shake of his head. "When will you two learn to get along?"

"Hey," Al answers, "I tried, but when Miss High and Mighty got promoted to Guardian, she couldn't get out of this place fast enough."

"Not everyone is made out for the Gates," Yeats says, patting Al's arm. "Especially the one that leads downstairs." Glancing at me, he adds, "I better deliver you to Peter."

"Tell the Bishop I said hello," Al says, and then looking in my directions adds, "Feel free to swing by and talk if you get bored hanging out with the goodie-goodies." As before, her head snaps back to the line of people waiting to enter the mouth of the cave. "Don't make me release the hound," her voice booms. "Trust me, you will be wishing for a fiery inferno when he gets done with you."

"Looks like you have your hands full," Yeats says, surveying the scene.

Al shakes her head in disgust. "Why is it when humans wage a war against each other in the name of religion, I end up dealing with a bunch of idiots?" She turns without saying goodbye and souls scramble out of her way.

"I like her," I say to Yeats as we make our way to where Hazel is waiting. "The dog, not so much, but Al's cool."

He laughs and I realize the sound doesn't hurt my head as much. "Alexandra has been Cerberus's handler since the beginning of time. She's seen everything and it's given her a sick sense of humor. Still, there are few who can see the best and the worst in a person like she can. Back before Peter arrived, she handled the flow of all incoming souls. Of course, there weren't as many people on Earth back then."

I look around at the multitude of souls, each speaking different languages and wearing clothes I've only seen on the news or on the National Geographic channel. "When Peter arrived, she got the short straw and now has to hang out at the mouth of Hell?"

Yeats nods. "Cerberus still had a job to do and without her controlling him, well, let's just say chaos would be redefined." We cross an invisible center line between Heaven and Hell and there is an immediate change in the energy. For one thing, people aren't trying to get out of line. Instead, it's like being in a mosh pit with people pushing you closer and closer to the stage. Yeats has no trouble navigating us through the crowd.

"Finally," Hazel huffs as we approach. She turns around and calls over the din of voices. "Peter, she's here."

"Why do I feel like Mom and Dad are dropping me off at the babysitter's house?" I mutter, feeling the eyes of everyone around us turn to look at me.

"Who is she?" I hear someone whisper.

Another voice asks, "Why does she get special treatment?"

"Is she an actress?" another soul groans. "Please tell me they don't get special treatment even in the Afterlife."

"Back of the line," somebody else calls and a chorus of applause follows. If they knew my story, I don't think they would be jealous.

"My dearly departed," an authoritative voice bellows from the front of the crowd. "You have not yet entered the Eternal Kingdom. Please do not make me send you back for a Judgment Review." The man motions for us to follow him to a side room next to the Gates. As we pass a scribe seated outside the door, he adds, "Let 'em in. This is a rambunctious lot. The sooner they acclimate, the better."

"Yes, Peter," the young man says.

This is the holy Saint Peter. He looks more like Ryan Reynolds's doppelgänger. Once the door closes I blurt out, "Can you really send them back for a review?"

His light brown eyes twinkle and it almost takes my breath away. "Technically, yes, but I've never done it. I just like to scare the rowdy ones straight before I send them in. Plus," he says in a conspiratorial tone, "did you see the looks on their faces? It was priceless."

Okay, Saint Peter being a hottie I can handle, but a prankster? This I didn't see coming. I feel a blush spread across my cheeks. Oh no. This is not happening. I simply can't be crushing on a guy who's been dead almost two thousand years.

"Uh, yeah," I finally manage. "Good one."

"Peter," Hazel says briskly, "Azrael wants RJ to stay here while we try to figure out how to handle her situation."

"That's cool."

She looks at him in surprise. Maybe she's expecting more of a fight or something. "Okay then, we'll be back as soon as possible." And with that, she and Yeats fly off, leaving me alone with Peter and nothing even remotely intelligent to say.

He's studying me, his eyes probing mine for something. When the scrutiny gets to me, I blurt out, "What?" Like I said, I'm at a loss for witty comebacks.

"I'm just trying to figure out what all the fuss is about."

I look at my feet. "What do you mean?"

He gives me a curious look before shaking his head. "A Tribunal hasn't been convened. There hasn't even been talk about getting them together."

"You mean recently?" I ask quietly.

"I mean ever." He opens the door and waits for me to walk through. "I hope you're worth it," he adds and breezes back into the Gates, which is now empty.

"Where'd everyone go?" I ask, looking around in surprise.

"Inside," is all he says before letting out a sharp whistle.

From the other side of the space, Cerberus bounds toward us, all three tongues hanging out of their respective mouths. The creature skids to a stop in front of us and Peter scratches him under each chin. "Hey there, boy. How ya doing?" The dog flops down, rolling on his back and exposing his belly. "Not now, buddy. I've got some business to settle with your handler."

"Handler? More like warden," Al says, trotting over carrying two wooden boards. She hands one to Peter who counts out forty paces and then drops it in place.

"Definitely," Peter says. With a snap of his fingers eight small bags appear at his feet. He grins at me. "Didn't know I could do that, did you?"

"Quit messing with the poor kid's head," Al chastises. She places her board opposite his.

I glance at the board closest to me and gasp. The Guardians of Heaven and Hell are getting ready to play a game.

Chapter 9

I watch in amazement as two opposing representatives of Heaven and Hell sling bags of corn at small holes in wooden boxes while a dog with three heads groans harmonically in his sleep. This has got to be a joke. I clear my throat. "This is what you do when no one's around?"

"We used to play chess," Al says, heaving her fourth bag. "But then some college kids in one of those states in the middle of America came up with this and we got hooked."

Peter laughs as the bag skims over the edge of the target. "Yeah, plus chess took forever. A guy can die of boredom waiting for her to make a move."

I start to ask when they think my Guardian Angels will be back, but Peter holds up his hand. "Shhh. I'm throwing here."

"RJ, what's your story?" Al asks, as she starts her turn. The bag spirals out of control and Peter has to dodge out of the way to avoid it.

He shoots her a warning glare. "Don't start this again."

"Sorry," she says, but even I can tell she's not. "Go on, RJ. Tell us your tale."

I step farther away from them just in case their friendly game evolves into an all-out war and then tell them everything, starting with the fortune-teller and ending at the point when I was dropped off with them.

"That sucks," Al says, ducking out of the way of one of Peter's throws. The toss is definitely not an accident. "Hey!" she yells at him. "If you make it personal, it's a forfeit. You know the rules." He doesn't act like he cares, but his next toss lands neatly in the hole. "Show off. Next time we double the distance," she mutters before turning back to me. "What did the Reaper say?"

"That there was nothing he could do."

"There isn't," Peter agrees. "Someone much more powerful would have to handle this mess, and I can't think of anyone who would want to deal with it."

"Why not?" I huff. "I thought this was the place miracles came from."

"It is, but it's not like you can just plop back into your life. In case you forgot, you died. By now people are probably preparing your body for burial, assuming you aren't being cremated."

The idea makes my stomach turn and I struggle against the wave of nausea that rolls over me, but Peter keeps going. "In order to have what you want to happen, the Fates would have to rewind the entire world."

"But I'm not asking for the entire world to be reset. Just my life. I deserve a second chance."

"You keep telling yourself that," Al says, lining up her next shot. "From what I hear, the ruling on your Afterlife isn't cut and dry. Personally, if it were me, I would hang out here until your number's up. You could play the winner."

I can feel the color draining from my face. Is she saying I might actually end up in Hell? I mean, I know I haven't always been nice to people, but still. Hell? There is no way I can let that happen. "It's not like I've done anything really bad," I stammer.

"Oh really?" she says, returning back to her game.

"Yeah, really," I argue, not ready for this conversation to end. "It's not like I killed anybody."

This time it's Peter who speaks. "What about that boy in your high school?"

"What are you talking about?" I say, looking between the two of them.

Neither of them is playing the game now. "The boy in your school. The one who killed himself."

"You mean the guy in the bathroom? How is that my fault? He did that to himself."

Peter's eyes are gentle but stern. "But why did he do it?"

"How should I know?" I balk, still angry that they're trying to pin someone else's choice on me. "It's not like we were friends."

"No," Al agrees.

I'm speechless. Is she really trying to pin a suicide on me?

"In all fairness," Peter adds, "it wasn't just her."

"Right," Al says, stretching out the word. "Her *friends*. The difference is they're mean, self-centered people."

"Oh, and why do they get an excuse and I don't?" I ask, gritting my teeth.

"Because you're better than they are," Peter answers. "You were meant for so much more than you became."

Okay, now I'm getting tired of riddles and lectures. "Whatever," I say and cross my arms over my chest. I really wish Yeats and Hazel would hurry up.

With a sigh, Peter sits down on the ground and motions for me to do the same. "Everyone has a plan before them. They have a purpose. Each choice they make keeps them on their path or leads them off course."

"Okay," I say, still not understanding what he's trying to say.

"Well, you were pretty far off the path. In fact, you weren't even in the same forest you started in."

My shoulders drop. "But I still had my whole life in front of me. Maybe I would've changed."

"Maybe," he admits. "But for the first seventeen years you put yourself before others. You were more interested in being popular than being a good person."

"People can be both," I argue.

He shrugs. Wow. There is nothing like having Saint Peter insinuate that you suck as a human being.

"I could change," I mutter. "If I had more time, I could change."

"Yeah, or," Al adds, standing over us, "you could live out the rest of your allocated life, ring in a new millennium, and still arrive here with a first-class ticket to my line. It's not my call, but I'm not sure it's worth the risk."

"Al," Peter says sharply.

"What?" she snaps back. "It's my opinion. Even now, after everything she's seen, it's still all about her. People can change, but they have to want to. I don't think she has the desire."

Without warning, a bell rings. Peter makes a quick hand gesture and the boards dissolve into the floor, taking the corn bags with them. Cerberus is on his feet shaking his massive heads. The drool spreads several feet in every direction. Al gives a sharp whistle and in an instant Cerberus is at her side and ready for business.

"I could be better," I say to Peter, my eyes pleading for him to believe me.

"Hey, you're talking to the guy who denied his best friend not once but three times. I believe you can change. But Al's right. What you're asking for has never been done. The odds aren't in your favor, kid."

I watch the main doors swing open as souls begin to pour into the room. As the last one makes her way into the crowd, Hazel and Yeats swoop over them, dropping gracefully on either side of me.

Yeats looks at Peter and shakes his head. "The Tribunal has been summoned."

Before I can respond, Yeats and Hazel each take me by an arm and we shoot into the air on the way to my moment of truth.

"Good luck," I hear Al call over the rush of wind. "You're going to need it."

And deep down, I know she's right.

$\mathcal{C}hapter$ 10

Just about the time I get comfortable with flying, we're landing softly in front of a stone building with tall pillars supporting a steep roof. Since my arrival in the Afterlife, I've been in rooms of varying degrees of sumptuousness, but this is the first time I've seen an actual building.

"Wow," I say quietly. "It looks like the Supreme Court, only bigger."

"About this hearing," Hazel says, ignoring me, "if I were you, I wouldn't talk unless asked a question."

I stop her. "Don't worry. Peter and Al did a pretty good job of making it clear how big a deal this is."

"That wasn't their job," she mutters before asking, "What exactly did they say?"

Not wanting to rehash the breakdown of my apparently worthless life, I shrug off her question. "Just that it's going to be a hard sell."

Yeats clears his throat. "The Tribunal is made up of three angels. Azbaugh is one of the higher-ranking Angels of Judgment and he'll be running the show. Marmaroth is one of the Fates. He has the power to alter the course of time. The third member of the panel is Shepard, an Angel of Repentance. The three of them will have the ultimate authority over your past and future."

"It sure sounds like a trial to me," I remark.

"It is," Hazel answers quickly.

Great. Just great. I accidentally get collected by a Grim Reaper and end up the criminal. Could this get anymore unfair?

"Don't I get a lawyer?" I ask, half joking.

"Actually," Hazel answers, "you do. The angel Salathiel will speak on your behalf."

"Salathiel has a soft spot for hopeless causes," Yeats adds. "He'll put up a fight."

It's official. Everyone thinks my situation is hopeless.

"Who's going to argue that I be left to rot here until the end of my life?" I ask.

"Zachriel, an Angel of Memories," Yeats answers.

"Angel of Memories?"

This time it's Hazel who answers. "He has the ability to search through every memory that has ever been had. When he speaks, everyone, and I mean everyone, listens."

"He also has the gift of sight," Yeats adds.

"Huh?"

"It means he can see some aspects of the future. But he's not as accurate as the Akashic Records," Hazel adds impatiently.

Is that supposed to reassure me? Because it doesn't. Not even a little. My shoulders sag. "Azrael also said something about Death Himself?"

Again my two Guardians exchange a cryptic glance.

"Stop it," I demand. "Stop doing that thing where you look at each other like you're keeping a secret from me. I'm sick of it. I'm sick of people making me feel bad for something that's not my fault."

There are no sounds once the echoes of my words fade away. Yeats breaks the silence. "I would try to avoid doing that in front of the Tribunal."

"I'll keep that in mind," I say, taking in a deep breath. "So is he here?"

"Who?" Yeats asks.

"Death Himself."

"No, but I'm sure he will be." Hazel averts her gaze, and her unwillingness to look me in the eye does not inspire confidence.

"What about Gideon?" I ask in a panic. "He can tell them what happened."

Yeats shakes his head. "He's just a Reaper. The Tribunal won't listen to anyone except Death Himself."

"Who isn't here," I remind him. My knees buckle, and Yeats reaches down to catch my elbow.

"I'm so screwed," I moan.

"It doesn't look good," Hazel agrees.

My head snaps up at her. "I thought you were supposed to be my Guardian Angel. Aren't you on my side?"

"I am on your side. I just don't want you to get your hopes up when the odds are stacked against you."

"Because I'm just a spoiled princess who doesn't care about anyone but myself. Isn't that what you said earlier?" I mutter with a huff. "Why can't anyone see that I'm the victim here?"

Hazel surprises me by wrapping her arm around my shoulders. "I know how good you can be. I've watched you every day of your life. But what you can do and what you've done aren't the same. Not to mention, this is uncharted territory. You need to be ready to defend your life."

I groan. "How can I fight when everything is on the Tribunal's terms?"

"I'm sure Salathiel has a plan," she says with a tired smile.

Before anyone can say anything more, the door at the top of the stairs creaks open.

"Enter," a voice calls. "Enter into the Judgment Hall, Rowena Joy Jones. The Tribunal is waiting."

I lean over to Yeats. "Where's the guy who's going to represent me?"

He nods toward the open door. "In there."

I close my eyes. "I can do this," I whisper to myself. When my nerves settle, I add, "Let's go." Yeats and Hazel exchange another look. "What?"

"We can't go in," Yeats says, his wings hanging a little lower.

"Why not?" I demand.

"We are Guardians," Hazel says. "We cannot enter the Hall unless the Tribunal requests our presence."

I think I'm going to throw up. "So I'm on my own?"

She nods. "Salathiel will take care of you. You can trust him."

I raise a foot and take my first steps toward the looming entryway. My legs feel like they're made of lead. When I reach the top and turn around, Yeats and Hazel are gone. Just like that. I am alone.

"If I ever see that gypsy again, I'll kill her," I mutter.

"Oh, I wouldn't worry about her," someone says. I look up and see another angel. This one has long, stringy blond hair, like a surfer who's been in the water all day.

"Are you Salathiel?" I ask, tentatively.

He nods. "You can call me Sal. It's easier to say. Now, let's you and I have a chat, shall we? There's a lot to go over if we're going to rewrite your history."

I smile at his optimism, even though I know he's forcing it. "Sure. Should I start at the beginning?"

He looks at me with surprise. "Is there anywhere else to start?"

Once more, I tell my story. And like Azrael, he truly listens to everything I say.

"Well," he says when I finish, "it's not going to be easy, but I think we can do this. However, I have to know one thing before we proceed."

"What?"

"What are you willing to risk to go back?"

Willing to risk? Is he crazy? I have nothing left. I'm dead. "Anything," I say to him.

He holds my gaze for a long while. "Are you sure?"

No, but I'm not backing down. I've come too far to stop. I give him a swift nod before saying, "Yes."

He smiles. "Good. Because that's the only way you have a shot." And with that, he walks swiftly out the room and down the hall, leaving me standing alone. "You coming?" he calls back. "The Tribunal won't like it if we're late."

While his voice is light and cheerful, I have no doubt that the consequences of crossing the Tribunal will be severe. I spring into action and follow him down the hall and into the unknown. Behind me, the doors slam shut.

Chapter 11

The Tribunal Room is set up to look like a courtroom. Two tables face a large platform desk, and there is a galley where spectators can watch the proceedings. The seats of the gallery are empty, and I breathe a sigh of relief. It's nerve-racking enough to defend why I should get back the life that someone stole from me, but to do so in front of a crowd would probably kill me. That is, if I weren't already dead.

"We sit here," Sal says, directing me to one of the tables. My hands are shaking as I pull out the chair, and Sal gives me a wide, open smile. "Take a moment to calm yourself. The Tribunal would never have been convened if Azrael didn't see some merit in your situation."

The flutter of wings and swoosh of wind alerts me that we're no longer alone.

"Salathiel," the new arrival says. I spin around to find an angel with golden hair that reminds me of the sunset on a warm summer night.

A flash of irritation fires up in Sal's eyes. "Zachriel," he says curtly.

I give Sal a questioning look and he pulls me up by the elbow and leads me to a door. Once inside the small room, he waits until the door latches behind us before asking, "What did Hazel tell you about Zachriel?"

"Just that he can access memories," I say with a shrug.

He nods. "He'll use them against you if he can."

"How?" I ask. Why is it that almost everyone opposes me getting every single second of life that I had coming to me?

"You can never tell, but rest assured, he will. Be ready. No secret is safe with him around." He cocks his head to the side. "We better go."

I dutifully follow him, wondering if there is any chance I could run back to the terminal and stow away on the train back to the mortal plane. Of course, there is one fatal flaw in my plan. I have no idea how to find my way back to the terminal.

"The Tribunal will convene momentarily to discuss the matter of Rowena Joy Jones," a voice bellows. I look around for speakers or some other source for the sound but see none.

"Come on," Sal says through a comforting smile. With a sigh of resignation, I follow him back to our table. Zachriel is sitting in his chair, eyes shut and hands resting gently in his lap.

No sooner are we in our seats than the thunder of flapping wings forces me to cover my ears. The three angels Yeats warned me about land on the platform. Talk about making an entrance.

Without so much as a hello, the angel in the middle speaks. "We have been summoned by Azrael to conclude the matter surrounding this human's complaint."

Wait a minute. How can they conclude something before it begins? I look at Sal, but his eyes are fixed on the three authoritative figures.

"We will hear from Salathiel first." The angel doing all the talking must be Azbaugh. He has that bored yet hostile look I use when I have to do something I don't want to do. Plus, he looks judgmental and bossy. "You will present the situation as you know it. We will ask questions. Zachriel will close with his recommendation as to why the request to return this girl to her life should or should not be granted. Then we will make our decision."

Maybe it's my imagination but did he just emphasize *should not?*

"Wait," I say, leaning forward in my seat. "Don't I get to speak?" I mean the words for Sal, but the last part comes out a little louder than intended.

Sal puts a hand on my arm and clamps down hard. I turn toward him and there's this expression on his face that's a mixture of irritation and fear. "Quiet," he hisses.

Before I can say anything, Azbaugh's voice explodes across the empty room. "You will only speak when spoken to. Salathiel should have already explained this to you." He looks down his nose at me, and I feel the hairs on the back of my neck stand up.

When I glance back at Sal, he's looking straight ahead, unwilling or maybe unable to talk or even look at me.

"Furthermore," Azbaugh continues, "you will show respect while you are before us. We are not an elevated human spirit or a Greek dog sitter. We are angels of the highest orders. Make no mistake. I do not care whether your request is granted or not. I care only that order is restored. Do I make myself clear?"

I'm so mad and scared that I can't think let alone speak. Sal nudges me and the connection with another being jolts me back into the moment. "Crystal," I mumble.

"What do rocks have to do with anything?" Azbaugh says as his eyes narrow.

"I believe she means to say that she understands you, my Brother," one of the other angels intercedes.

Azbaugh looks at me and I can feel the weight of his stare. "Thank you, Shepard." To me he says, "Is that what you meant?"

I clear my throat, sit up a little straighter, look him in the eye, and say, "Yes, I understand."

He looks satisfied with himself. "Good. Now, Salathiel, are you prepared to present this human's case?" Azbaugh doesn't even try to hide his disdain for me. What? Did I make him miss a golf date? How am I going to get a fair trial when this guy obviously has it out for me?

I turn my attention to Sal as he explains my circumstances, including the collection of my soul and the admission of error by Gideon, as well as noting the reference of my long lifeline in the Akashic Records. He also points out how I have been mostly cooperative since my arrival and how all I'm looking for is a chance to finish out my life. His plea is passionate and by the end, I want to stand up and applaud, but of course, with the harsh eyes of Azbaugh cutting through me, I don't move a muscle.

"Zachriel," Azbaugh says, turning his attention to the other table. "What do you have to say on the matter?"

Zachriel takes his time standing. He stares at me with such intensity that it feels like he's peering into the deepest part of my essence. I shift in my seat, but his eyes never stray from my face. Then he looks away.

"I have seen her actions through her eyes. She is an average girl with little to no special aptitude."

Um, what? Never in my entire life have I been called average. And I have plenty of aptitude. Sal gives me a slight shake of the head and I sit back in my chair, biting my lip. I can't believe they're talking about me and I have no opportunity for rebuttal. And then a thought occurs to me. Is this what it's like to be on the receiving end of one of my tirades?

Zachriel continues: "In her mind, she knows she has done certain things that can never be redeemed, no matter how long she lives on Earth. She is shockingly callous in her treatment of others and easily manipulated by those she considers to be her friends."

The person he's describing sounds weak and pathetic. There's no way he's talking about me. And why doesn't he mention any of the good things I've done?

"She has accomplished some marginal success in her life," he adds. "There are acts of charity and moments where she seems on the verge of moving toward the path she's meant to be on."

Well, that's something.

And then he drops the bomb. "But those moments are few and far between. In my opinion, to recast the fate of the world for this soul would be a waste of time. There is no evidence to indicate that she would in fact make any changes in her life or that her continued presence among the living would make for a better society."

Is he calling me a waste of space?

"And so your recommendation would be?" Azbaugh probes.

He dips his head slightly, closing his eyes again. And then he looks directly at me. In a voice that is void of any emotion he says, "The risk of this request is too great while the benefit is minimal at best. I recommend the soul remain hidden in the Afterlife until the time and date of her Akashic death."

My mouth drops open. When I recover, I lean over and whisper to Sal, "Is he suggesting that I wait around here until whatever date I'm supposed to die in the future? Because that's bull—"

Sal cuts me off with a look that actually renders me speechless. "Would you please shut up?"

I want to reply, to tell him no, but I don't. Instead, I turn my head forward and watch as my future is debated like I'm not even in the room.

Azbaugh looks to his left. "What say you, Marmaroth?"

His counterpart on the Tribunal nods his head. "While I agree this is a grievous error made on the part of the Grim Reaper, as it will be I who must negotiate the hands of time to return this girl to the moment of her accidental death, I must carefully weigh her wants against the needs of the many. I have several reservations."

I sink deeper into my chair. I don't think things can get any worse.

"Were we to agree to her request, countless things, both good and bad, must be undone," Marmaroth continues. "Her return to the world will alter peace treaties and wars alike. Though her Akashic Record indicates time of death well into the future, the world is moving on without her. I cannot, in good consciousness, recommend a reversal of her fate without some indication that it will have a positive benefit on the human race as a whole."

I was wrong. It just got worse.

"Shepard?" Azbaugh says to the third member of the Tribunal. "What are your thoughts on the matter before us?"

There is compassion in the eyes of this angel and he looks directly at me when he responds. "I do not think this child is beyond salvation. Her life and perspective have been greatly altered by her experiences in the Afterlife. I would hate to deprive the world of a useful and powerful witness to the acts of mercy that the Creator is capable of."

I see Marmaroth nod thoughtfully and a slim bit of hope this might actually work in my favor flickers inside me. I sit up, meeting Shepard's eyes, begging him to say yes. He smiles at me and warmth spreads through my body.

That is, until Azbaugh asks, "This is all well indeed, but we have seen time and time before how the feeble human mind is incapable of holding on to the experiences they encounter beyond the mortal plane. How are we to know that, should she be returned, her time here will feel like nothing more than a dream to her?"

"Perhaps we can ask the muses to weave a pattern into her life that will keep these moments fresh in her subconscious," Sal suggests. "If they can inspire writers to create masterpieces from words and sculptors to carve beauty from stone, surely this is not outside their capabilities?"

"The fundamental flaw in this idea is that it still weighs heavily on this girl. She has already shown poor judgment throughout her life," Zachriel interjects.

I really don't like that guy. Not as much as I hate Azbaugh, but he's running a close second.

Speaking of my tormentor, Azbaugh raises a hand for order. "While you have not been officially recognized to address this Tribunal, you raise a valid point." He turns to Sal. "What say you in response?"

The look of surprise on Sal's face does not fill me with confidence. "I think," he begins and then stops. "Well, you are right in the fact that the mind is feeble."

I'm screwed.

"But you are wrong in the idea that there is no chance of redemption. To return to Shepard's analogy of the sculptor, this girl is not the finished piece, but rather the block of stone waiting for the rough edges to be chipped away and sanded to reveal her true potential."

Okay, maybe I'm not screwed. Sal is on a roll.

"Zachriel's suggestion that her past will dictate her future is unfair and lacks little evidence. In fact, if we were to pull up twenty random lives, I'm sure we would find several who were able to overcome their early beginnings to become civic leaders and moral compasses for the human race. Who is to say this girl does not possess that quality?"

"If you take another twenty lives," Azbaugh responds, "I'm sure you will also find those who were given a life of privilege and became absolutely nothing. They became simply a drain on everyone around them."

Sal squares his shoulders. I can see he's trying to get the courage to say something important. Come on, Sal. We're dying here.

And then he does something that might shock him more than it does me. He challenges Azbaugh. "Your pessimism in the human race is clouding your view of what is right and just. This soul has been, by all accounts, robbed of any chance of betterment. She was made to be a sacrifice by someone gifted with sight and must now bear a cross that was not hers in the first place. To not send her back would deny her mercy."

I sit in awe of my champion, but only for a moment.

"Mercy," Azbaugh roars, "is not the matter before this court! This is about the impact her whimsical request will warrant and whether the risk of altering the past is worth it. Mercy is only a factor once a decision has been rendered. Now, unless there are any further comments *from the Tribunal*, we will vote."

And with that, my champion sits down in defeat. Unable to look at me, he waits for the verdict.

"Marmaroth?" Azbaugh asks. "What is your decision?"

He shakes his head. "I cannot, in good faith, agree to the unknown and countless changes that the world will endure if we agree to the alteration of this girl's fate, no matter how much I would like to see her have another chance. I vote no."

Azbaugh nods in approval. "Shepard?"

The angel is quick to the point. "By denying her a chance at redemption, we deny her existence. I vote yes. We should send her back, no matter the cost, because it is right and just."

I can't be sure, but I think Azbaugh rolls his eyes. When he looks at me, however, they are steady and empty. "As this Tribunal has voted in a tie, it is my job to decide your fate. While I do not doubt the infallibility of the Akashic Records, I must conclude this experience occurred for a reason and so I must—"

I can't sit still any longer while these angels shred my very existence. If Sal isn't going to speak up for me then I have nothing left to lose. Pushing my chair back so fast it clanks to the floor, I shout, "Stop it! This isn't fair, and you know it. You can't erase my future because you don't think my past was good enough." Sal is standing at my side, trying to pull me back, but I shake him off. Some defender of the underdog he turns out to be. "You can't determine I'm unworthy to exist after just five minutes."

"Silence!" Azbaugh thunders and a slight movement of his wings raises him a tad higher than the others. "I have made my decision. There is nothing more you can say in this matter. Your petty pleading is insulting."

Just as Azbaugh is about to deliver what is undoubtedly my condemnation, the doors behind us open. Light shines in behind a broad-shouldered being that looks as much like an angel as I do. His hair is brown with loose curls that hang over the tips of his ears and his eyes, which are scanning the room, are so dark they look black. But his hair, eyes, and obvious lack of wings aren't what make him stand out. No, it's the bright Hawaiian shirt and Bermuda shorts he's wearing that catch my attention.

Azbaugh watches him stride to the front of the room, stopping a few feet before the bench. No one has to tell me that there's no love lost between these two. The Angel of Judgment looks down at the new arrival with contempt but his intimidation is returned with palpable arrogance. Who is this guy?

"I believe I have the right to say something, seeing as how it was my Reaper who started this whole mess."

And then it hits me.

This is Death Himself.

Chapter 12

"Nice of you to join us," Azbaugh says with venomous disdain.

Death Himself is undeterred by the angel's open hostility. "Life in the death business doesn't run by a timetable. So, where were we?" Death Himself asks before he produces a black leather recliner out of thin air and drops down into it, flipping the footrest up and leaning back. I half expect him to snap a tub of popcorn into his lap like he's settling in to watch a movie.

Azbaugh doesn't look happy with Death Himself's theatrics. "*We* were about to deliver our verdict. So if you don't mind—"

"Actually, I do mind," Death Himself says. "You see, it's my department that has been called into question, and after reviewing the evidence, I have concluded that, in order to maintain the integrity of my Reapers, RJ should be returned to her natural place in time."

"That is not your decision," Azbaugh challenges. "We have been charged with this matter and it is in our opinion that the costs far outweigh the remote chance that Ms. Jones might actually amount to something of importance."

Death Himself continues, undeterred. "I don't answer to you, and you don't rule over death. That is my jurisdiction."

Azbaugh looks like he isn't about to give up authority over my life without a fight. "While that may be true, you do not have the power to interfere with the stream of time without our approval."

A slow smile spreads across Death Himself's face. "Well, then, it seems we are at an impasse."

Azbaugh glares from Death Himself to me and back to Death Himself. A chill runs through me and I get the feeling he could walk into a pen of puppies and start kicking without any remorse.

"And just what do you propose?" Azbaugh asks, his teeth grinding together. It sounds like nails on a chalkboard multiplied by ninety.

"A test," Death Himself suggests. "One that will allow RJ to set her life back on the path she was meant to be on."

"I'm listening," Azbaugh replies, but the way his eyes narrow tells me he couldn't care less about the proposition.

"A guide will be assigned to take her back to a moment in her life when she made the choice to be less than she was meant to be. Assuming she makes the right choice, the timeline will be reset and RJ will return to the land of the living."

Azbaugh shakes his head. "Just because she makes one change doesn't mean she's learned anything."

"No," Death Himself agrees, "but it will set her life on a different course."

"I'm not convinced," Marmaroth interjects. "Yes, her life will change, but life is a series of decisions that define us. One change when she is young can be nullified by an action when she's older."

Azbaugh nods in agreement. "This is a foolish proposition meant to disrupt this hearing. I suggest—"

Marmaroth interrupts. "Perhaps five points spread throughout her life span would be more sufficient. Since each moment will ultimately build on the previous one, we can be assured that a solid foundation has been laid out for a worthy life."

Having people talk about me like I'm not in the room is humiliating. Risking the wrath of Azbaugh, I speak up. "Can I say something?"

"No," Azbaugh says. At the same time, Death Himself answers, "Yes."

The two stare each other down until Azbaugh finally relents. "What?" he snaps.

Wringing my hands together, I ask, "Was I really that horrible? I mean, if I had lived the long life I was supposed to have, was I going to turn out to be a horrible person? Because the way you talk about me, you'd think I was destined to be a serial killer."

The Tribunal is quiet, as is Zachriel. Even Sal avoids my eyes.

"You're kidding," I say. "I'm a criminal?"

Death Himself laughs and he continues doing so until tears roll down his cheeks.

"I really don't think I said anything funny," I say with a huff.

He shakes his mane of hair and I can smell the salt water and sand perfuming the air. "It's not you, really. I just love it when the angels are rendered speechless." He wipes his eyes and stands, walking to face me across the table. He kneels down and looks me in the eyes. "They aren't speaking because they don't know. When Gideon collected your soul, your Akashic Records became undecipherable. The only reason Hazel knew your actual death date was because of her status as your Guardian Angel. The Tribunal is basing their decision on nothing more than a lot of what ifs."

"Isn't there anything you can do?" I ask.

He shakes his head. "Not really." I feel the blood drain from my face. "On the bright side," he adds, "since I have decided to be a part of this process, they can't condemn you without my agreement. It's our version of checks and balances."

Well, that's a relief. A spark of hope is growing again.

He smiles and his eyes crinkle with laugh lines. "Now, let me finish this negotiation and then we'll get you out of here, alright?"

I take a deep breath. "Okay." I really hope he knows what he's doing.

He winks and then stands to face the jury of angels. "Five points over seventeen years seems excessive. It's not like we have eternity to make the final decision. Well, we do, but I'm sure you have other matters to tend to. Besides, there's a swell heading for the Banzai Pipeline. I'd hate to miss those waves. I propose we split the difference. Three points of my choosing based on the moments where RJ's life veered too far off course."

Hold up. Is Death Himself making this deal because he would rather be surfing? Please tell me someone is messing with me and an actor with a camera is going to come out and yell, "Gotcha." Needless to say, no actor appears and I don't see any cameras.

What I do see is Shepard's smiling face and I swear the entire room lights up. "I think this is an excellent plan. The question is not whether Ms. Jones has been treated in an unjust manner, but rather if her character is worthy of such unprecedented action."

"I still don't like it," Marmaroth says. "Even though she would only be slipping into the moment, this interaction will change the course of the future."

"That's the point, isn't it?" Death Himself argues. "Those changes should answer your concerns about whether she will retain the lessons she learns. When she is sent back permanently, I'm sure Zachriel can ensure her old memories are replaced by the new ones. She will become the person created by those changes in her past."

"She still might relapse," Azbaugh points out. "There's no guarantee."

Death Himself groans. "The fundamental flaw of free will. Don't blame me. That's the Big Guy's thing. You should bring it up with Him. I'm sure He would love to debate the merit of this design feature one more time."

Zachriel stands, obviously ready to move on. "Actually," he says in an even voice. "If the memories are uniquely hers and the impacts of her actions are built in to her character, it is unlikely that a complete relapse will ever occur. I would, however, caution the Tribunal about allowing Death Himself to pick the times without any parameters. He is known for being quite conniving."

Death Himself grins and shrugs. "He's right."

The thought of the Tribunal being in charge of this wager fills me with dread. Shouldn't Death Himself try to put up a better fight? Or is he worried about missing the big waves?

"Fine," Azbaugh says. "How would you suggest we frame the parameters?"

"Four stipulations. First, the events must take place in chronological order. Second, at least one of the moments must occur during the first nine years of life. Third, each moment must be a part of the new life stream and not the old. Finally, I would require that each event be at least six months apart."

"Is that all?" Death Himself asks.

Absently, I twist Sandy's ring around my finger. I feel comforted, like she's with me or at least cheering me on from the Lobby. Death Himself looks a little too confident—as if he's winning a game no one else knows they're playing. I really hope he's on my team and not just using me as some pawn.

Zachriel looks pensive. He's probably wondering if he's walking into a trap. "Yes," he says, drawing the word out. "I believe those parameters will allow Death Himself the flexibility to adequately test the girl without giving him free reign to manipulate the experiment."

The Tribunal exchanges a series of glances. Finally, Azbaugh asks, "Are there any objections to this test?"

No one speaks. I start to clap, but Sal lays a hand on my shoulder and shakes his head. I sit back.

"I have a few stipulations of my own," Azbaugh states. "If, at any time, the girl fails to correct her life trajectory, the test will end and she will remain in the Lobby, or wherever Azrael wants to put her, until such time that the Akashic Records indicate her human death."

"I have no objection," Death Himself says.

I do. Is he saying that if I don't satisfy their expectations, I could actually spend who knows how long with all those catatonic souls?

"In case anyone wonders, I don't like this," I whisper, hoping he will hear me. He doesn't or at least he pretends not to.

"RJ will remain in my custody during the testing period. I would hate to burden anyone further," Death Himself adds, feigning humility. "I will also arrange for the guides that will accompany her on each of the three tests."

"She will, at no point, be left unaccompanied," Azbaugh insists.

Death Himself gives a quick nod. "You have my word."

"And no one speaks to any of the souls or beings unfamiliar with this situation," Azbaugh adds, his warning loud and clear. "I reserve the right to end this test should *any* of the terms be violated."

A gag order? Are you kidding me? Saint Peter said everyone was talking about me already. There's no way the news of my situation is going to fade into the clouds.

"Do we have a deal?" Death Himself says, boredom slipping in between each word. I notice he doesn't actually agree to the condition.

"I'm going to regret this," Azbaugh says. "But yes, we have a deal."

I jump out of my chair and this time, Sal doesn't even try to hold me back. I race around the table and throw my arms around Death Himself, who seems completely unprepared and unmoved.

"I'm sorry," I say breathlessly. "I'd almost given up, and then you came and forced them to give me a chance. Thank you so much."

He eases himself from my grasp and takes my elbow, leading me away from the disapproving trio. "Don't thank me yet, sweetheart. This deal may sound like a lifeline, but let me assure you, it isn't. In fact, I'm pretty sure there will come a time when being stuck in the Lobby will seem like a vacation."

"Not likely," I scoff.

He pushes open the large doors that lead to the steps. Once we're outside, he stops, spins me around, and says, "You're pretty arrogant for someone who was about ten seconds away from never feeling the grass beneath your feet or the sun on your face again. There are a lot of things in this situation I don't control, so you better take it seriously."

"Like what?" I ask.

He gives me a questioning look.

"What can't you control?" I ask again.

"I may be able to pick the moments, but the Fates decide when you enter into the action."

"So?"

"The Fates take their direction from Marmaroth."

"Yeah, but I thought he was on board?" I say as desperation begins to expand in my stomach.

"That doesn't mean he wants you to succeed. The sooner you fail, the less work he has to do to fix this mess."

"Oh." I know Marmaroth wasn't excited about me going back to my life, but the idea that he would set me up to fail knocks my confidence to the gutter.

"It's not too late," he says, giving me a hard look. "You can still decide to wait until they call your name in the Lobby. No one would blame you if you did. It's the easy way out."

I think about his suggestion. I could go back to the Lobby and hang out with Sandy, playing pranks on the new arrivals. But then I will never see my mom or dad again. I would never know what it was like to love someone so deeply that I'm willing to wait for him for eternity. I'm not ready to be dead.

"No," I say with resolve. "I may be a lot of those things the Tribunal said about me, but I'm not a quitter. Whatever Marmaroth throws at me, I can handle."

Death Himself flashes me a grin of approval. "Well, alright then. Let's go change your future, shall we?"

Chapter 13

With a flick of his wrist and a snap of his fingers, Death Himself transports us to his domain.

We stop in front of a building that looks more like a fraternity house than the global hub for all Grim Reaper activities. "Here we are, home sweet home," he says, leading me up the stairs and through the door.

Once inside, I see the entire first floor is one giant library. And it definitely doesn't smell like a frat house—thankfully. It smells like a wood burning stove.

"You live here?" I ask, glancing around. Clusters of Reapers are sitting together at huge wooden tables, their heads bent over thick silver binders.

"More or less."

I look over the shoulder of a nearby figure and see a bio page complete with mug shot. Is this how they know who their mark is? Maybe Gideon should have done a little more homework. I turn to ask where my file is, but Death Himself is already halfway down the hall.

He moves like the wind and I practically have to sprint to catch up with him. "Slow down," I plead.

"Can't. Hitting Pipe this afternoon, remember?"

Wait. He was serious. Death Himself is a surfer? "You're going to catch a wave at a time like this?"

He ignores me, and I have no choice but to follow him down a narrow hallway and into an office with a large stone fireplace.

"Do you get cold?" I ask in surprise at the roaring blaze that's built up inside.

"Nope." For all his eloquent words in front of the Tribunal, Death Himself really doesn't talk much.

"So, what happens now?" I ask, flipping through a stack of files on a table.

He pulls down a gold binder from a high shelf and flips it open, ignoring me. After a few minutes, he turns toward the fire, picks up a stone, and whispers something over it before chucking it into the flame.

"Is that the fires of Hell people are always talking about?" I ask, peering over his shoulder to get a better look. "It's not that impressive."

He spins around, giving me an annoyed look. "Do you ever stop talking?"

I want to tell him I would if someone would clue me in on the plan, assuming there is one, but a knock at the door stops me.

"Come in," Death Himself says.

A moment later, Gideon is standing in front of the desk.

"Is it all arranged?" Gideon asks, ignoring my slight wave.

Death Himself nods. "It went off just as we planned."

"How many interventions do we have to set up?"

"Three."

Gideon looks impressed. "That's all?"

Death Himself glances up with a cocky smirk. "They started out with five, but Zachriel worked his magic and got them down to three."

"He must have gotten my message," Gideon says. "I had to go through back channels to avoid Azbaugh's spies. I was afraid it wouldn't reach him before the Tribunal convened. Did he get the terms we wanted?"

My jaw drops. They set me up.

"Of course."

"And Marmaroth?"

"He's the same old son of a . . ." Death Himself stops talking and looks at me before adding, ". . . gun he's always been. I swear, for angels who have nothing to do all day, they sure get all high and mighty when you give them the slightest bit of power."

"What about Shep?"

"Perfect as always. In fact, the only one who almost blew the whole plan out of the water was Sal. I thought you said he would be able to handle his role."

Gideon straightens his shoulder against his boss's rebuff. "I said he would be able to represent her and keep his mouth shut when you showed up. The guy can't act to save his wings."

"Wait a minute," I say, interrupting the verbal ping-pong match. "Are you saying you wanted me to go in front of the Tribunal? That you planned this?"

"Look who just showed up to the party, Gideon," Death Himself says, sarcasm hanging on each word. "Of course. The only way to beat the system is from the inside."

"But why?"

"Because you couldn't keep your big mouth shut. Since your arrival, you've been running all over the Afterlife boo-hooing about your poor death—about how Gideon collected your soul by accident—and that all you want to do is go home. Do you have any idea how much trouble you've been causing us, Dorothy?"

"RJ," I say instinctively.

Death Himself snaps his fingers. A book appears in front of him and he shoves it toward me. "Read this. Maybe it will keep you quiet for a minute."

"*The Wonderful Wizard of Oz*," I read aloud before looking up. What's he trying to say? It wasn't a natural disaster that sent me here. It was a gypsy.

"My life isn't a novel," I pout.

"Or maybe it won't keep you quiet," Death Himself says in a low growl.

His latest jab at my situation makes me miss Sandy. At least she saw me as something more than a problem. I twist her ring on my finger and wonder if she still remembers why she's waiting in the Lobby.

When I glance up, Death Himself looks like his head is going to explode. Apparently he doesn't like to be ignored. Guess he knows how I feel now. Gideon pipes up to defuse the situation. "Relax, boss. We got this."

"But how did you get those angels to support me if they didn't believe in my case?" I ask, pushing around Gideon so I can look at Death Himself.

He laughs. "Do you really think they care? I hate to be the one to burst your bubble, but they don't." A grin spreads across his face. "Huh. Turns out I didn't hate bursting it. You want to know why? Because up here, favors are currency and you're costing me a fortune. Now, if you're done bugging me, I have to wrangle up your guides who are going to cost me even more. Trust me. I cannot wait to see you waltzing around Earth. Better there than here."

"Why don't I take RJ and fill her in on how this is going to work?" Gideon says, grabbing my arm and practically yanking me out of Death Himself's sight.

"Good idea," Death Himself says, turning his back on us.

"Come on," Gideon hisses as he pushes me through the door. When we're out of earshot he says, "I'm starting to wonder if there is something seriously wrong with you."

"I thought he cared about what was happening with me," I answer, and even to my ears, the words sound lame.

Gideon's eyebrows shoot up in surprise. "You thought Death Himself, the one who answers only to Azrael, would give an ounce of interest in you compared to the billions of souls he watches over every day?"

Well, when you put it that way . . .

But Gideon isn't done. "You can't possibly be that narcissistic." I feel tears welling up in my eyes but he doesn't seem to notice. Or maybe he doesn't care, because he just keeps talking, his voice getting louder and louder. "I told you I would figure this out, didn't I? I told you to keep your head low and not to make a scene."

"Yeah, and then you left me," I snap back. "What was I supposed to do?"

"Not run your mouth off to anyone in the Afterlife who can hear."

Okay, he has a point. "If he's so mad at me, why did he show up to my defense?" I ask.

My question is greeted with Gideon's howling laugh. "That has nothing to do with your situation."

"Of course it does," I argue.

"You are delusional. He isn't trying to save you. He's trying to save me."

I step back in shock. "Why you?"

"Because, princess, in your sad tale of woe, you name me as the Reaper who snags your soul."

"Big deal," I snarl.

He shakes his head slowly, tapping his forehead with the palm of his hand. "It's a very big deal to *me*. Your story makes me look incompetent. Azrael doesn't like mistakes. He brought the hammer down and ordered me cast into Hell."

"You're kidding," I sputter. I hadn't meant to get anyone in trouble. "But how does my case going in front of the Tribunal help you?"

Gideon lets out a weary groan. "Death Himself stood up to Azrael—said I was one of the best Reapers he had and that to replace me would be next to impossible. Azrael made him a deal. I can keep my position if we make you, and this whole situation, disappear in a way that makes everyone look good or . . ." his voice trails off.

"Or what?" I press.

"Or Death Himself will take the downward spiral with me, and his position will be reassigned to another celestial being."

Understanding hits me like a brick wall. "Meaning Azbaugh?"

"None other."

"So that's why he wanted me stuck in the Lobby for the next seven decades."

Gideon nods. "Azbaugh knew you would complain to any semiconscious person who arrived on the train and then word would spread like wildfire and before anyone could blink an eye, there's a vacancy in the Death department. No one, well almost no one, in the Lobby is supposed to be able to hear you. But since you were able to wake up the biker, it's possible you have the ability to communicate with the dead. Death Himself didn't want to take any chances with you causing any more problems."

"And that's why he hates me," I say, my knees buckling a little.

Gideon catches me by the elbow and leads me over to a chair. "He doesn't hate you. To be completely honest, I don't think he cares one way or the other about you. But he does want the best end result so he can prove to Azrael that he's capable of solving problems on his own. For the entire span of human existence, Death Himself has run his department without anyone keeping tabs on him. He gets souls collected and transported here where he passes them off. When you showed up demanding to go back, a giant spotlight started shining on all of us. As you can imagine, he's not too happy about it."

"What does he mean about calling in favors?"

"You heard what he said about favors being currency, right?" I nod and he continues. "Clearing this up is going to make him, how do you say it, broke."

I slump in my chair. "And the guides are going to cost him even more, aren't they?"

"We can't have angels or Reapers leading you through the tests. It would create all kinds of chances for biases. The only alternative is to use souls."

A shiver goes through me. "But haven't they already crossed over or whatever they do? Why would they help me?"

"Favors," he says. "Who do you think picks the welcome committee for the new arrivals? Who do you think assigns souls to the different jobs up here? Death Himself is going to be in serious debt by the time this is over. That's not a position he likes to be in."

"This is bad, isn't it?"

"Well, it's not good," he agrees. "But the bright side is that you and Death Himself both want the same end, regardless of the reason. He's going to do whatever it takes to help you succeed because it's in his best interest to. But he can't assign just any ghost to be your guide. It has to be one connected to your life. They need to have a vested interest in the outcome of your choice."

"And that's why it costs favors?" I ask.

"If they were just any random three spirits, it wouldn't. My boss could snag them before they cross over. But since the request is specific, he will have to appeal to Saint Peter for the release of the souls and then convince the souls to take part."

I brighten up at the idea. "Peter likes me. Surely he'll help me out."

Gideon snorts. "Peter likes everyone. It's part of his charm. But no one does anything for free and three specific souls are going to have Death Himself owing Saint Peter for eons to come."

"I didn't mean to screw everything up," I say, hiding my face in my hands. I wonder if he's using some angel voodoo to make me feel bad. "I just want to go home."

Gideon sits down on the arm of the chair with a long sigh. "I get it. And I think deep down, and we're talking *really* deep down, so does Death Himself, but this is going to be a tough road, for us and for you."

"What happens next?"

"When your first ghost arrives, he or she will escort you to the point in your past that you're meant to change. You'll get one shot at it. Each ghost can help you as much or as little as they want. We might be able to summon their souls, but we can't control them. You've hurt a lot of people over your life, even if you don't know it. There's no telling how much they'll want you to succeed. Some of them might even want you to fail."

I take a couple cleansing breaths. "Any last words of wisdom you want to offer up?"

"Yeah," he says with a snort. "Don't be you."

What am I supposed to say? He has a point, but he's still a jerk. The lights flicker overhead and any witty comeback dies on the tip of my tongue.

"Looks like your first guide is here," he says, standing to leave. "I better get going."

Maybe it's the not knowing what's going to happen, but the words that come out of my mouth surprise even me. "Gideon," I say, reaching out for his robe. "I'm really sorry about all the trouble I've caused."

He smiles. "How did that word 'sorry' taste?"

"Like lemonade without sugar," I admit with a grin.

He chuckles before adding, "Oh, and just so you know, the gypsy didn't die from a falling piano." He pauses and I stare back, waiting for the next bombshell he's going to drop on me.

"It was a tuba." And with that he's gone, leaving me to wait for whatever happens next.

Chapter 14

I never understood how silence could be deafening until now. This is the first time since I reviewed my life that I've been alone and I don't like it. Sitting back in the chair, I spin the ring, switching it from my right to left hand. I think back to Sandy and wonder if she's still getting into trouble in the Lobby. When I try to picture her in my mind, the painful buzz starts up somewhere in the back of my brain and I shut my eyes, wishing for it to go away. I know better than to try to think about my old life, but I didn't know the Lobby was off limits, too.

With no other distraction, I think about the ghost who should arrive and whisk me off to replay my life like some over-told Christmas story. Except it's not a story. It's real and apparently I'm not the only person who stands to lose everything if it ends badly. No pressure or anything.

The mist around me begins to swirl as it takes on a slightly pinkish tint. I shut my eyes, then open them wide to make sure I'm not imagining the change. I'm not. In fact, when I look up, I see a woman with long red hair that falls in waves against her pale, radiant skin. Instead of a white robe like almost everyone else I've seen, she's wearing a sheath dress that perfectly matches the hue of the air around us.

"Hello, RJ. It's nice to see you," she says as she approaches. "I'm Angelica."

"Of course you are," I mutter under my breath and her bright green eyes widen slightly. Remembering Gideon's warning about souls being able to help me, I quickly add, "I meant hi."

"Of course you did," she says, and though her smile is perfectly in place, I can't miss the slight hint of bitterness in her tone. She's pretty in a willowy way and somewhere, in the far reaches of my memory, I know I should recognize her. I study her but just when I think I'm going to make the connection, the humming kicks in and I stop. That's when it hits me that I've become the dog in Pavlov's experiment.

An awkward silence follows as I wait for her to say something. Angelica, on the other hand, seems content to simply stare at me. I shift uncomfortably under her gaze before asking, "I guess you're my first spirit guide?"

"Apparently."

That's all she's got for me? Isn't she the one who's supposed to tell me what to do to fix my past so I can get back to my present? Where are the pearls of wisdom? Can't she at least muster an inspiring "go get 'em, champ" speech? No. She just watches me, and while everything about her *looks* pleasant, I have this gut feeling that she hates me and has every reason to. Finally, I can't stand it anymore and blurt out, "I'm sorry, but is something wrong? Have I done something to irritate you in the whole minute you've known me?"

My question is met with a cool smile. "Of course not, RJ."

Even though she only says four words, I don't believe any of them. I know passive aggressive when I see it. I've made it an art form. What I don't know is why I'm on the receiving end.

So I say, "Fine, if there's no problem, maybe you could fill me in on what I'm supposed to do next?"

She sits next to me, tucking the edge of her dress under her, and then stares off into the mist.

My faith in Death Himself's ghostly selection is fading fast.

Finally she says, "The moments of your life are passing by us." I expect her to pause so she can deliver her explanation in a flowery prophecy. Much to my relief, she doesn't. "Eventually, it will slow down and you will be able to see the memory unfold. Be ready. Your soul will be pulled back into the mortal plane and you'll only have a few seconds to figure out how you are going to respond. Your future will be entirely in your hands. I cannot interfere."

"That's it?" I ask, not completely sure she's telling me everything I need to know. "No offense, but it sounds a little too easy. I mean, if I go back and do the opposite of what I did the last time around, there's no way I will fail."

"I wouldn't make that assumption if I were you. It's true you will want to avoid the same choices as before, but that may not be enough."

"Why not?" I ask. "Doesn't it make sense that the opposite action will result in the opposite outcome?"

"It can," she begins, her voice soft, almost like a lullaby. "Or it can result in far worse consequences. It's not enough that the end result is different. It needs to be better."

"How am I supposed to know if it's going to be better before I change the past?"

She lets out a long sigh and I feel a pang of sadness. It's the same sound my mom gives me when her patience is running thin. "Everything you do has a consequence. Good, bad, indifferent, there is always a price to pay. The question is: who pays? Sometimes making the right choice means you might lose something that seems important at the time."

She looks pointedly at me and I know she's trying to tell me something.

"But what's the point of doing all this if my life is going to suck when I get back?"

"Look," she says, slapping her hands on her thighs. All evidence of her cool exterior is gone. "You've done some crappy things in your life—"

"Who hasn't?" I counter.

"You're right. Everyone has regrets. But you have been given the chance to go back and change them. These points in your life aren't random. They mark a time where your selfishness and ambition were more important to you than doing the right thing."

"I don't need a lecture from some dead chick," I mutter. I can feel the hairs on the back of my neck stand up as the air crackles with tension.

"On that we will agree to disagree," she says calmly.

And now the gloves are off. "Do I know you?" I ask, unable to figure out why she's being so rude. "Seriously, Angelica, if I did something to you, tell me what it was so I can say sorry and move on."

A hollow laugh trickles over her lips. "There is nothing you need to say to me."

"Then why are you so angry?"

As soon as my accusation fills the space between us, I see Angelica regain her composure. "Anger isn't something that lasts long up here."

"Really?" I answer, unconvinced. "Because you seem to be channeling it pretty well."

This time, she gives me a wry grin. "What can I say? I'm stubborn. That's something we have in common."

The wind stirs and the energy in the space changes once again. "It's happening now, right?" A shiver runs down my spine. "Is it possible that I could screw things up more than the first time?"

"Yes," she says, and I look up to see compassion in her eyes.

"So what do I do?" I ask, wishing I hadn't spent so much time arguing with Angelica and more time gathering as much information as possible.

"This is your journey, not mine. I can't tell you what to do. But deep down, there is good in you. Remember what I said about doing the right thing."

"It's not always the easy thing to do," I repeat, letting the words wash over me as the mist in front of us begins to shimmer. Slowly, a familiar world begins to take shape. We're standing in the middle of the playground near my house. It's a bright morning and the place is packed.

"Can they see us?" I ask.

She shakes her head.

"What's happening?"

"Just wait," she says, staring at the scene, her eyes searching for something or someone.

And then I see myself. I'm eight, and my family has just moved in to our new house. I don't know anyone, but every day I come here, hoping to find a friendly face. That's when I see Abby Richards, the first best friend I ever had. I watch her walk up and whisper something in my ear and the next thing I know, we're catapulting ourselves off the swings and racing down the slides like we've known each other our entire lives.

Time speeds up a little and I watch the summer sun give way to the bright colors of early fall. Abby's parents are sending her to the Catholic school across town, but every afternoon, at 3:15 p.m., we meet on the merry-go-round until the sun ducks behind the trees. On this particular afternoon, I meet my first mean girl. She's a sixth grader named Claudia, and from what I remember, she did everything she could to make Abby miserable. No matter how hard Abby tried to stay out of her way, it didn't work. I think the whole fight between Claudia and Abby began earlier in the day, at school, but now it's about to make an encore performance at our sacred place.

A few minutes later, Claudia's friends arrive. I was expecting this. Every queen of the playground needs loyal subjects to do their bidding and more importantly, they need people who fear them. Once she has an audience, Claudia begins following Abby, taunting her in a loud, cruel cackle. "What's the matter, Blabby Abby? No teacher here to protect you now? Are you scared?"

I hear my voice rise above the din of the laughter. "Ignore her, Abby. She's just trying to make you mad. Come on, let's go to my house."

And then, like a roller coaster ride, time rushes forward before a jerking stop. It's winter. The park is deserted. I've almost forgotten about Angelica, but when I glance over, her face is a tapestry of pain and sadness. I start to ask her what's wrong, but the running footsteps crunching against the fresh snow stop me.

It's Abby. She's crying and looking down the street toward my house. She's waiting for me and instantly I know what's about to happen. I watch in silence as my child-self races to the merry-go-round. I wrap Abby up in my arms and she begins to sob. My face is easy to read: I have no idea what is going on. At least I didn't. Not then. I do now.

I try to turn away, but Angelica stops me with a crisp, "Pay attention."

Taking a breath of resolve, I turn back just as Claudia shows up with a dutiful lackey in tow.

Seeing her tormentor stomping toward her, Abby tries to hide her tears, but it's no use. The tigress has found her prey weak and vulnerable, and she is ready to pounce.

"What's the matter, Blabby Abby? Did you skin your wittle knee?"

"Leave her alone," I say, but Claudia either doesn't hear me or doesn't care.

"You know, Jenny," she says to her follower, "we never really dealt with Blabby Abby after she got us busted for smoking."

"Nope," Jenny answers. "We never did."

"I said leave her alone," I repeat.

That's when Claudia notices me. "Shut up."

I watch the fury rise up inside me and I can see something in me snaps. I start to move toward her, my hands curling up, ready to strike. But Jenny, ever the bodyguard, pushes me to the ground.

"Stay where you belong, wimp," Claudia says. "Try to get in my way again and I'll ruin what pathetic reputation you have at your school with one phone call."

Out of the corner of my eye I see two more figures enter the playground. Ah, there they are. The rest of the entourage.

"Hi, girls," Claudia calls out. "It looks like we found our narc."

"Nice," one of the newcomers says.

"I was grounded the entire week of Christmas because of you," another girl says, standing inches in front of Abby, whose eyes are trained on the ground. "Did you hear me?" the girl adds before poking Abby hard in the shoulder with her manicured nail.

I try to get up, but Jenny is faster than she looks. "Stay out of it," she warns, kicking my legs out from under me.

"Now, girls," Claudia says and three sets of eyes turn toward her, but mine stay trained on Abby who looks like she's going to pass out. "I think it's time to show Blabby Abby how we deal with babies who can't keep their mouths shut."

I watch, waiting for the punch, but it never comes. Instead, I feel a tug at my belly button. I look down and see a silvery cord. I glance back up in confusion at Angelica a moment before my soul is hurtling toward the scene. I stop for a split second before my seventeen-year-old spirit slams into my eight-year-old self.

Chapter 15

I can't even begin to describe what it feels like to crash into your own body. I'm not talking about the initial shock. That wears off pretty quickly. I'm talking about the disconnected feeling. All the hours of dance and tumbling for cheerleading are wasted. In this situation my arms and legs refuse to do what I want. I feel like a stranger in my own skin.

I shake my head, trying to dislodge all the information I'm going to need for this test. I don't know how long I have.

"Did you say something?" Claudia sneers down at me.

I pick myself up off the ground, my still-developing body giving me the balance of a newborn calf. I don't remember being this short. I step back to take in Claudia and for the life of me I can't figure out why we were afraid of her. Sure, she's bigger than us, but only because of her baby fat. Without her friends, Claudia would be a frumpy girl with wild hair and bad breath.

"What's your problem?" I ask in a squeaky voice. "Why do you have to pick on kids who are littler than you?"

"Oh. Somebody must have found a little courage while she was flapping around on the ground." Claudia takes a few steps forward, leaning in close, and I turn away. Her breath really *is* bad. "I warned you about staying out of this, didn't I?"

One second ticks by and then another. I don't know what I'm supposed to do. I want to punch her smug face right in the nose, but given the fact that Claudia is almost a foot taller than I am and has a good twenty pounds on me, it's probably not the best choice. Plus, I'm outnumbered.

Instead, I push past her and race over to Abby. Her eyes are wide with wonder and fear. "What are you doing?" she whispers when I offer my hand to help her stand.

"What I should have done before," I answer, before I can stop myself.

Her eyebrows knit together in confusion, but she doesn't ask any questions as she takes my hand and lets me hoist her up.

"Now, let's get out of here," I say.

"What about them?" she asks. The fear in her voice shatters my heart. The older me is getting mad. Little kids shouldn't be afraid to come to a playground.

"Forget them," I say, loud enough for Claudia and her friends to hear. "They don't scare me."

"Oh really?" The words register in my brain just before I go sprawling across the blacktop. The knees of my new jeans rip and I can smell the blood oozing from the scrape. I remember these. They're my first pair of designer jeans. Mom brought them back from a business trip to New York City.

I stagger to my feet before spinning around to face Claudia. "Do you have any idea how much these cost?" I growl.

"Like I care," Claudia retorts. The glint in her eyes is pure evil. I'm pretty sure I've had the same one in my eyes on several occasions.

I don't think Claudia expects to have a fight on her hands and the idea is bringing out the worst in her. I motion for Abby to follow me. "Come on."

"Are you stupid? I told you to stay out of this. Now it's time for you to learn your place," Claudia says with a hateful laugh. She motions to her friends and I watch Jenny and the other girls circle in front of us. I have to admit, they're doing a good job of stopping our retreat. They remind me of a pack of wolves closing in on an injured deer.

"I'll distract them. As soon as you can, make a run to my house and get my parents. Whatever you do, don't come back without them," I whisper to Abby.

"But they're going to kill you," she whispers back.

"Wouldn't be the first time today," I mutter. To Abby I add, "I can handle them." Turning back, I hope what I'm saying is true.

Before she can argue, I spin back to Claudia. "Did you have something to teach me?" I try to send out as much confidence as my scrawny body can manage. It's not much, but it does get their attention.

"Hold her, girls," Claudia says.

Now it's time to see if this body will respond to some evasive maneuvers. I dodge past Jenny and head toward the other end of the playground, away from Abby and my best escape. My speed surprises both of us as I race to the far end of the playground. The gate that's normally open during the summer is sporting a lock and chain. I hear Claudia laughing like a hyena behind me. "Stupid kid."

Out of the corner of my eye, I see Abby dart out of the playground and sprint toward my house. "Yeah, I'm the stupid one. But I don't have to bully people to feel good about myself," I say, full of bravado. I don't know if it's because I won't have to nurse the wounds in the morning or because I'm pretty sure she's not going to kill me, but I'm not afraid of Claudia. "Do you get some sort of sick thrill out of picking on people?"

Claudia's eyes narrow and I realize that I sound more like my mom than an eight-year-old kid on the playground. I try to put on a look that's a mixture of surprise and fear and hope she isn't smart enough to get suspicious because the truth is, this girl could break me like a tooth pick. Luckily, Claudia's rage is still focused on Abby. Well, lucky for me, anyway.

"She got us in trouble," Claudia said, opening and closing her fist.

"You got yourself in trouble," I counter. "Smoking is dumb."

She steps forward. Her hand is tightly clenched in a fist. "Did you just call me stupid?"

"Technically, I called you dumb, but it's the same thing." I watch Claudia motion to Jenny.

I don't have time to move before the girl locks my arms behind my back. I struggle to get away, but I forget how strong she is.

"Let me go," I demand, shifting from side to side, struggling against her grasp.

"Hey," Jenny says, looking around. "Where's Abby?"

Everyone looks around the playground for her. Except me. I'm looking at Jenny's bright pink tennis shoes. With every ounce of strength I have, I lift my foot and crash it hard in the center of her orange laces. She howls out in pain. It serves her right. Orange and pink do not go together. They never have, no matter what anyone says.

I race past Claudia, bending low to ram my shoulder into her gut.

"Ouch!" she gasps. But a moment later she recovers and is in hot pursuit. Her legs are longer than mine but I almost make it to the front of the playground entrance before she catches up. Grabbing the hood of my coat, she yanks me back, and once again I'm looking up at the starless sky.

"I'm done talking," she growls.

I watch as she raises her fist back, ready to smash in my face. And I don't react. I don't try to protect my face. I just watch her fist as it moves in slow motion. First back and then picking up speed as it nears my nose. And then I do the only thing I can. I roll out of the way and her hand smashes into the blacktop. I think I hear the tiny bones breaking in her hand, but I'm too busy scurrying out from under her to care. With their leader howling in pain, the rest of the girls are paying more attention to her than me. I race toward the entrance and run full force into the wool coat of my dad.

"What's going on here?" he asks, looking between me and Claudia.

I glance behind him and see Abby crossing the street with my mom. From the look on her face, someone is in a lot of trouble. I just hope it isn't me.

"Um, I think she broke her hand?" I say, pointing toward the group of girls.

"What did you do?" my mom asks me, rushing over to Claudia.

"Nothing," I answer. "I mean, when she was going to punch me in the face I moved, but I didn't touch her, Mom. I swear."

She pauses for a moment and looks at Claudia. "Is this true?"

I don't know what Claudia says, but I see the disappointment fade from Mom's face and pride sweep in. "Well, we should get you home." She helps Claudia stand up.

"I'll get the car," my father says.

I can't believe they're being so kind to the girl who tried to beat me up. But a few minutes later, our tormentors are driving away with my father who's on the cell phone with Claudia's parents. I wonder how he's going to explain their daughter's condition.

My mom takes my hand and leads Abby and me back to our warm house. It isn't until I'm in clean PJs and sitting in front of a cup of steaming hot cocoa that I find out about Abby's mom and the car accident that took her away from her family.

That's when the silver cord tugs and I'm soaring into the night sky away from the tears and sadness.

I land with a thump next to Angelica. When I look up, her eyes are brimming with tears and joy.

"You did very well," she says, pulling me into her arms. "Thank you." Her embrace is warm and nothing like I would expect from a ghost. But there's something else about it that triggers the humming in my brain. Something familiar. It smells of lilacs.

I step back to look at her. She has the same red hair and big blue eyes. How did I not see it before?

"You're Abby's mom. But I don't remember you looking so . . ."

"Young, relaxed, fabulous?" she asks, tossing her ginger locks over her shoulder.

"Well, yeah," I admit. Abby's mom was always rushing out of the house in a flurry of activity. She never let her hair down—literally or figuratively.

She throws back her head and laughs. "I like you, RJ. I haven't always liked you, but I like you now."

"Because I didn't stand up for Abby?" I ask.

She nods. "Yes. I understood why you ran that night at the park. You were a kid. But I could never figure out why you didn't go back. You just left her to face those girls alone."

"I'm sorry," I say, hoping it doesn't sound as lame out loud as it does in my head. But there's nothing else to say. I don't know why I didn't go back, either. I think it was Claudia's threat to ruin my chance of being popular. And I honestly didn't think they were really going to hurt Abby.

"There is no need to be sorry anymore. You made up for everything just now."

I blink back the tears from my eyes. Her forgiveness is more than I'm ready for. "How did I do that?" I whisper.

Angelica hugs me again. "You saved my family."

"I didn't—"

She tucks a strand of hair behind my ear, cutting off my argument. "But you did. After my funeral, your mother stepped in to arrange for local churches and business leaders to bring meals to my house so that my husband, a widower with five children, didn't have to figure out what to make for dinner. She persuaded the mortgage company to give him a three-month grace period on the house payments. She also made sure my entire family was given time and space to grieve. And she kicked them in the butt when it was time to pick up the pieces and start moving on. For that I will always be grateful."

"All because I helped Abby?"

She nods her head. "My husband was broken after my death. If not for your mom, well, I've seen the future they would have had and it wasn't a good one."

I bite my lip and look away. She may know what happened to her kids in the old lifeline, but I don't. Abby and I never spoke again after that night. Her dad lost his job and they moved in with her grandmother in Tulsa. "What happened with Claudia? Did she stop harassing Abby?"

Angelica's smile widens even more and I'm afraid her face might split open. "With you by her side, my daughter will never have to worry about being picked on again."

The tears are falling freely now and I wipe them off with the back of my hand. "You mean we're still friends?"

"Yes. You're not as close as you used to be, but once a year you meet up at the playground for a mini-reunion," Angelica says, giving me another gentle smile. Off in the distance, a chime rings and she stands. "It's time for me to go."

I reach out for her, not wanting her to leave. "So, did I pass?"

She pats my hand gently before placing it in my lap. Before backing away, she touches my cheek. "It's not my decision, but if they ask me, I'll tell them you aced it."

And then she's disappears. And I'm alone. Again.

Chapter 16

I don't know how long I wait for the next ghost to arrive, but it feels like forever. After a while, the white mist takes on the dark appearance of storm clouds, and even though I can't feel any change in temperature, a cold shiver runs over me. Through the dense fog I see a figure approaching, and when the shadow emerges, a boy with eyes the color of gooey honeycombs glares down at me. Why does it seem like everyone in the Afterlife is mad at me? Okay, sure, I probably wouldn't win a Miss Congeniality title, but I can think of tons of people who lived worse lives than I did. Hitler springs to mind.

"You ready?" he growls, shoving his hands deep into the pockets of his black jeans.

I can't stop staring at him. He is the definition of hotness. The dirty-blond hair topping his tan, square face is tousled like he just woke up. I move closer to get a better look at him, but he shrinks away.

"Have we met?" I ask.

He shakes his head but doesn't answer. Instead, he turns and walks away.

"I knew Angelica. Well, sorta. So it makes sense that I would know you, too."

"You don't know me," he says, not even bothering to look at me.

"Well, can you at least tell me your name?"

"Trevor."

The hostility coming from him hits me hard. Yeah, I probably did something to him. Death Himself must have had a blast picking out the ghosts who hate me almost as much as he does.

"Where are we going?" I ask, following behind him.

"I thought you wanted to get back to your life."

Sarcasm sucks when I'm not the one dishing it out. "Yeah, but I could use some words of wisdom or something."

He stops short and I almost run into his strong, lean back.

"You want a pep talk?" he asks, turning slowly to glare at me.

"Um, I guess. Sure."

"Because I'm not warm and fuzzy. Not like Angelica."

"Yeah, I get that." What is this guy's problem?

"Fine. My advice: don't be you." I can feel the color drain from my face and a look of satisfaction appears in his eyes.

He turns sharply and walks away.

"Hey!" I yell after him.

He stops but doesn't turn around.

I'm shaking as I walk toward him, my hands forming fists. "Who do you think you are?" He doesn't answer. "I'm talking to you," I yell and grab his arm, spinning him around.

He turns his head away, but I'm not about to let him avoid me any longer. I take a step closer, daring him to look at me. "You don't like the duty of escorting me around, fine. I get it. But you don't know anything about me, so quit being such a jerk."

"You sure about that?" he asks, stepping back, but at least he's looking at me again.

"What?"

"Forget it." He begins to walk away.

This time, I fall in step with him.

"What do you mean? I thought you said I didn't know you."

"You don't. You never took the time."

"Whatever," I say, throwing my arms up in frustration. "Keep your secrets. I'll do this without your help. And then you can move on and be out of my life."

"What life? You're dead, remember?"

"That's temporary."

"Right," he says, and I can hear the laughter in his voice.

"Look, whatever your problem with me is, I don't care."

Trevor spins around, towering over me. He's not keeping his distance anymore. In fact, if he were any closer, I'd have to grab onto him to keep from falling backward.

"My problem," he hisses, "is that you might actually get a second chance to ruin even more people's lives."

"Ruin lives?" I laugh. "Don't you think you're being a little dramatic?"

"What? You think every spoiled princess who croaks in her prime gets a do-over at life?"

"I wasn't supposed to die. It was an—"

"I know. An accident. The whole Afterlife knows. You think gossip travels fast on Earth. Trust me, it's nothing compared to this place," he says, waving his hand in the air.

"At least someone is concerned with my situation. Customer service up here is horrible."

"Trust me. No one cares whether you go back or not. What they're really interested in is whether you're going up or down. Did you know you could place a bet on it? It's like Vegas before the Super Bowl and in case you're wondering, the odds are not in your favor."

My mouth drops open but no words come out.

His lips twitch into a sneer. "Speechless? I bet that's a first," he says, stopping suddenly. "We're here. Just like you wanted."

I look around and take a deep breath. "Uh, this doesn't look any different than where we just were."

"Oh, so now you're an expert on the inner working of the universe? My mistake." His eyes pinch together and he runs his hands through his hair so fast I think he's going to pull some of it out.

"Fine. Where are we?"

"Take a look," he says, swiping his hand through the air. The haze fades back as if someone is sucking in a deep breath. What remains is a movie screen–size patch of clear air.

"RJ Jones, this is your moment," my spirit guide whispers in my ear, his breath unexpectedly hot against my skin. "Don't screw it up."

Images begin to flash and I don't need him to remind me about the details. I know exactly when we are. It's my sophomore year and I'm trying to impress Dave, the varsity quarterback with an arm like a laser-guided missile. We're standing in the hallway near my locker after school on a Friday. I can tell because I'm wearing the horrid varsity cheerleading uniform, which means I must still be passing all my classes.

I remember this day because tonight, after he wins the big game with a last-minute touchdown pass, Dave is going to kiss me. Even now there's a flutter in my stomach. Not because I like him anymore. He's kind of a jerk, but he's also ridiculously hot. More importantly, he liked me.

"Why isn't the universe doing that yanking thing?" I ask. Trevor is looking down the hall, his eyes following something or someone. I follow his gaze. That's when I see him.

I watch as the gangly figure comes closer. His arms are full of books and the top half is threatening to topple to the ground. Not a single thing is different from my first timeline. I thought the park incident was supposed to have a ripple effect.

"I thought things were supposed to change after what I did for Abby," I whisper.

"They only change if you do," is his dull response. "Looks like you didn't learn your lesson."

I look back at the group. He's right. Everything is the same as I remember it. Well, one thing is different.

Felicity and I really were best friends during our sophomore year. Not frenemies, but honest to goodness friends. We did everything together. But now, she's giving me a death stare. I rack my brain thinking what I could have done to her. At first, I draw a blank, but then, like the last piece snapping into a puzzle, I remember. During the summer, while she was away visiting her grandmother, I was forced by my parents to give back to the community, meaning I worked as a camp counselor for the Parks and Rec day camp along with Felicity's boyfriend, Jacob. One night, after a particularly brutal day of herding kids around from one activity to another, several of us headed out to a fellow counselor's farm for a bonfire.

Jacob was a junior and while I thought Felicity could do better, he had a car and I needed a ride. So, after a quick shower and change of clothes, he picked me up and we headed out to the country. I should mention that this was the first time I'd ever been offered a beer and I didn't want anyone to think I was a baby. So I took it. It was so gross I almost puked. But Jacob, being the gentleman that he was, got me a wine cooler. Some gentleman. Before the end of the night, my best friend's boyfriend was trying to kiss me. Okay, not trying. I actually let him.

The next morning, I felt horrible and not just because of the pounding headache. I couldn't believe what I had done. And, in an effort to be the good friend, I confessed everything to Felicity. She was mad, to say the least, but eventually she said she knew I didn't mean it and she wasn't mad. In my gut, I knew she was lying, but I wanted to believe it was true. She broke up with Jacob. He hooked up with someone else and ended up a baby-daddy before graduation. In hindsight, I probably saved her, but judging by the evil eye she's giving me now in the hallway, I don't think she sees it that way.

The clatter of books slamming to the floor catches my attention. My head snaps back and there he is, his beet red face hitting hard against the ground.

"Nice job, dork," Dave laughs, kicking one of the books down the hall.

The entire group erupts in laughter.

"Seriously," Felicity says, a sneer spreading across her face. "You almost scuffed my Louis Vuittons."

He tries to gather up his things, but only succeeds in dropping his glasses. I close my eyes as the heel of Dave's shoe smashes them. The crunch sounds like a bomb going off in my ears, followed by hysterical laughter bouncing off the rows of lockers.

The boy's face is on the verge of breaking into tears as he picks up his last spiral notebook.

"I can't watch," I whisper.

Trevor snorts. "Why not? Isn't this the perfect life you're so eager to get back to?" he asks. "This is my favorite part."

I turn back just in time to see Dave swing his arm around me. "What do you say, RJ? Is this loser bothering you?"

I get ready to jump into my body. Nothing happens. I hear myself say, "He so is. Scurry along, little cockroach."

Again, the crowd laughs like a pack of wild dogs.

"Maybe I should squash him," Dave says. "I think I would be doing the world a favor by ending him."

I look back at Trevor. "I know who that kid is. He's the guy that kills himself in the bathroom." A second ticks by. And then another, as realization dawns on me. "We didn't make him do that, did we? I mean, we didn't force him over the edge, right?" Trevor looks at me with empty eyes.

I turn back to the scene. Now, instead of laughter I hear cackling. I can see everything through the boy's eyes. And I can feel how he feels. The humiliation. The embarrassment. The anger.

"Send me in. I have to stop this. It's probably gone too far already, but I have to try."

"Not my call," he answers. There's grit in his voice. "The Fates are calling the shots. If they want you to go in, you will. Until then, you're stuck with me."

The scene changes before I can answer. This time the same boy is sitting on a bench in the quad scribbling furiously on a sketchpad. There's a flash of movement off to the side and then it happens again.

But this time, when the pull comes, I'm ready.

Chapter 17

The jolt doesn't seem as bad as before and it only takes me a few seconds to adjust to my physical body. I even manage to avoid screaming—which is a good thing because once my brain and body connect I realize I'm walking next to my English teacher.

"If you can get me the paper by Monday, I can give you partial credit," Ms. Walters is saying.

"Uh, sure. Thanks," I mutter, as memories from the new lifeline begin to replace the old ones.

She stops in the middle of the hall, forcing a freshman to swerve in order to avoid a collision. "RJ, this is important. If you don't pass my class, you're going to be on academic probation. That means no cheerleading. No homecoming dance. And you will be kicked off the court. You will be barred from all school activities of any kind, period. You need to take this seriously."

Oh right, I'm failing three classes. "I know, Ms. Walters. I'll get it done. I promise." I don't know why, but there's a part of me that cares about disappointing her. Maybe something is different about me. Who knows, maybe I am evolving.

"Monday morning," Ms. Walters repeats before slinging her heavy bag and walking toward the parking lot.

I take a deep breath before heading toward the next stop on my road to redemption.

As I walk silently up behind the boy with the sketchpad, I wish I could remember his name. "Um, hi." Pathetic conversation starter, I know, but it's the best I've got under the circumstances.

He wraps his arms protectively around his sketchbook. "What do you want?" he growls.

"I, uh, I thought we could talk."

"What? Are you here to make fun of me again? Where's your ogre of a boyfriend?" He glances around the quad nervously. I can't blame him. It wouldn't be the first time one of my friends set him up for public ridicule.

"About that. I'm sorry."

He snorts. "No, you're not. If you were sorry, you would have stopped them."

"I should have. I wanted to. I really did, but—"

"But what?" he spits. "Don't patronize me. You saw old Daniel sitting alone and thought you'd get in a few more low blows to let me know just how much of a waste of space you think I am."

Daniel. That's his name. But he has a point, and I don't have an excuse. "What are you working on?" I ask, trying to save this conversation and my chance at getting my life back.

"None of your business."

Clearly whatever I'm supposed to change isn't going to be easy. I crane my neck to get a better look. "Are those your drawings?"

"How do you know about them?" he asks defensively. I notice his grip on the book tighten slightly.

I shrug. "I was sitting behind you last week when it was raining." He keeps staring at me. "You know, when everyone was hanging out in the auditorium before school."

"Yeah, I think I got hit by a couple spitballs from your boyfriend."

"He's not my boyfriend," I say defensively. He gives me a curious look. Okay, yes, earlier today I was probably hanging all over him in the hall, but that was then. This is now.

"Right. He's just a friend. Look, what do you want from me?" he sneers.

I can't believe how hard it is to think of the right thing to say. "I guess I just wanted to talk."

"What? Did you lose a bet?"

Wow. He really is hostile. That's when I realize I don't know the first thing about trying to make amends with someone who doesn't at least pretend to like me. I take a deep breath. "I came over here to say I'm sorry and you . . ."

"You said you were sorry. You can go now."

A sharp whistle from across the quad makes us both turn. "RJ, come on."

I stifle a groan. Felicity is sauntering toward us with Penny and Lyndsey in tow.

"Are you coming?" she says, looking straight through Daniel to me.

"Coming where?" I ask, shifting uncomfortably on the cold cement bench.

"Did you forget? We're all going to Marinara's for pizza. Dave's waiting for us." Her lips spread into a sneer. "Who's your friend?"

She's not going to let this go. "Uh, this is Daniel," I answer.

"Huh. I thought his name was Splatter."

I jump up from my seat. "What did you say?"

She takes two steps toward me until we're less than a foot apart. "Well, that's what my stepbrother calls him. Dave thinks he would be better off as splatter on the pavement." I sense Daniel tense up at her words. Did we really do this to him? Did we really make him so scared that just the mention of Dave makes him nervous?

"Shut up," I try to say in an even, calm voice. I fail miserably.

"What's gotten into you?" she says with venom oozing off each word. "He's a nobody. Why are you defending him?"

"Because he's not a nobody."

"Relax. I didn't know you had a new BFF."

I shake my head in disgust. "At least he's real," I mutter.

"Excuse me?" Felicity says over Penny's gasp. "You know what, forget it. I hope you enjoy your downward mobility. It's going to be a lot of fun to watch."

I move even closer. "Are you threatening me?"

"Who would ever threaten the queen?"

"Well, maybe I don't want to be the queen anymore." From the far reaches of my mind, I feel the urge to take it back and I wonder if it's the old me struggling to regain control. I bet this is what it feels like to be taken over by an alien body snatcher.

She gives me a tight smile and gleefully says, "That can be arranged."

"Oh, big deal. Now I have to find another place to sit in the cafeteria. I think I'll live."

Her smile widens, but it's far from friendly. "Oh, I don't think that will work. We can't have you becoming a social martyr for the losers of the school to rally around."

I give her a look of shock and then start to laugh.

"What?" she asks, crossing her arms in front of her chest.

I try to stop laughing. "I'm just surprised you know what a martyr is."

Without missing a beat, Felicity leans close. The smell of her peppermint gum is so strong my nose starts to tingle. But her breath is still better than Claudia's. Why do mean girls like to get in your face so much? And then I remember doing the exact same thing when I'm trying to intimidate someone. I also remember it being highly effective. "You would be surprised at what I know."

Behind me, I hear Daniel stand up. "Forget it, RJ. You don't have to defend me."

I swivel around to face him. His face is bright red and he's slumping over, broken. The sadness in his eyes tugs at my heart. I turn back to Felicity but she's walking toward the parking lot, her cackle grating on my nerves.

"Dang it," I say, turning back to Daniel who's shoving his sketchbook into his bag.

"What?" he asks, wiping his face with the back of his hand.

"Well, I can't be sure, but I think Felicity is off sealing the coffin on my popularity and there's a very good chance that Dave is going to leave me here without a ride home."

"Your friends would do that to you?" he asks.

I shake my head. "I wouldn't exactly call them friends, not anymore, anyways."

"Still, you didn't have to get in a fight with her."

"Are you kidding?" I say with a laugh. "I've wanted to tell her off for a year. You just gave me a good reason." My words ring with truth and I can feel my new timeline finally catching up with me.

He smiles and takes his sunglasses off to clean them.

"So, do you have a car?" I ask.

His head snaps up and when I see his eyes, my heart skips a beat. "Why?" he asks with suspicion.

"Um, well," I begin, but I can't break eye contact with him and it's distracting. "It's just that, um, like I said, Dave was supposed to take me home."

"So, you need a ride?" he asks, and I think I see a smile starting to form.

I give him my most sincere smile. "Kinda. I mean, unless you want to leave me, too, which I would totally understand, seeing as how my people make your life a living hell on a daily basis. It would be a fair retaliation."

"Huh," he says. "But I thought they weren't your people anymore?"

I laugh and look down, my flirting skills kicking in. "I guess not. I'm in high school limbo."

"Welcome to my world," he says, and even though he's smiling back at me, I can still feel his pain.

"Daniel, I am really sorry. For everything I did and everything I didn't do. It wasn't right."

"Forget it," he says, looking away as a blush spreads across his cheeks.

"No. If I can help it, I won't forget."

He looks back at me. "What do you mean, if you can help it?"

I force a nervous laugh and reach out to touch his arm. For a moment, I think he's going to pull away, but he doesn't. "Never mind. So, about that ride? Think you can help a stranded girl out? I would hate to hitchhike. Today doesn't seem like a good day to die."

I mean it as a joke, but his eyes cloud over and I know where I've seen them before. But it couldn't be who I think it is. "No," he says, a slow, mischievous smile spreading across his face and I think he's going to tell me I can find someone else to act as my chauffer. "I don't think it's a good day to die, either. Come on."

"Seriously? Thank you so much. I'll pay for gas," I offer, giving him my most pitiful look.

It must work because he laughs. Not one of those uncomfortable ones people give when they want to disappear. But a laugh that starts in the gut and rumbles through the body until it bursts past the lips.

As we walk toward the parking lot, I ask, "What's your middle name?"

"Why?"

I shrug, trying to play it off like it's a random question. "Just curious."

He gives me a quizzical look before answering. "It's Trevor."

Chapter 18

Like the last time, the silver cord tightens and pulls me out of my body and the nanosecond it takes to get back to the Afterlife is all I need to put two and two together.

"Daniel!" I scream, searching the mist in desperation. "Where are you? Daniel. Trevor. Whatever your name is. Answer me."

"He's not here, dear," a calm voice says behind me.

I spin around, eager to know what is happening. Did I change things? Is he still dead? But all the questions disappear when I meet the baby blue eyes of my Grams. Without a word I hurl myself into her waiting arms and hold on tight. All the emotions I've been holding back rush forward. It's been so long since she died and there are a lot of things I want to say to her.

I start with the most important. "I love you," I say, as the words trip over each other and mix with sobs. "I've missed you so much."

She strokes my hair. "Shh, child. There is no need for tears."

Her words only cause me to cry harder. She pulls me closer and begins rocking me like she did when I was a child, and, for a brief second, I wonder if staying here, with her, wouldn't be such a bad idea.

"It's a horrible idea," she admonishes me.

I look up at her in surprise. "How'd you know what I was thinking?"

Instead of answering she asks, "Do you remember when you were a little girl and your mother would bring you over after school?"

"Yeah, you always had cookies ready for me."

She nods. "And as you got older, you started to play a little game, didn't you?"

My eyes grow wide. "Yeah, but I never told you about it."

"No, but you did, didn't you?"

I nod, speechless for a moment. "I would, uh, try to predict what cookie you were going to make. I thought I was psychic or something."

Grams shakes her head. "Sorry, my dear, you are completely normal. But you and I do have a connection I've never been able to explain. I always knew which cookie you were thinking about."

"That's so weird. Maybe you're the mind reader."

Grams throws back her head and her familiar laugh fills the air. When she's done, she smiles at me. "Maybe we both have a sixth sense when it comes to each other."

I grin. "It's probably because I'm your favorite grandkid, isn't it?"

She just pulls me close again and holds me so tight I can barely breathe. Even though I can't feel it, I sense the warmth that only a grandmother has. Finally, I pull back and look to her for answers. "Grams, where did Daniel go?"

"I would suppose he's back on Earth."

Relief washes over me. "He's alive? That means he didn't kill himself?"

Nodding her head, she looks at me with pride. "No. After he took you home, he thought about it. He left your house and headed back to the school. But as he was sitting in his car, he got a text from you. Do you remember what it said?"

The memories of my old and new lives are still mingling in my brain. "I think so. Didn't I ask if he wanted to be my friend?"

"Almost. I think it was more like, 'Since I probably don't have any friends left, do you want the job? I'm high maintenance and kind of a pain, but if you're interested, press one. If you aren't, I understand.' Does that sound right?"

And even though I'm not completely sure who the new me is, I know that's exactly what I would say. Sorting through the different timelines is starting to give me a headache so I ask, "Did he answer?"

She looks at me with twinkling eyes. "He did."

I wait for her to finish. When she doesn't I prompt her, "And?"

"He wrote one."

"What did he do after he sent the text?"

She picks up my hand, patting it absently. "He started the car, drove home, and the next morning was waiting in your driveway to take you to school."

"Wow," I say. "That's pretty cool."

"That's one way to put it. The two of you became very close."

"Did we date? Because when he was Trevor, he was freaking hot, and if he turns out to look anything like that, I could see it happening."

She shakes her head, but I see a glint of amusement sneaking into her eyes. "It's amazing what having good friends can do to a person. By the time your senior year comes around, he will look like that, but you will never date."

I groan. "What? Why not?"

"His heart will be won by someone else," she says with finality.

Figures. I hope it's not Felicity. "Since Trevor is alive and kicking, then, did Death Himself send you here to meet me?"

"Oh, I wouldn't say that exactly. When I heard my granddaughter was the one causing a fuss up in the Afterlife, I came to find you."

"Grams," I say, giving her a hard look, "are you AWOL from Heaven?"

Without missing a beat she says, "Who says I went to Heaven? I was quite a hell-raiser, in my day, I'll have you know."

I study her carefully. "Nope. I'm not buying it. You probably had a VIP ticket waiting for you when you arrived."

She laughs again, the sound wrapping me in a cocoon of happiness. I lean back against her, wishing I was small enough to climb onto her lap just so I can be a little closer to her. "Hey, Grams," I say, still feeling the tingle of joy on my skin. "I was wondering something."

"Hmm," she murmurs, absently stroking my hair.

"Were you proud of me?"

I expect her to laugh but she doesn't. Instead, her hand freezes in place. "Well . . ." she starts, but her words trickle off.

The warm air is chilly now. I sit up straight, a strand of my hair catching on her fingers. "Grams?" I whisper. Her hesitation cuts me like a knife.

She snaps out of her thoughts and stands up. "Here's the thing about the Afterlife. Once you cross over, you can't lie. Not even white lies."

"So you weren't proud of me," I deduce.

"The truth is never simple," she begins. "I'm proud of the woman you are becoming now, but the girl you were before your death made it harder to stand up and cheer for you."

I don't need a pulse to know that my heart is breaking— no, crumbling. Grams, my rock, the one person I thought would never turn on me is now telling me she doesn't like me. Or didn't like me, and all I can say is, "Oh." What else is there?

She sits back next to me and takes both of my hands in hers. I try to pull them away but she's stronger than I remember. "I know it sounds bad, and if I could lie, I might be tempted. But you have to realize, the woman you were turning into was selfish and mean. I know it's not all your fault, but sweetheart, it's true. I love you more than anything. I always have. But you asked the question and I can't lie."

"You already said that," I say flatly.

She lifts my chin, forcing me to look at her. "Whether you know it or not, you've made some pretty big changes in your life. First, you stood up to a bully who was bigger than you. By doing that, you started to develop the courage to stand up to your friends, which is much harder. I can't begin to tell you how much those two choices have changed you."

"So now that I'm someone different, you love me more?" I ask, turning my back to her.

But Grams won't let me get away that easy. She spins me around, refusing to let me ignore her. "You listen to me, young lady. Do not for one moment think that I didn't love you. I always have and I always will. That has never changed. But that was not what you asked. You asked if I was proud of you. Not then. But the girl you are, the woman you are on your way to becoming, that is who you were meant to be. Not some carbon copy of her friends. And definitely not someone who makes herself feel better by making others feel worse. You are meant to be an original, like you are now."

I sniff back the tears. "Why didn't you say something? I would have changed if you had called me out. I always wanted you to be proud of me."

She pulls herself up and I hear her knees creak. "Curse of the form I chose to see you in," she says with a wry laugh. "The old ailments come with the look. But don't worry. It just sounds bad. I don't feel a thing."

My smile is weak, but at least I can manage one. "I didn't mean to be a disappointment," I say, looking up at her, pleading with my eyes for forgiveness. "I guess I just got so caught up with being popular. I think, somehow, I lost myself."

"That's the wonderful thing about losing something. You can always find it again if you look hard enough."

What is it about Grams's wisdom? It's brutal and honest, all the while filling me with hope.

"A moment ago you asked why I didn't say something to you," she says. "Maybe I should have. I hoped you would find your way on your own because you knew it was the right thing to do, not because you wanted to make me happy."

I know exactly what she's saying. And she's right. I would have done anything she told me to do. "You know," I say, forcing my smile, "I am the original. Everyone else was the copy."

"So true," she says, tapping me lightly on the cheek.

A comfortable silence falls between us, but I know it can't last forever. "I still have one more ghost from my past to deal with, don't I?"

She nods. "I'm not sure where she is, though. It's not like her to be late."

"You know her?" I say in surprise.

Grams grins. "Oh sure. Everybody knows everyone around here. There are no strangers in Heaven."

"So you did go to Heaven," I tease. "Is Grandpa there, too?"

Her smile grows wide and it looks like the wrinkles on her aged face fade away. "If he wasn't, do you think I would be?" The air around us begins to turn a stunning shade of yellow. The soft hues cast a glow over us like the early rays of sunrise. "Looks like she's here," Grams adds, turning to leave. I reach out and hold on to her arm.

"Wait. Don't go yet. I'm not sure I can do this."

She turns back and rushes to my side, kneeling before me. "My dear, you have no idea how capable you are. You can do this." In her eyes I see another look of pride and I realize that, before today, it's been a long time since I've seen that look directed at me.

I feel the tears falling again and I reach up to touch her cheek. "I love you."

Now there is sadness in her eyes. "I love you, too, Rowena Joy. But this test will end soon and with any luck, the Tribunal will see fit to send you back to finish your journey on Earth." She looks off in the distance. "I can't stay any longer. They'll come looking for me soon." She lovingly removes my hand, placing it gently in my lap. "We will see each other when the time is right, and while it will not be soon enough, I will always love you. Remember that."

Tears are falling even faster now and I close my eyes to hold them back. When I open them, Grams is gone and standing in her place is a girl about my age. I know her. Not in a you-look-familiar kind of way. I actually know her. In fact, I saw her a few days before my ill-fated trip to see the gypsy. The last time I saw her was the day she died.

Chapter 19

"Madeline?" I ask hesitantly. "Is that you?"

I expect her to rip off my head for what my friends and I did, but instead she smiles and rushes up to me. "RJ, I'm so happy to see you!" she cries and wraps her arms, not her hands, around my neck. Shock paralyzes me. "How are you?" she squeals. "I couldn't believe it when Death Himself told me you were here. At first I was so upset you were dead, but when he told me about the Tribunal, I jumped at the chance to help out. I think he was a little surprised when I told him I didn't want any favors to do it." She leans closer. "Rumor has it Daniel drove a hard bargain, but I'm glad he finally agreed." She winks at me and continues talking a mile a minute. I'm still trying to get over the fact she isn't punching me in the face.

When I can finally put words together I ask, "You're not mad at me?"

Confusion clouds her face. "Why would I be mad?"

"Well, um, you know, because of the party," I stumble, still bracing for an attack.

But she just laughs. "I guess your memories are still catching up with you."

I shrug. "I guess." Either Madeline is a great actress or she's really not mad. Though I'm still cautious, I feel the tension in my body easing.

"Then let me fill you in. Follow me. I hate this cloudy open air business they have around here." She leads the way to a door, opening it for me to walk through. I barely cross the threshold when I stop short. In front of me is a coffee shop. I mean, an honest to goodness, barista-wearing-green-smocks-and-smiling-at-us-as-we-walk-in kind of coffee shop. I can even smell the fresh ground coffee lingering in the air.

I look at Madeline in surprise. "You've got to be kidding me. There's coffee in the Afterlife?"

She giggles. "Only the fair trade variety. I thought you would like it. And it's not just in the Afterlife." She nods toward a door on the far end of the room.

There's a sign that reads, MEMBERS ONLY.

"Who are the members?" I ask, taking in the scene of people sipping lattes and talking.

"Souls who have crossed into Heaven."

Now I'm looking at her. "You're kidding?"

She shakes her head. "It's a new perk," she comments, leading the way to the counter.

As tempting as a caramel macchiato sounds, I have to ask, "Don't I still have that whole fix-my-past thing to deal with?"

She nods. "Yep, but what is it you say? There's always time for coffee?"

I do say that. "So, we just order?"

She rolls her brown eyes and links her arm with mine. "It's not rocket science. Everything is pretty much the same as on Earth." She gives the barista a bright smile and rattles off her drink of choice before turning to me. "What do you want?"

I hesitate for a moment before ordering my drink and then follow her to a pair of oversized brown leather chairs. "Don't we need to pick up our drinks?" I ask. I know it sounds lame, but seriously, this chick should hate my guts and the fact that she's hugging me and wanting a little girl time is freaking me out.

"Shayna will bring them."

Hearing her name, one of the baristas looks up and gives a slight wave. "Don't tell me the souls behind the counter are part of a work release program from Hell? Why would someone want to spend eternity making coffee drinks for people when they could float on a cloud or something?"

She looks thoughtful. "I suppose if you were a philosopher contemplating stuff that would be one way to spend your time, but it doesn't sound like fun to me. I would rather be interacting with people instead of being alone, wouldn't you?"

"Yeah, I guess. Wait, so everyone works up here? What about resting in peace?"

She's trying not to laugh at me. I can see it. Except, she's not really laughing *at* me. For the first time, I consider the idea we might be friends. The details are still a little fuzzy, but I don't think Madeline is pretending.

"No one has to do anything," she says, her smile as bright as ever. "After all, we've already served our time on Earth, doing what we have to do. Once we get here, how we spend our time is up to us. We get to do the things that we're passionate about."

Shayna appears at that moment with our drinks. I glance down at the foam and find my initials floating on top. "Let me see if I understand this," I say, turning to Shayna. "What did you do when you were alive?"

"I was a doctor," she says matter-of-factly.

"Okay," I say slowly. "Now you brew coffee?"

Her smile is blinding, even brighter than Madeline's, and I wonder if they hand out whitening strips to people when they arrive. "When I was in med school, I studied in a place like this," she says, waving her arm around the room. "The whole time I was plowing through my reading, all I could think was how awesome it must be to work as a barista. The people who worked at the café always seemed like they were part of a family. Of course, when I mentioned the idea to my dad, he went ballistic. I was expected to follow in the family business. And that's what I did."

"What do you think he would say now?"

Her eyes flit upward for a second, the smile still beaming. "He's one of my best customers." She laughs all the way back to the counter.

"She's young," I notice. "Wonder how far along she was when she died?"

"Forty-five, I think. It was a heart attack brought on by stress," Madeline answers casually.

I almost spit out my drink. "She does not look like she's in her forties," I blurt out before slapping my hand over my mouth.

But Madeline doesn't seem to notice. "We decide what age we present and under what conditions."

"Like your hair?" I ask. "When did it ever look like that?"

She reaches up to smooth the perfectly straight strands. "When I got my first wig," she answers. "You helped me pick it out."

I know it's taking a long time for all the new memories to integrate with my consciousness or whatever, but I'm pretty sure helping a girl with cancer pick out a wig would deserve instant recall. It doesn't and I'm drawing a blank. "Um, I don't remember doing that."

"You will," she says before taking a sip of her coffee. "This is the first time anyone has ever gone back to repeat their past. Even Death Himself isn't sure how long it will take him to make all the arrangements for your return. In the meantime, he asked me to entertain you until your memories catch up with you. He said something about you needing a solid understanding of your new reality before starting the last test. But who knows with Death Himself. The guy marches to a different symphony."

"So my first babysitter is Saint Peter and my second is Madeline Quinn," I say under my breath.

"It's not babysitting when we're friends," she says, looking a little hurt.

Here's my chance to get some clarification. "You mentioned that we were friends, but I still don't know what you're talking about. I remember that we threw the benefit auction and all, but that doesn't make us besties or anything. Besides, I . . ." I take a deep breath before adding, "I stole all that money we raised for your family and threw a party."

Why couldn't that memory disappear?

Madeline leans forward, her voice soft and low. "Listen to me. You aren't the person you used to be. You made some mistakes, but you fixed most of them. And you paid a pretty high price, don't you think?"

Her words trigger a few of the new memories. I close my eyes, grasping at all the details I can. "I'm still hanging out with Felicity?" I ask in surprise. Her face tells me it's true.

She nods solemnly. "You tried to break away, but then, all of a sudden, you were hanging out with her again. When we asked you about it, you wouldn't explain why. We still hung out, but it was like having a secret friend."

That doesn't sound like me. Or it didn't. The humming erupts in my head as I try to dig through the jumble of memories. "I can't remember why, either. But I know I don't like her."

She shrugs. "We thought she was blackmailing you but could never figure out what could be so bad that you would run back to her."

That reason leaps to mind without any urging. "My mom," I start. "My mom was having an affair. Felicity said if I didn't start hanging out with them again she'd tell everyone, starting with my dad."

"But she couldn't stand you," Madeline says. "Why would she want you back in her circle?"

"To do her dirty work while she kept her hands clean." The veil is lifting and whatever's been keeping me from recalling these memories finally breaks. Everything comes flooding back in waves. Every memory. Vacations I took.

New friendships that started after choosing Trevor—I mean Daniel—over Felicity. It's an entirely new life.

I sit my cup down as the room begins to spin. I would gladly take the buzzing in my head to this. "I think I'm going to be sick," I say and close my eyes. It doesn't help.

"You can't be sick here," Madeline assures me. "It just feels like it."

"It's too much, too fast," I choke. My head begins pounding as my old and new pasts fight for their place in my mind. I feel like my gray matter is going to squeeze out of my nose any second now. And then, as quickly as it came on, the pain stops.

I can hear Madeline talking to me. "RJ, are you okay?"

Everyone in the coffeehouse is watching me but no one offers to help. They seem as dumbfound as I feel. "Yeah," I say, sitting up. "It was just . . . wow . . . that sucked."

She picks up my cup. "Drink this. Maybe it will help."

I lift it to my lips and take a tentative sip. To my surprise and delight, the sweet and bitter taste chases away the last few spots of pain. I gulp down a few more sips before looking at her. "I thought people couldn't lie here."

She looks at me in confusion. "I didn't lie."

"You said I didn't steal the money for the fundraiser we threw to help your parents out. But I'm pretty sure I did. It may not have been my idea, but I didn't stop it." I groan when I remember the pending court date I have in December. "Too bad the whole you-can't-lie-in-the-Afterlife isn't admissible for my defense on Earth."

Madeline looks like she wants to say something but instead sits back and takes a long taste of her drink. "Do you remember us being friends now?"

This makes me smile. "I do. It happened not long after I started hanging out with Trevor, I mean Daniel." I sit up and grin at her. "Wait a minute. The two of you dated. You must be the girl Grams mentioned. The one Daniel's heart belongs to," I tease.

Love radiates from her entire being and the outpouring of energy makes my skin tingle from the intensity. "Sorry," she says, looking at me shyly as she struggles to reign in her emotion. "I only do that when I think of him."

Madeline reminds me of Sandy and I gently tap the ring. It's the way they aren't afraid to show how much they love. I search my brain for even a moment of that feeling but come up with nothing. I hate to admit it, but even with the possibility of getting to go back to my life, I'm jealous of two dead girls.

"Hey, Madeline," Shayna calls. "It's time. You guys better take off."

"Thanks," Madeline tells the barista before turning to me. "You ready to finish this?" I follow after her and plop my cup into the trash can. Madeline holds the door open and gestures for me to walk through. I glance at her to smile thanks and when I look up, I realize we're walking into Felicity's living room. This is the last place I want to be, especially with Madeline. This is where I gave her a reason to hate me forever.

My stomach lurches when I see myself. I look sad and pathetic and I know there are about a million places I would rather be than here.

"Hey, RJ," Felicity says. "I need the debit card. There are a couple vendors who still need to be paid before we figure the final tally."

"Which ones?" I ask, thumbing through a stack of receipts. "I thought I'd taken care of everything already."

"Don't worry about it," Felicity cuts me off with a wave of her hand, like she's swatting a gnat. "It's not a big deal. I can take care of it this evening and get the card back to you in the morning."

"Okay," I say. I watch myself reach into my bag and fumble with my wallet. I fish out the card and start to hand it over.

That's when I feel the familiar tug of the silver cord. This is gonna be bad. I just don't know for whom.

Chapter 20

Instead of fighting the pull, I give over to it completely and this time touchdown really isn't that bad. I see the debit card in my hand and I know what I have to do to.

"You know what?" I say, releasing my dormant queen bee just a little. "You've done so much with planning everything, why don't you just text me the businesses and I'll take care of it for you? That way you don't have to go out again." I give her my biggest smile, which gets a look of surprise from Felicity. I guess she hasn't seen this side of me in a while. I'm probably going to hear about it when I get back to the Afterlife, but for now, it feels nice to use my power for good.

A heartbeat later, Felicity is giving me a smile of her own and this one is dripping with annoyance and a warning. "No," she says. If you ask me, her voice is a little sharp and tight, and I'm not the only one who notices. A couple of people at the table are looking back and forth between the two of us. "I have a study session later. It's on my way."

Since when does Felicity have study sessions? The girl breezes through high school on her pouty lips and a file of tests left over from her sister's high school days. "It's no problem," I assure her. "This way, I'll have all the documents I need and I can hand it over to the school bookkeeper in the morning."

The room is silent. Now everyone's eyes are darting between Felicity and me. No one stands up to the queen. It's the first unwritten, deny-if-someone-ever-calls-you-on-it rule of popularity. "Give me the card," she hisses.

I look at her, my gaze steady as I say, "No."

I didn't think the room could get any quieter. I was wrong.

"What did you say?" Felicity asks. She's practically foaming at the mouth.

I push my chair back and stand up, squaring off my shoulders. "I said, no."

I expect her to sprint around the table like a barracuda. But she surprises me and stands still, except for her face. Under the surface, her muscles twitch and contort as she tries to remain cool and calm. "Give me the card, RJ, or I swear, I'll tell everyone."

And there it is. The warning that should force me back into my seat after handing her what she wants. But I'm not going to take it. Not when I've come so close to getting my life back. "Tell them what?" I dare her. "That my mom is having an affair? Call me crazy, but I'd be shocked if you haven't already told everyone in this room." A quick glance around the table confirms my suspicion. They're all looking anywhere but at me.

The surprise of calling her bluff only lasts a minute before Felicity is on the offense. "Now it's just a matter of time before the whole school finds out. But I think I'll start with a call to your dad. I'm sure he would love to hear about the extra activities your mom's been indulging in."

"That's not my problem," I say with a shrug. "She's the one who has to answer for her actions, not me." And with that one statement, this has become a battle between two queens. One who's fighting to hold on to what she has and one who has nothing to lose. If I don't change things now, Felicity will finish school and become a trophy wife to some loser ex-jock and I'll be in limbo for who knows how long. I just hope I don't live to regret challenging her. I don't want my dad to find out about my mom from Felicity, but I can't allow her to have any power over me anymore.

"Listen, Felicity, just let it go. Let me go. You don't like me. I don't like you. Your power to make me miserable is gone. Let's just call this a parting of ways and move on. Life is too short to spend in a passive aggressive cage match with each other."

She lets out a cackle that sounds like the call of the starving baboons they show on Animal Planet. "I should have left you in squalor with your low life friends. But I felt sorry for you. You went from ruling this school to barely being noticed."

"Do you really believe I think you took pity on me?" I scoff. "My friends, my real friends, are not losers. In fact, the only loser I see is you. You had to blackmail me in order to have someone willing to do your dirty work. But you know what?" I ask, watching her face turn fifty shades of red.

"What?" she seethes.

"I'm better than that. I realize now that I don't need fear to get people to do what I want."

"You've lost your mind," she spits back. "No one fears me. Everyone here loves me."

I cross my arms over my chest and lean back slightly. "Really?"

"Yes," she says, and I honestly think she believes what she's saying.

But the memories of my new past are well implanted in my mind and while I'm not proud of them, they're mine and nothing is going to take them from me again. Not if I can help it. "Then why did you tell me to put tequila bottles in Penny's car after she was nominated for homecoming queen?"

"What?" Penny says, snapping out of her bystander trance. "That was you? I got suspended. They kicked me off the court."

Felicity shakes her head and points at me. "She's lying."

"Am I?" I ask, scanning the faces for any sign of doubt. "Or am I finally showing everyone who you really are?"

"You've been like this ever since your social meltdown!" Felicity yells, moving around the table. I resist the urge to step back.

"Like what?" I ask, meeting her vicious stare with one of innocent calm.

"You've been trying to worm your way back in. And when I take pity on you and accept you back into our circle, you repay me with lies. Can anyone say, jealous much?"

This is exactly what I expect her to say. It's what I would say if I were in her shoes. One of the most important rules of being on top: use jealousy to explain why anyone would dare stand up to you.

I'm sure she expects me to stoop to her level, but instead of my blood boiling and steam coming out of my ears, I smile. "What do you have that I could possibly be jealous of?"

"That they choose me over you," she says, pointing to everyone watching us. "The only place you had to go was down and boy, how the mighty have fallen. All the way down to the bottom feeders of the social ladder. That Daniel guy is a freak. Leave it to him to hook up with a girl who's probably going to die before we graduate."

The room is silent again but this time it's from shock that even Felicity would say something so cruel. While no one in the room really knows Madeline, I don't think anyone has anything bad to say against her.

I push my way around the table until we're only inches apart. What do you know, it's not just the bullies who can pull off the in-your-face move. "Let's get something straight, you narcissistic egomaniac. No one picked you over me. I left. I made the choice. I picked me. So hold on to your fantasies if you need to, but don't bring Daniel and Madeline into this. They are five times the person you can ever hope to be. They know what's important. It's friendship. And in case you didn't know, that's about having someone's back instead of stabbing them in it."

I gather up all my stuff as quickly as I can and head for the door.

"Wait," she calls, and for a moment I think maybe, just maybe, she's going to have a change of heart. But even before she opens her mouth, I know it's wishful thinking.

"Leave the fundraiser stuff," she orders.

I turn around slowly, shaking my head. I see Dave standing behind her. Is he supposed to be the muscle? It doesn't matter. There's nothing they can do to me now. I've come too far to back down. "I don't think so. In fact, I think I'll drop these off in Principal Kauffman's office in the morning. He can make sure every *single* penny gets to the Quinns in time for Madeline's next treatment. We wouldn't want her to miss it because you wanted to frame me for theft or something crazy like that."

Dave's head snaps toward Felicity and I'm guessing he's made some promises to people about the party. She ignores him and instead keeps her eyes on me. "Wow. Now you're paranoid," she responds.

Here's the thing about people who spend their life putting on a fake face for everyone. There comes a moment when that face begins to crumble. I see the moment where Felicity first begins to implode. And I have two choices. I can go in for the kill, or I can be the bigger person. I really want to end her. But I don't.

"It doesn't matter what you think about me. It doesn't even matter what you've done." I can't believe what I'm about to say to her. "Felicity, I forgive you for everything. Everything you've done and everything you intended to do. I forgive you."

"I don't need your forgiveness for anything," she hisses.

"Doesn't matter. The forgiveness is mine to give." And with that, I turn on my heel and walk calmly out the door. Keep myself from being implicated in a crime? Check. Be a better person? Check. Get my life back? Let's hope so.

As the latch catches, I hear Felicity's heels clacking against the wood floor. I'm almost to the sidewalk when she yanks the front door open. "You're finished, RJ. I will ruin you. Everyone will know the truth about you."

At that moment, I snap out of my body and find myself sitting on a bench next to Madeline. "You're here," I say, still a little off balance from the body swap.

"Of course I am," she says brightly. "Where else would I be?"

"But I got the money to you in time, right? Felicity and Dave couldn't frame me for embezzlement, so I wasn't locked up for the trial. You should still be alive."

"RJ, what you did, standing up to Felicity, it was awesome. But it had nothing to do with my death."

"It had to have made a difference. It just had to," I cry out, burying my head in my hands.

"It did. It made a difference in my *life*."

I look up at her, unable to hide my confusion. "What is that supposed to mean? You're still here. You're still dead."

She nods. "Well, obviously. The treatment didn't work, but that's not because of you. It never was. It was my time. No treatment, no begging for mercy, no good deed could change that. But the last few months were incredible. I spent time with my friends and had more romantic dates with my boyfriend than any one person deserves. And I laughed. Because of you."

"How is it because of me?"

"Just think. What do you remember?"

I close my eyes, trying to clear my mind of all the anger I've been holding on to for years. "After I left Felicity's I went to school and handed over all the books to the principal so a check could be cut to your family." I open my eyes and look at her. "While I was there, he said that several businesses and individuals had agreed to match what we made. That brought the total to more than enough to help your family out and provide for the treatment."

She's smiling and there are tears of happiness in her eyes. "It was much more than enough. After the next round of chemo failed to make a difference, I decided I was done. My parents were able to take time off from work and spend it with me. Not hooked up to monitors, but at our home, surrounded by the people who cared about us. You have no idea what a gift that was for me and for them."

"I'm glad," I say, but my tone doesn't match the words. "But you're still dead. I didn't change that. I know you say it was your time, but it's not fair." I turn my head, unable to meet the gentleness in her eyes.

Madeline isn't about to let me ignore her. "Stop feeling sorry for me. This isn't about what's fair or not." She pauses and I think she's done until she yells, "Look at me!"

I turn quickly toward her. I don't remember Madeline ever yelling anything. Ever. "What?" I snap back.

"Don't do this to me. I don't feel bad that I'm dead. You can't begin to understand the pain I was in."

"But you were always happy," I say, knowing that, of all my lame comebacks, this has got to be the lamest. "I mean, you never let on how bad it got."

"Because there was nothing I could do about it. I was eight when I was diagnosed. I spent more than half of my life with cancer looming over my head. I went through a bone marrow transplant only to have a relapse two years later. I had two choices. I could fight and make the best of it, or I could curl up and let the disease consume not just my body, but who I was. I chose to fight for as long as I could, so don't you dare feel sorry for me."

I stare at her in shock. In all the memories I have of her, none of them even come close to this kind of emotional outburst. "Feel better?" I ask, not sure what else to say.

She runs her fingers through her hair. "You know, I do. I never got to say any of that when I was alive. I was more concerned about what other people were thinking and putting on a brave front. Thanks."

"No problem." We look at each other and then burst into laughter like only two soul friends can.

"Hate to break up the party," a voice booms from behind us. I don't have to turn around. I know Death Himself has come for me.

Chapter 21

"Not yet," Madeline begs. "She's not ready."

I turn around slowly to face Death Himself as he responds to Madeline. "I'm sorry, but they are." He touches her gently on the cheek and I'm drawn in by his unexpected compassion. Too bad it's not for me.

But when he turns to face me, it's still there. "Come on, kid."

Before I can move, Madeline leaps at me, pulling me into a tight hug. "I'm going to miss you," she whispers. Releasing me, she turns to Death Himself and shakes her finger at him. "You better fight for her."

He holds up his hands in surrender but there is an underlying chuckle in his voice when he answers, "I'll do my best."

"I'm counting on it," she mutters, giving my hand one last squeeze before whispering, "Tell Daniel I'm okay. He's trying to be strong for everyone, but he's hurting so much."

What is it with girls wanting me to pass along messages? First Sandy wants me to talk her fiancé's parents into letting him die and now Madeline is asking me to provide comfort for her high school sweetheart. When I hesitate she adds, "Promise me."

I nod my head quickly. "I will. I promise." And from somewhere deep inside, I get the urge to hold up my pinkie.

Madeline giggles when she sees me and quickly laces her thin finger with mine. "You remember our pinkie shake."

"No," I answer truthfully. "It's more of a gut thing. I just knew I was supposed to do that."

She smiles. "When I was sick, after the bone marrow transplant, you would come into my room and tell me about what was happening in school. I'll never forget how you looked covered from head to toe in a blue hospital gown."

Her description triggers something, and I remember the attire, including the booties over my shoes. "You were really tired. I never knew if you were listening or sleeping."

"I was listening," she assures me. "I heard every word."

I feel the waterworks starting up again. "When I would leave, you would hold up your pinkie just enough for me to slip mine underneath. That's how you said goodbye."

Of course Death Himself picks this moment to interrupt us. "This is touching and everything, but we need to go. I can't have you blubbering like an idiot before the Tribunal."

Madeline and I both roll our eyes in perfect unison. I give her one last hug before taking a deep breath. "I'm ready."

He offers me the sleeve of his cloak and I take it. Madeline disappears like a shimmering mirage and the next thing I know, we're standing in front of Judgment Hall. I'd like to say it looks less intimidating than before. I'd also like to say I'm less nervous about standing before the Tribunal. But if I did, both would be lies. After all this time and who knows what changes await me back in my old life, I really, really want to go back. The thought that the Tribunal might reject my appeal makes me sick.

Death Himself tries to make me feel better. "You know they expected you to mess this little test up, right? Especially that last one. But you didn't."

"It wasn't as hard as I thought," I admit.

"The test itself, no. It's what you, the new you, learned from the whole experience that matters. You know how Zachriel can see into your memories? Well, they're going to expect him to dig around in that brain of yours and find any indication that you will turn out like your old self. If he uncovers anything, and I mean anything, that indicates you will, Azbaugh is going to make sure your request is denied. You'll spend the rest of your lifeline in the Afterlife."

For the record, Death Himself sucks at pep talks. Trying to hold on to my last sliver of hope, I ask, "But if they turn back the hands of time—"

"Don't you get it?" Death Himself interrupts, looking at me like he's not sure how clueless I am. "They already did. Your fate has been cast by your actions. You have already changed your outcome. Now you have to hope it was enough."

I hadn't thought about that. "So the future has changed and I'm still a part of it. If they keep me here, how will my death be explained?" I ask, hoping for a loophole.

"Kids go missing all the time."

I decide this might be a good time to change the subject. "Why did you pick the moments you did?"

"Because they were the ones where your life was about to go off course and lead you away from the person you are meant to be."

"You mean, it's all about what I learned along the way?"

"Pretty much. How'd that work out for you?"

I shrug. "I guess we'll find out, won't we."

Death Himself shakes his head. "You really don't inspire confidence. You know that, right."

"Look who's talking." A figure walking toward us distracts me. It's Sal.

He gives Death Himself a nod as he approaches. "Nice of you to be on time for once."

"Hey, no problem, buddy," Death Himself says as he slaps Sal on the back. "You ready for this?"

Sal doesn't answer. Instead, he turns to me. "I've reviewed your life journey. I must say, I'm impressed. There are some big changes."

"I wish I could remember them all," I admit. "There's still a lot of stuff that's fuzzy."

"It'll come," Sal assures me. "But we don't have any time to wait. The Tribunal is prepared to rule on your appeal and wash their hands of it. Even with everything you've accomplished, this is still going to be a tough sell."

I nod in agreement. "I think I'm ready."

"Good," he says, leading the way up the stairs. "And just for the record, a lot of people here are pulling for you to win."

"Really?" I ask. "I'm surprised anyone cares. Besides, wasn't there supposed to be some type of gag order?"

"Are you kidding? No one can keep a secret around here."

I look around self-consciously but I don't see anyone or anything. I breathe a sigh of relief as we near the entrance of Judgment Hall. Sal pauses, his hand on the door. "I should also mention that the room is going to look a little different from before."

"How so?" I ask, as we walk through the door. He motions with his eyes for me to turn around. When I do, a thousand faces peer back at me. Angels are seated in the balcony while souls fill the seats on the floor.

The first person my eyes focus on is Grams, sitting in the front row directly behind my chair. On one side of her is Angelica and on the other is my grandfather. Madeline sits next to him at the end of the row. I glance up and see Yeats and Hazel sitting in the first row of the balcony.

Sal gives me a slight shove and I walk numbly into the room. As I pass the back row, a hand reaches out and stops me. It's Saint Peter.

"Al wanted to be here," he explains, "but no one was willing to babysit the mutt, so she wanted me to tell you to knock 'em dead."

"Thanks," I choke out. "Why is everyone here?"

"Some want to see you crash and burn."

From my mouth comes a sound that is a cross between a single chuckle of surprise and the last dying breath of a water buffalo. This makes Saint Peter smile with delight.

"Others are curious," he continues. "But most of us are here to make sure you get a fair trial and get your second chance."

"Come on," Sal hisses. "You do not want to make Azbaugh any madder than he will be when he sees this circus."

I let Sal propel me to a chair and focus my eyes over the crowd of heads as they twist to get a good look at me. When I sit down, Grams reaches over the rail separating us from the audience and squeezes my shoulder. "Everything will work out exactly as it should," she says, trying to reassure me.

It doesn't work.

A moment later, the flapping of wings captures everyone's attention, and I look up at the dais in time to see the Tribunal descending. Azbaugh's eyes are staring straight through me like he's wishing my very essence into oblivion. As he pounds the gavel to bring the crowd to order, I'm starting to wish the same thing. What if I lose? What if everything I did turns out to be pointless? What if they don't see enough good in my life?

Great. Now I sound like Death Himself. If the Tribunal rules against me, maybe I can work for him. That'll be payback. The thought almost makes me smile.

Chapter 22

"We are here to discuss the appeal of Rowena Joy Jones," Azbaugh calls out over the din of the crowd. He says my name as if the words taste of ash, and I shudder under his direct glare.

There's no question about how he's voting. Slowly, he turns to look at Sal. Unlike the first time I met him, my representative looks like he's ready for battle. His wings are extended slightly, giving him a wider stance, and when he addresses the Tribunal, his chin juts out just a little. His confidence rolls over him and I think some of it rubs off on me.

"I am prepared to present the actions Ms. Jones demonstrated during the test assigned to her by the Tribunal. I believe you will see her outcome far exceeds the concerns expressed in this very room when last we gathered." He gives me a nod to stand and I'm on my feet in an instant.

You know that confidence I had a minute ago? Yeah, well it's gone. Azbaugh leans forward, peering down over the dais. "You seem rather sure of yourself, my Brother. I guess we might as well adjourn, seeing as how you have already deemed her actions worthy of the complete reversal of history."

The room is silent and I sneak a look over my shoulder to see if the room has emptied out. It's still standing room only. Turning back, I see Sal's wings dip slightly. Oh no. He is not allowed to buckle under the weight of Azbaugh's scrutiny. I start to reach for the sleeve of his robe to show my support, but Sal surprises me when he raises his head and meets Azbaugh's jeering eyes. "We are also prepared to present witnesses who will testify on RJ's behalf."

"You forget, Brother, it's not for you to dictate the terms of this Tribunal. We are not a court of public opinion. That is a human concept. We will deal with fact and nothing else. All other information is subjective and thereby irrelevant." Azbaugh looks at the other Tribunal members and I can tell by the way his chest puffs out that he's expecting them to support him.

Instead, he meets with challenges.

"Actually," Shepard says, "I, for one, am interested in what the souls have to say. Their reflections, though not completely objective, can be nothing less than the truth."

"I will concede this point," Azbaugh replies slowly. "But they are also champions of the girl. There is no one here to refute her value."

Sal clears his throat. "I think that is an indication of the changes RJ has made. After all, her actions made it possible for one soul that harbored ill will toward her to repeat his own life-changing moment and as a result, the boy still walks on the mortal plane." He looks down at me with a cool smile.

"By saving him, she has already made a positive impact on the future of the world. The boy may be destined for greatness that would otherwise have gone unfulfilled."

"Your sentiment is without proof," Azbaugh scoffs. "It's merely speculation, which is exactly why I think we should confine ourselves to what we know to be true."

Marmaroth interjects, "This has never been about truth, Azbaugh. There is no doubt that this girl has been wronged. This Tribunal has been charged with determining if the positive impact of her return outweighs the negative. The history of the world has already been altered. The question is, will her return be worthy of what has been done. And that is not something that can be judged by truth alone."

"Since the souls in question currently have access to both timelines of memory," Zachriel chimes in, "they will be able to provide us with reliable information about changes to her character. This will lend credibility as to her future motives."

Hold up. Does this mean my Grams has to take the stand and answer questions about how I was in the first timeline and how I am now? I feel a lump form in the pit of my stomach. I don't think I can handle hearing what she, or Madeline for that matter, has to say. I'm not the only one who's surprised by this suggestion. Judging by the quick glance Sal gives Zachriel, this is news to him, too.

Azbaugh has that puppy-kicking look again. "This is ridiculous," he says, the muscles in his neck throbbing.

"Look, Azbaugh," Death Himself's voice booms behind me. I spin around to find him lounging in a chair next to Angelica. When did he get here? "It's not that hard," he continues. "You let a few souls talk, you listen, you decide if a valid case has been made for RJ to return to the land of the living."

The Angel of Judgment taunts him, "And why would I listen to you? Your position does not award you any power in this chamber. The memories will provide us with all the information we need. Your services are no longer required."

"Actually," Death Himself says, rising to his full height, "that's not true. You see, you may have the memories of the experience RJ had on Earth, but those she obtained while here are not part of her permanent memory and as such Zachriel is unable to access them."

"This is true," Zachriel pipes up, and Azbaugh studies him through suspicious eyes.

Azbaugh shakes his head. "And why would these be relevant?"

"I'm glad you ask," Death Himself says with his familiar cocky grin. "While they will not remain a part of her memory, they may become part of her subconscious."

"Get to the point," Azbaugh spits.

"Only those present at the time of the tests can vouch for immediate changes to her character. Combined with Zachriel's assessment, I believe you will have a full understanding of how RJ has not only met the challenge placed before her by this Tribunal, but has exceeded all expectations."

There is a murmur of support from the room. I hide a grin behind my hand.

"Enough!" Azbaugh roars. "We do not need to waste time with personal accounts. Let us take a look at her Akashic

Records. If she has truly changed her life, all the answers to our questions will be found there."

"We can't," Sal states matter-of-factly.

Azbaugh looks like he could shoot fire from his eyes. "And why is that?"

Sal sits up a little straighter. "They've been sealed, pending the outcome of this review."

"Oh really?" Azbaugh snarls. "By whom?"

The doors of the Hall swing open, crashing into the pillars. I look up, expecting the ceiling to come crashing down as a result of the force. Striding down the aisle, his millions of eyes looking around wildly, is Azrael.

"By me."

Chapter 23

The entire audience gasps at the same time. I hear a hundred voices whispering his name as he strides by me.

"This Tribunal set a task before the human soul and you will give her a fair chance to stake her claim," his voice booms.

I want to stand up and cheer, but he turns to me and I can't move. "You also have a responsibility to determine whether her efforts are worthy of an unprecedented reward. If you grant it, you accept that there may be future claims from others who feel they were unjustly collected."

The lump in my stomach doubles inside and the urge to celebrate disappears. So that's what this is about. No one wants to be the first to set precedence. Especially one that involves upheaval in the Afterlife.

His next charge takes aim at Death Himself. "I have a sneaking suspicion this is not the first time an error of this type has happened and I daresay it is unlikely to be the last."

He doesn't wait for a response and Death Himself doesn't attempt to offer one. Instead, Azrael turns back to the Tribunal and adds, "But, my Brothers, do not let that be your guiding motivation in your decision. You are right to say this is not a court of law." Azbaugh looks smug. "It is much greater. It is one of humanity. Do not discount the testimony of those who have first-hand experience with it."

And that's it. Azrael delivers his cryptic warning, then marches down the aisle and out the doors. After what seems like forever, the room erupts as everyone starts talking about the surprise appearance.

"Did that really just happen?" a soul nearby asks.

"Azrael just laid down the law," another confirms.

My head begins to swirl as the chorus of voices grows louder.

"I've never seen anyone talk to Azbaugh like that. It was great."

"He deserves it. Who is he to bully that girl?"

I plug my ears with the tips of my finger, trying to drown out the noise.

But one voice can be heard over every other. "Silence!" Azbaugh bellows. His face is bright red, and if I thought he was against me before, now it's not even a question. Sal better figure out a way to get me out of this mess.

When everyone is quiet, Azbaugh closes his eyes. The next time he speaks, his voice is tight with control. "We will begin. I will hear from witnesses, but only from those who have had substantive interactions with Ms. Jones since her arrival. Once that is done, I will ask for Zachriel to sort through the new memories and determine if they are likely to guide future actions in a positive and, more importantly, productive direction. The Tribunal reserves the right to question all witnesses before they are dismissed."

Sal speaks up quickly. "That's sounds fair and just, Brother."

"I have no objection," Zachriel says.

After the public chastising from Azrael, Azbaugh looks a little less full of himself, but not much. "Salathiel, you may begin."

Sal slips around the table and turns to face the crowd. "I would like to call Angelica to give her witness."

All eyes follow Angelica as she walks gracefully to the waiting chair. There's no need for anyone to swear an oath since perjury is impossible.

"Angelica," Sal begins, sounding like any number of lawyers on TV, "were you acquainted with RJ during both timelines?"

"Yes," she says, looking directly at me. "She was my daughter's best friend."

"You were also her guide for the first task of her test, correct?"

Again she answers, "Yes."

"How would you describe RJ during each of the time frames that you knew her?"

Angelica gives Sal a questioning look. "Are you talking about the time I was alive?"

He nods.

"She was exactly the same. A little shy at first, somewhat timid, but when she and Abby were together, it was like someone set off a giggle bomb."

"When did that change?"

Sadness floods Angelica's delicate features. "The night I died, I suppose. Obviously I wasn't there anymore."

"I believe your witness should only encapsulate the time you were alive," Azbaugh directs.

Angelica doesn't look at Azbaugh but instead waits for Sal to continue. "At what point did you next come into contact with RJ?" he asks.

"I was her first guide," she answers.

"How did that come to be?"

Angelica looks over my shoulder before answering. "Death Himself asked if I would help him on a special assignment. He said there was a girl whose soul was collected prematurely and he wanted to know if I would assist her in the task the Tribunal has assigned."

"And what did you say?"

"Well, obviously I said yes or I wouldn't be here now."

There is a light ripple of laughter behind me and even Sal smiles. "Of course. Did Death Himself tell you who the girl was?"

Angelica shakes her head. "No, and I didn't ask."

"When did you realize who RJ was?" Sal asks, his wings spreading just enough so he doesn't sit on them as he leans against the table.

"Death Himself showed me a clip from the girl's life review so I could have an idea of what was going to happen. That was when I realized it was RJ."

Now I get it. That's why she was so mad at me when I first met her. She already knew I left Abby alone with those girls.

Angelica is staring at her hands and Sal moves to her side. "When you found out it was RJ, did you have any second thoughts about assisting her?"

"Yes."

I know she can only tell the truth but the word still hurts and I wish there was something I could do to erase that moment from all timelines.

"But only for a second," she adds quickly.

"And what made you change your mind?"

"Because they were only children and children make mistakes. I could see RJ was scared, though I wasn't sure if it was the physical threats or the social ones that motivated her behavior."

Sal nods. "Is that the only reason? Because you thought she deserved a second chance?"

She smiles sadly. "No. I wanted her to stand by my daughter instead of running away."

"Why?" Sal asks.

"I'm sorry?" she asks.

Sal looks at her with tenderness. "Why did you want RJ to change the past so badly?"

Angelica looks down at her hands. "After my death, my daughter stopped smiling. She stopped being the little girl who would gather up dandelions and present them to me as if they were the finest roses Mother Nature ever created. She became a shell of the girl she should have been. She was lost, sad, and afraid." She looks at me and I sink low in my chair. "I wanted my daughter's life to be better. If RJ could change Abby's future, then I could finally stop worrying about her and find peace in my death."

Azbaugh interrupts, "That's very sentimental, Angelica. You are such a devoted mother. I imagine you would do anything to help your daughter, wouldn't you?"

Angelica's head snaps up. "I'm not sure I understand what you're implying." I can see the fire in her eyes. Azbaugh has awoken the mama bear.

He doesn't seem to care. "Did you attempt to influence Ms. Jones's decisions?"

"No. I didn't think that was possible. Since I was her first guide, Death Himself had given me very detailed instructions on what she needed to know before the first test began. I couldn't change them, even if I wanted to."

"And you refrained from lecturing or shaming her into making a choice that would better serve Abigail?"

Angelica looks guilty. "Not exactly," she begins. "I thought I would be able to talk to her like any other soul. I've done some work with the counselors, especially when mothers of young children arrive. I thought I was prepared for what I was going to see."

"But you weren't, were you?" Azbaugh continues to question.

"Do something," I hiss at Sal. "Isn't he badgering the witness or something?"

"He can't do anything, Ms. Jones," Azbaugh says. "As a member of the Tribunal, I am entitled to ask any question I see fit. It would serve you well to remember that." He turns back to Angelica and while his voice softens ever so slightly, he is still doing his best to intimidate her. "Please, answer the question."

"No, I was not."

"And you did lead her."

"A little," Angelica admits.

"Thank you," Azbaugh says, sitting back in triumph.

Shepard clears his throat. "If I may, Brother, I would like to follow up with a question of my own." Azbaugh says nothing so Shepard continues. "Angelica, did you explicitly tell RJ that she needed to protect your daughter?"

She shakes her head. "No, I did not."

"Then what did you tell her?" Azbaugh interjects.

"I reminded her that all choices have consequences and that her challenge was to make better ones than she did her first go around. I told her that everyone has regrets and she's been given a gift to go back to the moments where she was the most selfish and do the right thing."

I sink down low in my chair. I can feel the stares of everyone in the room burning a hole in the back of my neck.

"Did you tell her what she needed to do in order to, as you said, 'do the right thing'?"

Angelica shakes her head emphatically. "Absolutely not."

Azbaugh looks like he's going to push this line of questioning even further, but Shepard smiles at Angelica and says, "Thank you. Unless there are other questions from the Tribunal, Sal, I believe you may continue."

A heartbeat passes before Sal speaks. "Before her first test, did RJ know how she was connected to you?"

"I don't believe so."

"And during your observation, what did you see?" Sal inquires.

"I saw RJ struggle at first. But there was also a point where she looked at Abby and it was as if a lightbulb clicked on. She sacrificed herself in order to buy time for Abby to go get help," Angelica explains.

"Why didn't she run for help?"

Angelica looks thoughtful. "I don't know. I believe that is a question only RJ can answer."

"We can retrieve that answer during the memory evaluation," Zachriel offers. Azbaugh nods his approval.

"I have one last question," Sal says. "What impact did RJ's decision have on your family?"

"I will not allow that question," Azbaugh roars. "Stick to the facts."

Sal looks a little shaken. "Let me redefine the question, then. Angelica, did RJ's decision have a positive or negative impact on your family?" Azbaugh opens his mouth to object and Sal adds quickly, "As compared to the first timeline?"

Angelica doesn't hesitate. "Positive. For all of them," she says, beaming with joy.

"Thank you," Sal says. "If there are no other questions, you may return to the galley."

Angelica looks expectantly at the Tribunal but Azbaugh dismisses her with a nod.

As she walks by, she gives me a wink and warmth spreads through my body. No matter what happens, Angelica's approval is almost worth an eternity in the Afterlife. Almost, but not quite.

Chapter 24

"Is there another witness?" Azbaugh asks.

Sal glances to the front row. "Gladys Jones will be our next witness."

I swing my head to face her but Grams looks right past me as she walks to the chair. After our conversation, I know I'm not going to like what she has to say.

Once she's seated, Sal begins. "Gladys, you are RJ's grandmother, correct?"

"I am," she says with a quick nod of the head. "Her father is my son."

"And what was your role in the test set before her by the Tribunal."

Grams looks briefly at me and then answers. "Death Himself mentioned that there might be need for someone to step in should Daniel's timeline alter. Who better than her grandmother?"

I notice that Grams doesn't mention she skipped out of Heaven to see me. I wonder if it matters.

Sal gives her a gentle smile. "And why would Daniel's past be altered?"

"Well," Grams says, her face expressing the annoyance she's clearly starting to feel with the line of questioning, "the only reason he would be unable to fulfill his duties would be that he never died."

Sal nods encouragingly. "And is that what happened when RJ went back?"

Grams smiles at me. "Yes. She connected with him and through a series of circumstances helped change his mind about committing suicide."

"So, she saved him," Sal surmises.

Grams looks thoughtful. "Yes, I believe she did."

"Gladys," Azbaugh says before Sal can ask another question, "were you privy to the scene RJ was being shown as part of her test?"

Grams nods. "I was able to observe from a distance. How else would I have been able to step in for Daniel?"

Azbaugh stares down his nose at her. "I would like some clarification on the setup. In the previous test, RJ saw the events directly leading up to the moment when she was transported into the scene. Did the same thing happen in this second test?"

Grams looks from Death Himself to me and back to Azbaugh. "No," she says, her voice barely above a whisper.

Azbaugh looks smug. "I'm sorry, what was that?"

I can't believe he's being so rude to Grams, and I'm about to say something, except she beats me to it. "Just because you are an angel does not give you the right to speak to me like that. I said no. You heard me. Everyone heard me. Now, what is your next question?"

I have to slap my hand over my mouth to keep from laughing at Azbaugh's face. I don't think he could be more surprised if Grams were to stand on the dais in a hula skirt and do a little dance.

"I, uh, I have just one more question." He pauses and looks at her. If I didn't know better, I would say he's waiting for her to give him permission.

And then she does. "Please, ask away."

I hear giggles in the back of the room and when I give a quick glance at the crowd behind me, I see I'm not the only one hiding a smile.

Madeline leans forward and whispers in my ear, "Your grandmother is so cool."

I sit a little taller, pride giving me the lift I need. I can't believe Grams is standing up to the angel like this.

Azbaugh clears his throat. "Could you please describe the scene that took place prior to RJ being transported into her test?"

"I believe," Grams says slowly, "it was an event that took place a few days prior. RJ and her friends were tormenting Daniel, teasing him and suggesting that he wasn't worthy of life."

My smile fades. Even now, after all I've been through, her version of the situation is humiliating. How did I become such a mean person? Is there something in my nature that makes me like that or am I just weak?

Sal rushes to interject. "How did the two timelines differ?"

"Well, they were completely different. The later interaction between RJ and Daniel never occurred in the first timeline. When they did meet, I saw in her a willingness to not just take a stand for what is right, but more importantly, she was willing to stand up to her friends. I love my granddaughter, but she has been keenly aware of her social standing since she was a little girl and has sometimes made choices based on the need to be liked rather than the need to be right."

"And do you think this is an example of how she has changed on a fundamental level?" Sal prods.

"I wasn't sure at first," Grams admits. "But then I had a chance to talk with her and I knew she was different. Talking to Daniel, getting to know him, was one thing, but when she came back, the look in her eyes told me all I needed to know. She was beginning to realize how her actions made others feel. When she came back, the first thing she did was call for him, worried he wouldn't know how sorry she was."

"Did this surprise you?"

This time Grams looks everywhere but at me. Finally she says, "It was the first time in many years that I felt like she was kind."

Grams always could be a little harsh.

"Thank you," Sal says. "If there are no further questions—"

"I would like to say something, if you don't mind," Grams announces and then continues before anyone can object. "I can't say that I have always been proud of the decisions my granddaughter made in her first timeline. She was thoughtless and used people to get what she wanted."

Did I say a *little* harsh? I meant brutal.

She continues, still avoiding eye contact with me. "I always chalked it up to be her trying to figure out where she fit in. But I never stopped hoping that she would find her way. Her untimely death made it possible for her to make right what she did. I believe she has been changed to the core by the encounters she has experienced in the new timeline. To take away her chance to make a difference a second time goes beyond unfair. It takes away the hope she has of redeeming herself. It's cruel."

"Anything else?" Sal asks, looking pretty happy with her passionate plea.

"Yes," Grams says, and now she's looking at me. "I love you."

If this were a court of law, Azbaugh would be calling Grams out of order, but it doesn't matter. I feel her love pouring over me from across the room.

"I love you," I whisper with a secret wink.

She winks back as Sal dismisses her. Instead of walking back to her seat, she makes a beeline for me and scoops me up in a tight hug. "I don't care what happens here, you have already made a difference in the future," she says into my ear. "You remember that. Sit up tall. No matter what anyone says, remember that you are a better person. No one can take that away from you. Do you hear me?"

I nod, tears slipping over my cheek. "Thank you, Grams. I promise I won't let you down."

"I know you won't, sweetheart."

"While this little scene is indeed touching, could we move on to the next witness?" Azbaugh asks, sounding bored. "I believe you were going to call upon the angel Yeats, right, Salathiel?"

Great. I hope my new self isn't as much of a pain in the butt as my old self.

Chapter 25

Yeats descends from the balcony and strides to the front of the room, his white robes swirling at his ankles. He ignores the chair and instead turns to face Sal. "I will tell you what I know," Yeats says.

"Brother, you have been a Guardian for many people both good and not so good. Would you agree?"

"Yes."

"What is your relationship to RJ?" Sal asks.

That's a silly question. Everyone knows he's my Guardian.

But Yeats answers with sincerity, "RJ is a charge of mine. I am one of her two Guardian Angels."

"In what other capacities have you dealt with your charge?" Azbaugh interjects.

This question catches me off guard. What other experience could he possibly have, you know, other than my entire life?

Again, Yeats answers the question matter-of-factly. "While RJ was alive, and prior to her acts direct by this Tribunal, I counseled another charge, a boy, whose death, according to the Akashic Records, was a direct result of RJ's actions."

"What?" I shout before I can stop myself. Out of the corner of my eye I see Yeats pivot toward me, a look of disapproval and warning registering loud and clear. I can't believe he has the audacity to give me looks of accusation when he just betrayed me in front of the Tribunal. Daniel isn't dead. He's alive. Why should I be held accountable for something that never actually happened?

"Rowena Joy Jones!" Azbaugh yells, slamming his hands down on the bench. I really hate it when he says my whole name. "You are a guest of the Tribunal. Unless you are spoken to, do not utter a word."

I can't stay quiet any longer, not when I'm being accused of murder and technically, Azbaugh is talking to me. I decide to push my luck. "But he said I killed someone. I'm pretty sure that's something I would remember doing in any timeline."

"Enough, Ms. Jones," Azbaugh repeats, his eyes glowering down at me. "I will have you removed and you will await our decision in isolation."

I slip back against my chair, clench my fists, and dig my nails into the palms of my hands. Which is about the time I remember I can't feel physical pain. All I'm left with is the emotional pain. Maybe that's why souls cry. Tears are a product of our emotions, aren't they? I set my mouth in a grimace and wait for Sal to continue.

"Please, Brother, you were explaining your second connection to RJ."

Yeats slowly turns his face away from me to look Sal in the eye. "Not long ago, one of my charges took his own life."

Sal nods, encouragingly. "And what was the name of this charge?"

"Daniel Trevor Wick."

While several of the audience members gasp or murmur their surprise, Sal remains emotionless. "What was his relationship with RJ?"

Yeats again looks at me and as he speaks, I am unable to look away. "According to Daniel, he believed her to be one of the tormentors whose unrelenting pranks and harassment led him to the decision to end his existence."

"And would you agree that, as a result of RJ's change, he did not, in fact, make this choice," Sal says, looking around the room as if searching for something or someone. "In fact, doesn't Daniel continue to walk in the mortal world?"

It's about time someone pointed this little fact out.

Yeats nods solemnly. "He has had a rough go of it, but yes. He is not only alive and well, but filled with purpose."

Sal walks behind the table and leans against the railing separating us from the spectators. "And what role in this new timeline does RJ play?"

"That is difficult to say."

"And why is that?"

I lean forward, wanting to know the answer, too. What have I done now?

"Daniel will go on to do great things. RJ's influence on his future is immeasurable," Yeats continues.

"Really?" Sal says, with mock surprise, and I suppress a laugh at his bad acting. He turns toward me and gives a conspiratorial wink before continuing. "Then why is it difficult to explain her role in his life?"

"First of all," Yeats begins, "there's the part where she reached out to him, when genuine friendship began. Because of that friendship, he was introduced to Madeline who became his girlfriend. Her battle with cancer ultimately led to his career choice in medicine."

"And according to the Akashic Records, what does his future now hold?" Sal asks.

Yeats smiles broadly. "Immediately following RJ's second test, I checked the Records. According to them, he will be part of a team that will eventually discover a cure for three different forms of cancer. Their results, when shared with other researchers, will lead to a significant increase in cure rates for most cancer patients. Eventually, when Daniel's days on Earth are done, the foundation of his research will lead to the early detection and eradication of most cancers."

"So," Sal surmises, "Daniel's work will literally save millions of men, women, and children from dying."

Yeats nods. "Not just that, but it will improve the quality of life for all those who love and care for those people."

"Excuse me," Azbaugh says, mocking Sal. "Are you insinuating RJ is responsible for curing cancer?"

Sal shakes his head. "I'm making no such claim. I am merely providing an answer to the question put forth by the Tribunal. By sending RJ back into her life, the world will, in fact, be better off than if she remains in the Afterlife."

"And Daniel is the only one who can discover this miracle cure?" Azbaugh asks skeptically.

"I'm sure someone at some time in history might make the same discoveries as Daniel's team." Azbaugh looks pretty pleased with himself until Sal adds, "But as the world waits for this discovery, how many more people will suffer and die from diseases that the boy has the ability to end?"

Azbaugh glares at Sal. I don't think he's buying it. "But the changes have already been made. Sending her back would not change the future anymore. Her impact has already been felt."

I sit back in surprise. I didn't think they would take the changes I made and use them against me. That's like asking someone to do a job, promising them money for the work, and then going back on the deal. If not for Azbaugh's warning, which still lingers in the air, I would say so. As it is, Sal takes another approach.

A slow, almost gleeful smile spreads over Sal's face. "Ah, yes. I was getting to that." He turns back to Yeats. "My Brother, Azbaugh raises a valid question. Is Daniel's future set in stone?"

An odd look crosses my Guardian's face. "It is not."

Shepard and Marmaroth raise their heads and peer down over the dais. Azbaugh's eyes narrow like a hawk's. But it's Sal going in for the kill that makes me smile. "It seems that his future is still tentative, barring the outcome of this decision."

"But how is that possible?" Sal asks, his smile stretching from ear to ear. "The Akashic Records are not fluid. They are fact, are they not?"

Yeats clears his throat. "In all my time as a Guardian, a charge's future has always been set. However, I do not believe RJ's role in Daniel's decision has taken place yet."

"Please," Sal says, his arm sweeping toward the crowd. Is it my imagination or is he getting more theatrical by the minute? "Enlighten us."

Yeats nods. "It is RJ who convinces Daniel to pursue his dream of being a doctor when everyone else says he can't do it. Her belief in him and his passion for finding a cure is the combination that makes his discovery possible."

There is a tremor of talking that grows with each passing second.

"Silence!" Azbaugh yells over the chatter. "There will be silence!" When no one listens, he opens his mouth and a deafening sound, something between a shriek and a sonic boom, comes out of it. Everyone, including the angels, cower low to the floor. As for me, I'm in the fetal position under the table, my hands pressing my ears tight against my skull. Finally the noise stops and I look up to see the steady, weathered hand of my grandfather reaching down to help me up. I accept it and stand to see people reclaiming their seats in silence. Except for one person, that is.

"I hate it when he does that," Death Himself mutters, straightening his bright orange Hawaiian shirt.

"I heard that," Azbaugh's gravelly voice rings out and more than a few souls flinch. He gives one last glare in Death Himself's direction before turning to Yeats. "Let me get this straight. Are you saying there is a conditional future in the Akashic Records?"

Yeats nods. "I have never seen something like it before. After holding council with several of the Akashic Record Keepers, the only rational reason is that RJ's future is undecided."

Sal interjects. "Is Daniel's life the only one with, as Azbaugh says, a conditional future?" He gives the Tribunal a triumphant look, almost as smug as Azbaugh's normal face. I can see now why Gideon picked him to defend me.

Yeats shakes his head. "No. In fact, almost every file shares this common trait."

"Are there any that don't have notations?" Sal presses.

Yeats nods. "Yes, but almost all of the Records in question have expiration dates prior to Daniel's decision to attend medical school."

Azbaugh speaks up before Sal can ask any more questions. "But not everyone in the world will develop cancer."

"This is true," Yeats replies, "but the Keepers theorize that, since cancer impacts not only the life of the patient, but all those who know the person, the impact has a ripple effect. Until her fate is settled, theirs cannot be. Remember, Brother, humans are sentimental creatures."

Azbaugh shakes his head. "Mortals," he says with contempt.

So it's not just me Azbaugh doesn't like. He hates my entire species.

Sal nods thoughtfully. "Why did people have a future at all if their lives were so tied to the outcome of RJ's appeal?"

Yeats looks a little less confident and I feel the bottom of my stomach drop. "They did not know the answer to that question. All they could do was posture a theory."

"You mean guess?" Marmaroth confirms.

Yeats gives a tense nod in response.

Seeing Azbaugh lean forward to speak, Sal steps up to ask the next question. "And what was their theory?"

"They believe the futures are based on the best possible outcome."

"Which would be?" Sal prods.

"Because RJ is referenced as a determining factor in Daniel's future, they believe in order for the majority of the futures to become solidified that RJ's appeal must be approved. Once she returns to Earth to complete her life journey, they expect the Records to right themselves once again."

"And were there any other possibilities?" Sal asks.

"This was the only theory the Keepers could agree on," he says with a shrug.

Sal turns to the Tribunal. "I have no further questions, Brothers."

Azbaugh looks first to Shepard and then at Marmaroth. When neither speaks, he gives a flick of his hand. Yeats stands and then walks across the room and exits through the back door. Not once does he look at me.

"And who will give witness now?" Azbaugh asks, boredom dripping from his words. "Please tell me you are almost done with this parade of cheerleaders."

"Just one more," Sal assures him. He turns to look at the front row. "Madeline Quinn will be our final witness."

Finally, someone I don't have to worry about throwing me under the bus.

Chapter 26

Madeline makes her way to the front of the room, fluffing out her skirt as she sits down. It settles around her like yellow petals on a flower. She looks up at Sal and says, "I'm ready."

Not even Azbaugh can look at her with contempt or scorn. Sal steals a glance at the audience before he speaks. "Madeline, please tell us about your experiences with RJ."

"Are you asking about our relationship on Earth or while she's been here?" Madeline asks.

"Start with your human life," Azbaugh advises and there's an unnatural warmth in his tone.

Madeline smiles brightly at him. "Of course." She turns toward Sal. "After RJ stood up to Felicity, all her friends gave her the cold shoulder. I felt sorry for her. I mean, no one wanted to hang out with her."

"Why is that?" Sal asks, but I already know the answer.

Madeline shrugs. "I guess because it was socially inadvisable. I mean, most people tried to fly under the radar of RJ and her friends, but when she was dethroned, Felicity was vicious. She went out of her way to attack anyone who gave RJ so much as a glance of pity." She pauses.

"Madeline," Sal says gently, "is there another reason she had no friends?"

She's quiet for a long time. Finally she answers, "Yes."

"What are you not telling the Tribunal, Madeline?" Azbaugh asks.

With a sigh, Madeline answers, "RJ didn't really have any friends when she split from the popular kids. She'd spent three years making a lot of people miserable. There were more than a few people happy to watch her fall from grace."

The room is completely silent. So this is what it sounds like when the bus lays you out flat.

"What changed?" Sal continues.

"Daniel. He left school for a little while. No one knew it, but he was getting treatment for depression. He came back four inches taller and twenty pounds lighter. His skin was clear and he had switched from glasses to contacts," she blushes as she describes him, which I completely understand. She's describing Trevor. "When he came back to school, he knew part of the reason RJ was an outcast was because she stood up for him. So he started hanging out with her."

Sal leans against our table and crosses his feet in front of him. "What did Felicity do when he returned?"

Madeline lets out a little laugh. "She was furious. She would call Daniel names, try to embarrass him, that kind of stuff. But Daniel didn't care. He was still seeing his counselor, so if things got too bad, he could talk it out. Eventually, her words and jabs stopped registering. After a little while, people started gravitating to the two of them."

"Why?"

Madeline looks at me. "Because they were fun. They would laugh constantly during lunch, completely oblivious of the evil glares her old friends were giving them. I have to admit, I was jealous."

"And why's that?" Sal asks.

Madeline looks sad, like she's remembering something about her past that's painful. "I spent so much time in and out of hospitals with cancer running my life that the friends I had when I was diagnosed eventually stopped coming around. And when I saw the former queen of the school hanging out with a cute boy like she didn't have a care in the world, I knew I wanted to be a part of their little group. But I was afraid that they wouldn't want to be friends with me."

Not have a care in the world? Wow. I really had her fooled.

"What did you do?" Sal asks gently.

She brightens. "One day, about a week before I was supposed to start prepping for my bone marrow transplant, I got this surge of courage. I figured if I could face the possibility that I might walk into a hospital and never come out, asking a couple people if I could eat lunch with them was going to be a piece of cake."

"And was it?"

She nods. "Yep, and there wasn't even a second pause before RJ was pushing her backpack to the floor and making room for me. A few days later, a couple more people joined us. By the time I went into the hospital, I had this amazing group of people to support me."

I can see that Sal is trying to phrase his next question carefully. "How good of a friend was RJ? Did she ever abandon your lunch crowd?"

My stomach tightens. I'd forgotten there was a very real reason I was nervous Madeline would attack me when we first met. Now I'm about to hear the story through her eyes.

"Not while I was there but one time when Daniel came to visit, he said RJ wasn't hanging out with him as much as she used to. He was really broken up about it. When he told me she was having lunch with her old crowd, I couldn't believe it. He said she looked miserable, but she still met them every day."

"Did this come as a surprise to you?" Sal presses.

Madeline glances over at me. "Not really. I didn't tell Daniel this, but every single night at seven-thirty, RJ would gown up and spend an hour visiting me. She never missed a night. But I knew she was hiding something."

"Did you ever ask her about it?" Azbaugh asks.

His voice startles her and I see a shiver run through Madeline. Azbaugh's eyes soften, but he waits for her to answer the question. "Yes. At first, she tried to avoid my questions. She made up some excuse about Daniel being too sensitive, but I knew she was lying. Finally, she confessed that Felicity was blackmailing her back into the group. Once the cat was out of the bag, she spilled the whole story." She pauses and gives me an apologetic look. She has nothing to be sorry for, but I brace myself for what she's going to say next. "RJ's mom was having an affair and Felicity had threatened to tell the whole school about it if RJ didn't start hanging out with her again."

I glance over my shoulder at Grams. Did she already know about my mom? Was she mad? Her eyes are staring straight ahead and there's no expression in them.

"Why would Felicity spend time with someone she didn't like?" Sal asks. I turn forward and watch my friend share all my deepest secrets with the Afterlife. I know she can't help it. She's just answering the question, but it still feels like a betrayal.

"There's a saying among the humans: you should keep your friends close but your enemies closer. RJ's apparent immunity to Felicity's attempts to ice her out made her a threat. Besides, Felicity needed her."

"For what?" Shepard asks.

Madeline takes a deep breath. "She said Felicity was using her leverage to make RJ do all kinds of mean things to their friends. She hated doing it, but she needed to protect her mom. I felt so bad for her. I mean, that's a lot for someone our age to deal with."

"What else did she tell you about Felicity and her friends?"

"She told me she'd suggested Felicity and her group throw a benefit for my family, to help them pay for my treatments and catch up on bills. I told her she didn't need to, but RJ insisted. She begged me to let her use her position for something good. I think she thought it might make up for all the mean things she was doing, or at least help balance the scale."

Sal walks around the table and sits next to me. "Did you finally give her permission to go ahead with the plan?"

Madeline gulps. "Yes. Maybe I should have insisted she get out, but I was selfish. I knew my parents could use the money. Dad's company was giving him as much time off as he needed but there was no money coming in. They were months behind on the mortgage. I thought this could be an answer to their prayers."

"When did you find out about the plan to frame RJ for stealing money from the fund?" Sal asks.

"After she went to the principal. I had been out of the hospital for a few weeks but my immune system was still weak and my doctors were concerned that I might develop an infection. We were supposed to try an experimental treatment but our insurance wouldn't cover it. She came to tell me that her group had raised enough for the procedure and that the school should have a check for my parents in a matter of days."

"And how did that make you feel?" Sal asks.

Madeline's eyes start welling up. "Relieved. I didn't tell RJ this, but we were running out of last chances. If this treatment didn't work, I was ready to stop. I was tired of fighting against something I couldn't beat. I had friends. I had a boyfriend." She looks at the audience. "Daniel and I grew close in such a short time. Really, I have Felicity sucking RJ back in to thank for that. Without her being around, he spent more time with me. Then, one day, he kissed me."

I swear I heard a collective sigh rise up from everyone in the courtroom, angels and souls alike. Madeline is holding them in the palm of her hand and she doesn't even know it.

I study Madeline. I know I adore her, but what is it about her that captivates everyone she meets? Suddenly, I feel overwhelmed with sadness. Even if I get what I want, she won't be a part of my life anymore. There is no changing her future.

Azbaugh looks directly at me as he asks the next question. "What was RJ like in the first timeline?"

Madeline clasps her hands in her lap and stares down at them, her chin dipping down to her chin. "She was evil."

Chapter 27

The entire room gasps. I'm pretty sure they've never heard Madeline say anything negative about anybody. I, on the other hand, crack up. Partly because it's funny and partly because of the look of absolute horror on Madeline's face. I wonder what it's like to be that nice.

"I didn't have a choice," she sputters. "It's this place." She looks at me with tears in her eyes. "I can't lie. But I would if I could. If it would help you. This isn't fair." She turns to Azbaugh. "You don't know her. You don't know how much stronger she is than the rest of them. She deserves a second chance."

While she's pleading my case, two thoughts go through my head. One: how could I have been such an idiot to spend so much time with my fake friends when there were real ones there the whole time? And two: I'm pretty sure Madeline's outburst is going to be the topic of conversation for centuries to come.

"Madeline Quinn," Azbaugh says, but there's no harshness in his voice like there is when he talks to me.

Wait a minute. How come when he says her name the walls don't rattle? I look at Madeline, seeing her, I mean really seeing her for the first time. A faint glow radiates from every inch of her body as if she is made of pure goodness.

"No," Madeline says. "You have to listen to me."

"Madeline," Azbaugh repeats. This time he's a little testier. "Please, calm yourself."

She sits back against her chair in a huff. When she locks eyes with me, I want to reach out and comfort her. But she's full of surprises.

"I'm so sorry," she mouths, and I'm pretty sure she's on the verge of a breakdown.

I shake my head and smile. "Don't be," is all I can whisper before the tears choke the rest of my words. How in the world did I ever get a best friend like her? Okay, sure, I had to make a lot of people mad and become a social pariah, but still, in the end I'm the one who got a better deal. "Whatever happens, I'll be okay. It's not like I'm a Chilean coal miner," I say.

Madeline lets out a giggle. "You're never going to let me forget my obsession with that mine collapse, are you? Do I need to remind you that I was stuck in my bed, post–bone marrow transplant, and there was nothing else on TV? *And*, it was nice to see that someone else was having a rougher time than I was. It was, no, it *is* a perfect mantra. You should get one for yourself and stop stealing mine."

The sensation that we're sharing a private joke floods over me. In my first life, a private joke always came at someone else's expense. But with Madeline, there's no viciousness, only comfort.

Azbaugh is clearly not happy with our banter and instead turns to Sal. "Are you finished with this witness?" he asks coldly.

Sal nods and turns to Madeline. "Thank you for your testimony. You may step down."

She slowly slips off the chair and looks from Azbaugh to me. I can tell she's thinking about doing something but isn't sure how the Tribunal will react. Finally, she makes up her mind and rushes around the table, throwing her arms around my neck.

I look at Azbaugh, my eyes wide with fear and surprise. And then the dam breaks. I stand and return her embrace. Once again, I'm struck by how peaceful I feel around her. I wish I could feel this way forever. But she reluctantly breaks away and I look up to see Yeats pulling her into the audience. His look tells me he's sorry and with a slight nod toward the dais, he redirects my attention to Azbaugh, who looks none too thrilled with my emotional outburst. I guess the Angel of Judgment doesn't like feelings clouding up the facts.

Sal comes back around the table and motions for me to sit. I tuck my hair behind my ears and do as I'm told. I'm too exhausted to fight anymore. Madeline was my last chance. And if her passionate witness doesn't convince the three angels that my life deserves a second chance, well, then I doubt anything will. I prepare for my turn before them.

"Zachriel," Azbaugh asks once the smattering of conversation from the galley dies down, "are you ready?"

I lean over and whisper to Sal, "What's happening?"

He tilts his head slightly, not taking his eyes off the dais. "Zachriel is going to sift through your memories to see if there is any evidence that your soul has changed after the experiences you've had."

"Wait, so I don't get to say anything?"

"Is there a problem?" Azbaugh calls out, irritation creeping into his tone.

Sal gives me a thanks-a-lot look and stands. "If it would please the Tribunal, I would like a few moments to discuss the next phase of the Tribunal's inquiry with RJ. Surely, my Brothers, you would have no objections."

Azbaugh nods and makes a motion with his hand. Out of the corner of my eye I see the wall to my right begin to shimmer and a door appears. Grabbing my arm, Sal propels me from the room.

When the door latches shut, he whirls around on me, exasperation filling the air. "Geez, RJ, can't you just sit there and let me do my job? The less Azbaugh hears your voice, the better. He doesn't like you."

"Really? I hadn't noticed," I snap. "This is my life they're debating. I think I'm entitled to have a say or at least know when someone's going to be poking around in my brain."

"No, you aren't. Believe it or not, Zachriel might be your best shot at getting out of here."

"What do you mean?"

"He knows what your life was like when you first got here. He's going to use that as a baseline and filter out what you have learned and predict with perfect accuracy what will happen when your conscious and subconscious merge again. He alone can give witness to the growth you have experienced.

"If all they care about is Zachriel's projections, what was the point of the testimonies?"

"That's what Azbaugh cares about," Sal agrees. "But Marmaroth and Shepard are swayed by other variables."

"Like what?"

"Well, for starters, most of the time souls are passive, preferring to cast off the chains of mortality and enjoy life after death. But several have temporarily relinquished their peace and entered into this three-ring circus. For them to become impassioned and take up for a cause will go a long way to get you the other two votes."

His eyes are pleading with me. I want to argue but I can't. I know he's got a point. I run my hands through my hair, twisting a few strands when I get to the end. "What do you think my chances are?"

"Azbaugh is looking for any reason to turn you down, but you already know that. I don't think he cares about whether you are a good person or not. To him, this has been handled wrong from the beginning and should be made right."

"And Marmaroth?"

Sal looks a little less sure now. "He's the wild card. You scored some major points with him when Yeats brought up the Akashic Records. All of those lives with questionable futures won't sit well with him. Add to the fact that they are most likely based on you being sent back, making the outcome all the more questionable if you don't, and I think he could swing the vote in our direction. But he may see sending you back as a slippery slope to more appeals being made by souls who are not ready to accept their death. That could be enough for him to vote with Azbaugh."

I take a deep breath and realize the room smells like the gardenia garden my grandmother had behind her house. It's not enough to make me relax, but my head is clearer. "After Zachriel does his thing to my head and gives his report, is that when they vote?"

"Yes, but Azbaugh will make them deliberate before rendering their verdict. You can bet he'll have prepared a pretty compelling argument to deny your request."

"And there's absolutely nothing I can do?"

He's quiet for a minute and then answers, "Maybe one thing. You've won over the crowd, but their opinion doesn't matter. It's the three angels at the front of the room that count. You have to make them realize that you recognize the seriousness of the situation."

"I can do that," I say with a nod.

"And you have to convince them that you've learned from your experiences. Make them believe your life and those of the people you harmed have value to the world."

I want to yell at him to stop lecturing me, but I can't. I know he's right. "If I can do that, everything should work out?" I could really use some reassurance right now.

"I can't promise you that."

Not exactly what I was looking for. "But we can hope, right?"

"Hope is a pretty powerful form of prayer," Sal says, his hand on the doorknob.

Absently I say, "I don't pray."

He pauses before responding, "Maybe you should."

Chapter 28

My return to the Hall is met with a sudden hush falling over the room. The three members of the Tribunal are standing together behind the dais, talking in voices that I can only describe as quieter than a butterfly's wings. When they hear us, they return wordlessly to their places.

Azbaugh doesn't even look at me. "Zachriel, you may begin."

I expect for him to come over and touch my forehead or something, but he doesn't. He just closes his eyes. And then I feel him. At first it starts like a subtle tingle, but the deeper he digs into my memories, the more it feels like tendrils carefully picking over every inch of my brain. I shudder, trying to pull back, but I feel a hand on my shoulder. I glance up to see Yeats standing next to me.

I don't remember seeing him when I came back into the room, but I'm glad he's here. His touch soothes me and I manage to stay calm through the rest of Zachriel's investigation. When my mind feels like my own again, Yeats moves away. Taking a deep breath, I look to Sal for reassurance.

"You did good," he says. "Not many people can go through such a thorough review without screaming. You didn't even whimper."

His approval does nothing to diminish the violation I feel. Since not all of my new memories have made their way to my consciousness, Zachriel probably knows more about me than I do. I look at him to find his eyes still shut. As though he senses me watching, they flutter open without warning.

Azbaugh looks at him carefully. "What say you, Brother?"

Zachriel is silent and still for a long time. When he speaks, his voice is flat, like he's in a trance. "I have reviewed the memories of Rowena Joy Jones. I have seen her past and her present. I have filtered out her memories of the Afterlife, though it was difficult as some of them have become embedded in her subconscious. According to all that is seen, I can say without hesitation that the unseen of her future poses significant improvement over the last timeline. The quality of her life has already been greatly altered by her actions." And with that, Zachriel stops talking and slumps in his seat.

I don't know what the Tribunal wants to hear, but all of that sounds good for me. I turn to fist bump Sal, but his eyes are still on Zachriel. I follow his gaze.

Can angels die? Because Zachriel looks dead. I mean, really, really dead.

Azbaugh doesn't seem concerned about Zachriel's sudden change at all. He isn't even looking at him. Instead, his gaze is boring into my soul and any happiness I feel about my success is quickly receding. He scrunches his face up until his eyebrows come together and a snarl skips across his lips. "My, my, aren't you a surprise."

I can't believe it. He's mad at me because I did what the Tribunal asked me to do? It's not like I'm trying to undermine his authority. But that's exactly what I've done. I glance at Sal who reminds me with his eyes to stay quiet. I fold my hands in my lap and the coolness of Sandy's ring takes me by surprise. Until now, nothing has felt hot or cold.

I focus on the ring until Shepard breaks the awkwardness settling over the crowd. "It would seem that we have all the information we need and the decision is in our hands, Brothers. Shall we convene for counsel?" Not waiting for Azbaugh's answer, he stands up and slowly unfurls his wings to their full length. The flapping starts as a gentle breeze, growing steady as he rises. When Marmaroth joins him, the air begins to swirl, but at least he's taking care not to stir up the wind too much. Azbaugh, on the other hand, doesn't seem to care about our comfort and shoots up, his wake leaving everyone struggling to stay upright.

"Oh, yeah," Sal says. "He's not happy."

I turn to him, feeling the blood drain from my face. "He can't refuse me. Not after what he just heard. How can he say I can't go back when everyone, including the mind invader over there, says I've changed? Geez. Even the Akashic Records are on my side."

"Because he's Azbaugh," Sal says in frustration. "Don't you get it? The Tribunal was called because Azrael said it had to be. But he does not determine the outcome. The Tribunal can do whatever they want and there is no one to overturn their decision. Azbaugh doesn't have to explain the reason for his vote."

"So this has probably been a complete waste of time," I sulk.

Sal shakes his head. "We were never trying to get Azbaugh's vote. It's the other two we're working on."

"Well, do you think we got them?"

Sal looks away. "I don't know."

I see Grams and Madeline huddling close together, whispering and giving me hopeful looks that aren't very convincing. Around the room, I meet similar faces staring at me. People want to encourage me but deep down, they're not sure what's going to happen. I begin to prepare myself for the worst. Maybe the Lobby wouldn't be so bad.

Turning back to Sal I ask, "What if they reject my appeal? What happens then?"

Sal doesn't answer for a moment. When he finally does, I'm not happy with his response. "They will make a recommendation to Azrael. Basically, they'll likely suggest you be hidden until your time is up."

"Why can't I just go back to the Lobby?"

"You've already proven that you have the ability to communicate with the newly deceased," he answers. "Azrael will want you kept out of sight of souls going through processing."

He's talking about the lovesick biker. Why didn't I leave that guy alone?

I force myself to pay attention to the rest of Sal's speech. "However, you haven't completed processing, so you won't be able to enter Heaven or Hell, either."

"Why does it have to be 'or Hell'? At the very least, I should get a free pass to Heaven."

He ignores me. "Something in between will have to be figured out."

"Maybe I can work at the coffee shop," I suggest, remembering how I was able to enter the space and interact with the barista. Wait a minute. What am I doing? Am I giving up? Am I seriously sitting here, contemplating what I can do to pass the time until my mortal time of death.

Sal seems to consider the idea. "It's a possibility. But as I said, that will be up to Azrael."

He glances over at Zachriel, who is starting to show signs of life again. "It's hard on him, you know," Sal says, and I'm not sure if he's talking to me.

"What?"

He glances at me and then back to Zachriel. "Going through memories. It's hard. I can't imagine how it is to explore a mind that is neither dead nor alive."

I glance at Madeline and she gives me an encouraging wink. Her support is a sad reminder that even if, by some miracle, the Tribunal sends me back, she will still be here. I won't have my best friend.

As if sensing my sudden sadness, Madeline reaches over the wooden rail and squeezes my hand. Instinctively, I squeeze back and the heat coming from her takes me off guard. Everything up here is the same temperature, but right now, in this moment, I can feel the warmth radiating from her.

"You know," I start, turning toward her, "I never asked what you do up here. I mean, other than helping me not screw up my future."

She beams at me. "Oh, I don't know yet. I haven't found my place." She pauses slightly. "But don't worry about me. I will."

A thought occurs to me and I turn back to Sal. "Can human souls ever become angels?" The question makes him uncomfortable and I watch him squirm slightly in his chair. "Can they?" I press.

"You know, you're pushy," he finally blurts out after I poke him in the arm to get a reaction.

"Well, you didn't answer me."

He looks up at Madeline, his lips puckering from clenching them together so tightly.

"You know," Madeline begins, "I'll just leave the two of you to talk about whatever." She turns and walks back to her seat. As she does, Sal relaxes.

"What gives?" I ask, eyeing him with suspicion.

He looks around to make sure no one is listening. "Okay, yes, humans on *very* rare occasions can be elevated to the rank of angel, but it's almost impossible."

"Why?" I ask.

Sal really looks like he would rather explain how babies are made than how a human becomes an angel, but he dutifully launches into a brief explanation. I suspect he's just trying to distract me from thinking about the verdict.

"There are several traits that a human must possess in order to become an angel. First, they need to be true of heart.

Maliciousness is something that does not come naturally to angels."

"That seems a bit unfair," I mutter, my eyes drifting skyward. After all, from what I can see, Azbaugh embodies malice with some wickedness to spare.

Sal glares at me. "You cannot pretend to understand the existence we have endured since before the beginning of time."

"You're right," I admit sheepishly.

I'm not sure if it's my honesty or humility that surprises him more, but Sal recovers and continues his explanation. "They also have to be pure."

"Pure? You mean like never having—"

"Yes," he says quickly.

Turns out, there is nothing more awkward than discussing sex with an angel.

"Okay, so pure of heart and body. What else?"

Sal ticks off the rest on his fingers. "Empathetic, loyal, trustworthy, eager to serve others, and the survivor of a life unlived."

The last one throws me for a loop. "Okay, I get the first four. Sounds like you're looking for a Boy Scout, which I get. But I don't know what you mean by a survivor of a life unlived."

"It means," Sal says, leaning closer, "that their life was cut short before the trappings of the human life could make them pessimistic toward the human condition."

"Huh?"

Sal rolls his eyes. "They aren't full of the societal desire to conform and be someone they aren't."

I nod my head. "You mean like me."

"Yes," he says, not bothering to sugarcoat his answer.

I look back at Madeline, her eyes bright and shining as she listens to something my grandfather is saying. "What about Madeline? She would be perfect."

"I cannot discuss this with you."

My eyes widen. "Is she a candidate or whatever you call them?" I grab his hand in excitement. "Oh, you have to make her an angel. Seriously, she would be perfect."

He looks down at my hand before carefully lifting it off his robe. "Even if she was, I couldn't talk to you about details."

"Oh, come on. It makes perfect sense. First, she meets every single criteria . . . not sure about the pure of body one, but I would put money on it that she is. And then there's the way Azbaugh reacts to her. I mean, I'm pretty sure the guy hates everybody and yet when she was giving her witness, he practically bent over backward to be nice to her."

He looks away, unwilling to meet my demanding gaze.

"She is!" I squeal, clapping my hands together under the desk.

"Stop talking," he orders.

I make a motion of zipping my lip and throwing away the key. "That is perfect. When?"

"You're not going to drop this, are you?"

"Nope."

"Fine. Yes, she is now being considered for elevation. But she has a choice to make."

"What kind of choice?" I ask.

Now that the truth is out, Sal doesn't seem to care about keeping the information to himself. "If she were to be elevated to the rank of angel, Madeline would have to agree to give up everything from her mortal life. When family members and friends arrive, she will not be able to greet them, at least not as human souls. Her memories will be sealed until such time as she wishes for them back."

"They can do that?" I ask in surprise.

Sal nods. "It doesn't happen often, though."

I want to ask him more and find out how soon Madeline will know if she's going to be elevated, but the whoosh of wings makes me forget.

Azbaugh's voice can be heard before his form is visible.

"We've reached our decision."

Chapter 29

Silence doesn't even begin to describe the sound in the room once the wings become still. I search each face of the Tribunal, hoping for some indication of how they're going to cast their vote, but each member reveals nothing—not even a hint of where they stand on the issue of my fate.

"That was fast," I whisper to Sal, who shakes his head.

"Not as fast as I thought it would be."

My eyes still on the angels, I ask, "Is that good or bad? Because where I come from, a fast deliberation normally means someone's about to do jail time."

Sal doesn't answer. And I'm not sure if that's because he doesn't know or he doesn't want to tell me.

I start to stand, like they do in the courtroom shows on TV, but Sal reaches out to stop me. He probably thinks I'm going to say something to get myself in trouble. Joke's on him. I'm pretty sure if I try to say anything, I'm going to throw up all over the place.

"We have heard compelling testimony," Azbaugh begins. "Some of it has been revealing, though it is my opinion that most of it has been emotional fluff. And while truthful, it does not instill me with the belief that setting a precedent of undoing death in such a manner is either wise or responsible. I also recognize that, by voting against this appeal, I am setting in motion changes that have long-reaching effects, but I believe that they will all work out in the end just as they are meant to." He looks directly at me when he delivers his verdict. "My decision is that we should not return Rowena Joy Jones to her timeline."

A chorus of disagreement meets his ruling, but all I can hear is the sound of the air being sucked out of the room. Sal touches my hand and I look up at him, my peripheral vision blurring until I can only see his mouth moving.

"We knew that was coming. There are still two others," he says. And then he turns back to the dais.

Azbaugh raises his hand for silence and though it takes a little longer than before, everyone eventually complies. "Shepard, please deliver your ruling."

Shepard, whose contribution to the Tribunal's inquiry has been minimal to this point, steps up, his voice ringing out clear as a crystal blue lake. "While I respect my Brother's decision, I do not share it. I think RJ has shown great strength of character in not only achieving the objectives set before her by this Tribunal, but also in her decision to pursue this matter in the first place. It takes much courage to stand up and demand something be done to right injustice." He smiles at me before continuing. "I do not doubt RJ has learned much, both through the tests and through interaction in the Afterlife. I do not share the belief that a human soul will be completely stripped of experiences when they cross from the mortal realm to the immortal and vice versa. I believe the core of what makes RJ who she is can only be made better by her time up here." He pauses to scan the audience. "Finally, human souls and angels alike have given witness to the power of RJ's future. In their own way, the Akashic Records have acknowledged the intricate nature of life and how we are all connected. I don't think RJ is special because the outcome of this Tribunal leaves so many other lives in limbo. After all, what is it they say on Earth? If a butterfly flaps its wings in one corner of the planet, does it not change the weather patterns somewhere else?"

There is a smattering of laughter but Shepard continues. "The human experience, their very existence, depends on their interconnectedness to each other. To knowingly rip those threads apart just because we don't like the issues in front of us is both childish and unrefined."

My jaw drops. Did Shepard just call Azbaugh out? I hope I don't forget that if I'm sent back to the mortal world. It has to be one of the most epic moments in the history of, well, history.

Azbaugh looks like he could spit nails but Shepard pays him no attention. "It is for this reason that I vote in favor of this appeal. I believe any other decision is reckless and unjust."

Wow. Remind me to look for Shepard if I ever need an angel backing me up. He might appear serene and pleasant, but he has no problem landing some nice sucker punches.

The room erupts in applause and Shepard looks around with genuine surprise. He smiles at the crowd and then at me. Out of the corner of my eye I see Sal breathe a sigh of relief. Of course this means that everything rests on the decision of

Marmaroth. Even now I can't get a read on him but that's not a surprise. I think angels tend to play their cards pretty close to the vest. Or robe.

Azbaugh looks expectantly toward the last member of the Tribunal. "What say you, Brother?"

Marmaroth stares at me for a long while. As each second ticks by, I begin to sink farther into the back of my chair. His decision is the only thing standing between me and my life. The better life. The life I actually want to go back to.

Finally, he speaks. "This is a very difficult decision. On one hand, Salathiel has given us a very compelling case. And I must admit RJ's performance in her test has exceeded my expectations. On the other hand, to mess with time is dangerous. If I were to have it my way, the issue would never have come to this. Perhaps someone else will find the cure for cancer. Perhaps not. As an angel, I do not concern myself with the issues facing the human race."

I fight back a wave of nausea. This is not going well.

"I am responsible for the passage of time, not what happens in it," he adds.

Yep, definitely not going well at all.

He continues, "But my opinion on this matter is also irrelevant. It is not for me to force my will on others." I perk up. "Azrael commanded we listen to this child's claim of injustice. She has given us ample proof that she is of stronger character than perhaps we first thought. The adaptation to her second timeline and the ease with which she changed the passing of her life gives me hope that greater things are yet to come from her life."

I resist the urge to high five Sal, who probably wouldn't know what I was doing anyway. The ping-pong match over my future still is making my head swim, but I think Marmaroth is on my side after all.

"However, the fact that her Akashic Records are sealed is troubling," he continues.

Maybe not. The match continues.

"If I am going to put my trust in the human child, I wish it were not on blind faith. But then again, is that not why we exist in the first place? Because we have faith to believe there is something more, something greater than ourselves?"

If they send me back, I have to remember never to take a philosophy class. I hear rustling behind me and I know I'm not the only one wishing he would just get it over with already.

"Yes, this is a difficult decision," Marmaroth says with a click of his tongue.

Azbaugh isn't looking so confident now. "But a decision you must give," he leads.

"As I am well aware," Marmaroth snaps. "You make an excellent point about establishing precedent, but I will not be rushed on this matter." He looks thoughtfully toward the ceiling. "If only there were some way we could see what her life has in store for her. It's undoubtedly changing, even as we speak." He looks at Sal. "Is there no way?"

Sal shakes his head. "I am sorry, but RJ's records are sealed until the moment she returns to the mortal plane or the time of her natural death."

"On Azrael's command, I assume?"

"Of course."

Wow. For a guy who hardly said two words during the proceedings, he sure has a lot of questions now.

Marmaroth looks over Sal's head. "Death Himself, I seek your counsel."

"And you shall have it," is the reply. My eyes follow Death Himself as he strides toward the dais, stopping in front of Marmaroth. "How may I assist you?"

The formal tone sounds out of place when coming from a man in clothes fit for a luau. But Marmaroth doesn't seem to care. "This issue before us is a result of an error by one of the Grim Reapers, correct?"

"It is," Death Himself concedes. "I accept full responsibility and I'm going to great lengths to make sure it does not happen again."

"Yes, yes," Marmaroth says, dismissing the humility. "You have a vested interest in the outcome of this, I would assume."

"I do."

"And what outcome do you think will serve us all best?"

Death Himself casts a sideways glance at Azbaugh. "There is only one among us who will be better served if RJ does not return to the new timeline, and he has made his position perfectly clear."

"What makes you say that?" Shepard says, taking notice of the carefully chosen words.

Death Himself stands a little straighter. "I have it on good authority that Azbaugh is eager to wield judgment first hand. He has been looking for a way to usurp my authority over the dead for some time now."

Marmaroth shoots a suspicious look at Azbaugh. "Is this true, Brother? Are your intentions less than pure?"

"They have been and always will be for the greater good," is all Azbaugh says.

Am I the only one who notices he doesn't answer the question?

Marmaroth looks back to Death Himself. "These are serious accusations," he says, leaning forward.

"Yes, Marmaroth. They are serious indeed. This is why I must come forth with all the facts now." He turns toward Azbaugh, who looks like he wants to leap across the dais and strangle Death Himself.

"Are you prepared to offer proof to support your claim?" Shepard interjects.

"I am. However, these proceedings are neither the time nor place. RJ deserves her verdict to be untainted by our ethereal squabbling."

Marmaroth nods slowly, his eyes turning toward me again. "And you believe the girl will continue the changes that have begun even when she leaves this realm and the memories fade?"

"I do," Death Himself confirms with a swift nod, and I think he really means it.

Turning to look at me again, Marmaroth, without emotion, says, "I agree."

Wait a minute. Did I just win?

Chapter 30

Judgment Hall erupts in pandemonium. I'm going back! I'm going to see my family and my friends again! I'm going to eat popcorn and watch movies and feel the sun on my face. I can't believe it.

Before the mob of well-wishers descend upon me, Sal rushes us back through the little door to the side of our table. This time, instead of a small room, I find myself back in the confines of Azrael's office. Death Himself is already there.

Azrael looks up with his millions of eyes and says, "Is it done?"

Sal gives a quick nod and then promptly disappears.

"Where did he go?" I ask.

Death Himself shakes his head. "He is of no benefit to you now. He has done his part to represent you but he has other work to do."

"When will this matter be completed?" Marmaroth asks.

"Soon," Azrael replies. "We must decide when the best time will be. Her return must be seamless but we must allow for her body and soul to acclimate. Suggestions?"

"Well, obviously it should be when she is alone," Death Himself asserts.

"Agreed," Marmaroth seconds. "But near the date of her collection. We want to make sure her memories are fully restored."

I look between the three of them and it dawns on me that I'm in the middle of an Afterlife war room.

Azrael looks back down at his desk. "I trust you will make sure the plan goes off without a hitch."

Marmaroth nods, accepting the responsibility. Azrael then turns to Death Himself. "And I see you couldn't refrain from exposing Azbaugh's plans."

"I was asked a question. I answered it. I couldn't exactly lie in Judgment Hall."

"No," Azrael replies, a growl emanating from his throat. "But you didn't have to be so honest." He pauses, looking at me. "Never mind," he says, shaking his head. "What's done is done. Back to the girl. Let's intersect her early in the morning on the day she originally met the Reaper. If we're lucky, she'll think this is all some dream and forget everything she's seen."

"But I don't want to forget," I blurt out before I can stop myself. If Azbaugh and his self-important power trip frightens me, then Azrael conjures up almost enough terror to bring on a heart attack.

"You have been catered to enough, human," Azrael says, his eyes—the ones that belong to him and him alone—turning black as coal. "And you would be well advised not to ask for any more favors." He begins to walk toward me and I back up until I bounce off the chest of Death Himself. "Furthermore, when your life is over and you return here to learn your fate, I suggest you do everything you can to avoid me. You have been a thorn in my side long enough. Understand?"

I nod my head, wishing Azrael would turn into his less disgusting form. Having the eyes of every soul on Earth looking at me isn't something I could ever want to get used to. "Yes," I say but have to choke out the word.

"Good," Azrael snarls. "The Afterlife is in chaos thanks to you. The Lobby, which is normally the quietest place around, is abuzz with stories of your refusal to accept your end. Of course, none of them mention the role the Grim Reaper played. No, they only talk about how you didn't want to go quietly into the light. The sooner you're gone, the sooner this world can get back to normal."

No wonder most of the people in charge around here hate me. I had no idea how much trouble wanting to set things right might cause. I start to apologize when Death Himself puts his hand over my mouth. He moves me out of the way, placing his body between mine and Azrael.

"I will see that she is on the next available train to the mortal realm," he assures Azrael. "Yeats will escort her on the return journey. When he returns, I will notify you."

"And Hazel?" Azrael asks.

Death Himself shakes his head. "Hazel is no longer on the Guardian path. She has taken a position more suited to her particular skill set."

"Meaning?"

"She is now ferrying the souls of the newborns to their new lives on Earth."

Azrael gives a quick nod of approval. "She will do well there. Is there anything else we need to discuss regarding this matter?"

"I do not believe so."

"Wonderful. I trust you and Marmaroth will be able to coordinate the reentry without any further issues."

Death Himself bows. "Of course."

I'm ushered out quickly and Death Himself closes the door firmly behind him. "Do you ever think that staying quiet would be the best thing for you?"

"I know. I'm sorry," I say. And I really am. "It's just that I don't want to forget. I don't want to be the girl I was before. That mean girl who didn't care about anyone other than herself. I want to be good. Like Madeline."

Death Himself throws back his head and howls in laughter. I cross my arms over my chest. "What's so funny?"

"My dear girl, you will never be like Madeline."

"Hey," I say, defensively. "I could be."

"No chance," he says. "She is a special soul, sent to change the world through her death. Even if you really wanted to, and I have a sneaking suspicion you don't, you could never be like her. From what I can tell, you are meant to change the world through your life, but the gentleness that she possesses, the part of her that has not become blackened by greed or lust or any of the other deadly sins, is already out of your reach."

"Thanks," I say, not even trying to hide my hurt feelings. Seems like no matter what, I'm doomed.

Death Himself rolls his eyes. "I forget how sensitive humans are. I wasn't trying to make you feel bad. But it's a fact.

Your contribution to the human race comes from the things you will experience. You have to get knocked down from time to time so you can serve as a living testament that you can always, no matter what, get back up and soldier on."

"So, I'm already damaged goods?"

Death Himself nods. "Pretty much. I could send you all the way back to your birth, but it wouldn't matter. The life journey path you are on and the one Madeline has completed are different. They always have been. Just be glad your journeys ran together for a while. In all honesty, she's a huge part of why the Tribunal listened to your appeal in the first place."

"What do you mean?"

He shrugs. "I probably shouldn't say anything, but since you'll forget about this by the time you wake up, what the heck. You know that little party you and your friends threw during the first timeline? The one paid for with the money raised to help Madeline's family out?"

I groan. "How could I forget? I still can't believe I did that."

"Well, lucky for you, you didn't. Not the second time at least. In the first timeline, after the party, when Madeline found out what you and your friends did, her heart was broken. Not for herself, of course, but for her parents. She couldn't believe people would pretend to care about her, about her family, and then steal from them. She felt betrayed. And that betrayal, combined with the fear of what was to come in the time she had left, melted together to create one angry, bitter girl."

"We broke her," I whisper.

Death Himself nods. "In a way. She was no longer pure of heart. She had learned to hate. Nice little lesson to get right before you're going to die."

"She would never have had a chance to become an angel, then."

Death Himself looks at me in surprise. "Who told you about that?"

Lost in thought, I answer without thinking: "Sal." Slowly I raise my hand to my mouth. "I wasn't supposed to say anything."

Death Himself just laughs. "Yeah, like I'm going to get the guy who just saved my job in trouble. Do I look like an idiot?"

I give his current outfit an up and down appraisal. "No, not at all."

"See, more proof you don't belong here. You're probably the only person who can get away with lying in this place."

I just grin. After all, sarcasm isn't lying. Not really. It's more like my superpower. "Why are you being so nice to me? The last time we were in the same room, I thought you were going to rip my head off."

"Two reasons. One, I'm no longer in the hot seat because of this whole mess, and two, you did good, kid. Better than I thought you would do."

"You thought I was going to fail, didn't you?"

"Let's just leave it at this: there were moments when I thought locking you in a broom closet for the rest of eternity was a good backup plan."

"Was I really that bad?" I ask, the sting of his comment hitting me in the gut.

"In the beginning, yeah, you were that bad. But you got better." He grins at me and reaches out to tousle my hair.

"Quit," I snap. "I hate that."

"I know," he says. "Some things never change."

"Funny."

"I thought so," he says, turning to lead me away from the Hall. "Now, how about we find your Guardian and get you on a train back to your life?" I don't follow immediately and he stops. "That is what you want, right?"

Of course it is. It's what I did all this for, isn't it? Then why am I afraid to put one foot in front of the other and leave?

Death Himself backtracks toward me. "RJ, we need to leave now. You'll miss your window."

I nod slowly, but still don't move. For the life of me, I can't think of any reason why I would want to stay, but I can't leave. And then it hits me. All this time, while the battle to send me back was raging on, I got to spend a little more time with Grams and Madeline. I'll even miss Saint Peter and Al and that smelly dog with three heads. I guess I like it here. It's starting to feel like home.

As if reading my thoughts, Death Himself grabs me by the arms and moves me forward. "Go. Now. After everything I've gone through, you are not allowed to change your mind. Heaven and Earth have been moved and at no point will missing your friends and family be an acceptable reason not to return to the living."

"But—"

"There are no buts," Death Himself insists. He then softens his tone. "There is only the life you are meant to live. You have to go back now. Everything is ready for you. Once Marmaroth sets out on a mission, there is no stopping him."

"What about them?" I whimper. "Grams and Madeline—"

"What about them?" he asks. "They were fine before you got here and they will be just fine once you're gone. Let's get moving. Yeats is waiting."

As we near the train, my fingers begin to tingle and I start examining them.

"It's the memory of being alive," Death Himself explains.

"What?"

He nods at my hands. "That sensation. It's your soul remembering what it feels like to be connected to your body."

"Oh." I look over my shoulder and think I see Madeline watching, but the more my eyes strain to see her, the more the wisps of air swirl around me, blocking my view.

"Yeats," Death Himself says as we approach the train, "here she is, delivered safe and sound."

"So it would seem." My Guardian turns to me and motions toward the door. "It's almost time to leave."

I look through the window into the train. It is crowded like before, but unlike my arrival, which consisted of mostly old souls, this crowd is full of Guardians cuddling what looks like rolls of blankets.

"What are those?" I ask.

"Brand new souls," Yeats says with a serene smile.

"Please tell me they aren't going to cry the entire way there," I say. "Because if they are, I'll wait."

"Just get on the train," he says with a laugh.

And I do, without anyone forcing me. As the doors close, I turn to find Death Himself still standing outside the door.

"What?" I ask.

"Keep your chin up, kid. Who knows, you might be back here before you know it," he says as the Soul Mover chugs forward and picks up speed.

I lean against the glass, but Death Himself is lost in the mist. I look at Yeats. "Hey, you don't think that was some cryptic message about my impending death, do you? Because I'm fine with not seeing this place or any of you for at least seventy years, maybe eighty, with the right diet and exercise."

Yeats shakes his head and lets out a deep chuckle. "It's Death Himself, RJ. No one can know for sure what he means. My guess is he's messing with you. You do kinda bring out the antagonist in him."

"Yeah, but do you think he knows something about my new life—and my real death?" I demand.

"I doubt it."

"What makes you so sure?"

"Because your Records are still sealed. Until your soul reunites with your body, no one, not even Death Himself, can view them."

Why do I get the feeling Death Himself can do whatever he wants?

"Maybe you're right," I say. Looking around, I notice the seats are white and pristine. "How come this train is so much nicer than the one we arrived on?"

Yeats glances up. "I don't know. This is my first time on the outbound express."

"It's because these souls are pure. They're clean and the train is a reflection of them," a familiar voice explains.

Chapter 31

I spin around to find Hazel standing near us, complete with a swaddle of her own.

"Hi," I say in surprise.

She smiles and I can see the change in her since she stopped being a Guardian. There's a gentleness in her face that wasn't there before.

"You look amazing," I say. Do angels care about their looks? I mean, they're all beautiful, but Hazel's transformation goes beyond surface level.

To my surprise, Hazel blushes. "It's less stressful delivering the souls than it is to watch over them and bring them back when their lifeline ends," she admits.

"Hazel was once a human soul, before she was elevated to angel status," Yeats says, taking both of us by surprise.

"Yeats," Hazel says, shifting the future newborn away from him. "I thought that information wasn't supposed to be discussed in front of the souls."

"I was just explaining your unusual assignment," he explains. "Besides, she already knows about the elevation process."

"Who told her?" Hazel demands.

"Um, hello. I'm standing right here," I remind them, but as always, they ignore me. I guess Death Himself was right. Some things never change.

"Sal did," Yeats explains. "She was asking all kinds of questions about Madeline."

"She knows about Madeline?" Hazel shrieks and every angelic face on the train turns toward her. She doesn't seem to notice and I get a sense of satisfaction that I'm not the only one she ignores.

"Relax," I tell her. "Apparently they have it set up so when I get back, I'll think this is just some crazy dream and eventually forget all about it."

And much to my surprise, she does seem to relax a little. "You know what? You're not my responsibility anymore. I trust Yeats. If he, or any of the other angels for that matter, wants to take chances with what you will or won't remember, that's up to them."

"Speaking of that, do you know who they're going to assign as my new Guardian?" I ask Yeats.

"I don't know yet," he answers. "For now, you're stuck with me. Just do me a favor and try not to cause too many problems when you get back."

The train is beginning to slow. I watch as the black outside the window gives way to gray and then eventually white. When it finally stops, the doors open and the angels, in solemn reverence, walk single file out into the mortal realm. Hazel is the last to disembark.

"Good luck," she says. "I knew you were redeemable." She rushes out the door to catch up with the others.

"Well," I say, turning back to Yeats, "this is it."

"End of the line," he jokes.

"What happens next?"

"When the doors shut, the connection between you and the Afterlife will sever, much like it did when your first timeline came to an end."

I nod. "And then what?"

"Hopefully, you'll rejoin your life just after midnight on the day of your first death," Yeats says, reaching out to place his hand on my shoulder. "With any luck, you'll be asleep, giving your mind and body enough time to re-form the connection. However, I wouldn't be surprised if you're still a little disoriented when you interact with others. There may be some residual interference from the first timeline, at least for the first day or so."

"What do you mean?"

"Some events will seem almost exactly as they did in the first timeline, but more than likely there will be some slight change. Those anomalies may take a little longer for your consciousness to identify and correct."

"For example?"

Yeats shakes his head. "I don't know. Like maybe when you go to open your locker, you'll use the combination from the first timeline instead of the second."

I think back to my locker. Before the collection, it was next to Felicity's. I hope things change enough so I'm not in the same hall as her.

"Okay, I get that," I say and then start to think about all the trouble this could cause if I forget who I'm friends with and, more importantly, who I'm not.

"You'd think, after all this time, I would get used to all your questions," Yeats says, throwing his hands in the air. "We're in uncharted territory and you hopefully won't remember this conversation when you wake up, so—"

"Yeah, yeah. I know. You want me to get moving."

"It's time," Yeats agrees.

I stand at the edge of the car, take a deep breath, and step onto the platform. Fear seeps through me and I spin around, yearning to get on the train and flee back to the Afterlife.

"What if I screw this up?" I ask Yeats.

"You won't."

"But how do you know?" I press. I take a step back toward the train but my retreat is cut short as the doors snap shut.

A slow smile spreads over Yeats's face. "Because I can see your future," he says before the door closes with a loud thud.

Chapter 32

I sit upright in bed, shielding my eyes against the bright sun. Is it morning already? I don't remember going to sleep and when I try to think about yesterday, a distracting hum kicks in my brain. I pick up my phone to check the time just as the alarm blares the latest boy band chart topper. Hitting the snooze button, I pull the comforter over my head, vaguely aware of the phone falling to the floor as the humming grows louder.

"RJ?" my mother calls from behind the door. "Are you awake?"

"No," I say, but the fabric muffles my response.

She knocks again.

"What?" I yell and immediately grab my head. "I'm up. Geez."

She doesn't answer, but I see the shadow of her feet from under the door disappear. Sitting up again, I yank back my hair in a messy ponytail, then lean over the side of the bed, searching for my phone. My fingertips graze the edge of the case. Just a little farther and I'm able to hook my pinkie around it. When I finally fish it out, a ring I don't remember seeing before tumbles out from beneath the bed. I vaguely remember Mom telling me last week that she had some fake jewelry I could use for my Halloween costume, but the diamond in the middle of the leaping dolphins looks pretty real. At that moment, the alarm on the phone rings again. If I don't get moving, I'm going to be late. Grabbing the clothes lying on the back of my desk chair, I plod to the bathroom and turn on the faucet in the shower. It isn't until I step out of the tub and wipe the steam off the mirror that I actually look at the clothes hanging on the back of the door. Why in the world would I ever wear a yellow polka dot pleated halter dress to school? I double check the date on my phone. I thought so. It's Halloween. What? Am I dressing up as Mary Sunshine?

A tap on the door distracts me and I wrap the towel around my body. When I swing the door open, my mom, who is also wearing a yellow ensemble, is standing in front of me. Usually, my mom only wears black power suits.

"How are you doing?" she asks, rushing to be the first to speak.

"Fine," I say, drawing out the word so she knows how strange she's acting.

I watch as she shifts her weight from one foot to the other. Her eyes are misty and she looks like she's about to burst into tears. "I just wanted to make sure you were ready for today."

What is she talking about? Why would she care? It's another crappy school day. A nagging feeling creeps in from somewhere deep inside. There's something I should be remembering, but whatever it is, my mind is fuzzy. I look back at the dress. Yellow. That means something, doesn't it? I'm drawing a blank and my head feels like there's a cage match raging inside. "I think I'm good," I finally answer, filling a glass with water and choking down two pain killers.

She gives me a quick nod. "I fixed your shoes up, just like you asked." She pauses, waiting for something.

Why would I ask her to fix my shoes?

"Um, thanks," I finally mutter.

Tears begin to well up in her eyes before they stream down her face. She reaches out and pulls me into a hug so tight I'm pretty sure at least one, if not both, of my lungs collapses. When she finally releases me, I tighten my towel and give her a little smile. What is her deal? Unless she . . . oh no . . . did Dad find out about the affair? Is that why she's so weepy? Is he leaving her? Is he leaving me *with* her?

I watch as she wipes her eyes before giving my arm a light squeeze and whispers, "I love you so much."

Crap. He knows.

"I love you, too," I say. She smiles and finally starts to leave my room. "Do you want a ride to school or is Daniel picking you up?"

"I'm good," I assure her, wondering why in the world Daniel would be picking me up. We haven't hung out in months. Or have we? There's that fuzzy feeling in my brain again.

Without warning, my head begins to spin and I have to sit down on the toilet to keep from throwing up. Once the nausea passes, I pick up the dress and consider hiding it in the back of my closet. The very thought conjures a strong negative reaction. For whatever reasons, I need to wear it. As the soft material slips over my body and the folds fall into place, so do my memories. I remember why I'm wearing yellow. My stomach lurches and I race to the toilet just in time for the pills to come back up.

Today is Madeline's funeral. And the reason Daniel is picking me up is to take me to the memorial they're having at school. The entire town will be there, including my mother. As for the unseasonable outfit, that was Madeline's rule. Everyone attending her service had to wear yellow.

How could I forget? It's not like every moment of the last four days hasn't been spent planning her service. Or crying in private. Or hating God.

On the floor sits a pair of black heels with yellow daisy clips. Daisies are, or were, Madeline's favorite flowers. After slipping them on, I finish getting ready in silence. Just as I'm putting the finishing touches on my makeup, the phone rings.

"Hello?" I answer, my voice echoing in my ears.

"Hey." Daniel's voice is flat without a trace of his trademark laughter. "You ready?"

"Yep." And by yep, I mean nope. Who can ever be ready to bury her friend?

"Okay."

I grab my purse and don't even stop for one last look to make sure I appear perfectly composed. This day is going to suck and no amount of mascara is going to change that. As I walk out the front door, my mother calls out, "We'll be there soon!"

I turn to answer but stop as I notice my father helping her with the clasp of her necklace. When he's done, he kisses Mom lightly on the head and she turns around, letting him pull her into a protective embrace.

Maybe he doesn't know about her betrayal. Or maybe he does and the thought of attending the funeral of his daughter's best friend is making them push that aside for now. After all, they aren't the ones putting their kid in the ground. This thought strikes me as ironic, but as soon as the idea enters my brain, the fuzzy hum starts up again. Whatever's going on, I don't have time for it. I shut the door softly, trying not to interrupt their moment, and walk to the waiting car at the curb.

I feel a familiar rush of comfort when I see Daniel. I know the weeks I was MIA in our friendship, the time I was hanging out with Felicity and her people, were hard on him and it's always tense when we're first around each other.

Daniel unlocks the door just as I touch the handle. I slip into the seat and stare straight ahead. There's nothing left for us to say to each other that hasn't already been said. We are beyond kind gestures and empty condolences. The only positive thing to come from Madeline's death is that it has brought the two of us back together.

This morning, Daniel does what he does best. He distracts me from my pity by taking shots at the only person in the world I actually hate. "So," he says as he pulls away from the curb, "what do you think Felicity is going to wear? Feather-skirted cocktail dress?"

I smile. It's not quite a laugh, but better than I expect. "Don't forget the plunging neckline and glitter stilettos."

"Of course." The corners of Daniel's mouth turn up. Not enough to resemble a real smile, but enough to give me hope he will get there someday. "Did you know she actually called Madeline's mom to see if she wanted her to speak at the service?"

My mouth gapes. Leave it to Felicity to think she could try to steal money from someone and still ask for a moment in the spotlight.

"You're kidding," I say in disgust. Then I remember how I almost became an accomplice in her scheme. How could I forget something like that? It must be shock.

"Not even a little. I was there when she called."

I shake my head. "Does she really think the Quinns don't know about the stunt she tried to pull?" We sit in silence for a while. Probably because we know this is about the point in the story where Madeline would jump in and tell us to be nice. Or maybe it's because there's really nothing worth joking about on a day like today.

"Do you have the letter?" he asks as the smile slips from his face.

My mind is asking, "What letter?" but I feel my head nod and my hand pat my purse.

"And you really think you can get through it without crying?"

I shake my head. What letter are we talking about, and why do I feel like I've been taken over by a body snatcher?

"Yeah, I can't imagine what it will be like to carry the coffin, especially after you read her last words," he admits. "To know she's there, but not there, you know?"

Oh no. He's talking about the letter Madeline left for me to read at her funeral. I've got to get it together. First, I forget that it's the day of her burial and then I forget one of her final wishes. "She'll be there," I tell him absently. And in my heart, I believe the words I'm saying.

He hits the steering wheel with the palm of his hand. "Cut the crap, RJ. This is me. She won't be there. She'll never be there. Not ever."

"Pull over," I command, and, surprisingly, he does so without question.

The car shudders a little when he cuts the engine. I turn to him, ready to assume the role of Madeline's best friend. "We have to get through this day. For her."

"How?" he shoots back. "When the memorial is over and it's just those who knew and loved her most at the graveside, how am I supposed to get through it? I thought someday I would be watching her walk down the aisle on our wedding day. Instead, I'm going to be rolling her down the aisle in a mahogany box. Tell me how I'm supposed to get through it."

I sit back in surprise. "You never told me that."

"What?"

"That you wanted to marry her."

He scoffs. "Well, there were a lot of things we talked about while you were making up with Felicity and her clones."

"Hey!" I cry as his words pierce my heart like an arrow. "You don't get to be mean. Not to me, and not today."

Immediately he looks like he regrets what he said. "I'm sorry."

"Don't worry about it," I say with a sigh.

We sit in silence and wait for him to calm down enough to keep the car on the road. I can almost hear the minutes ticking away.

"I'm good now," he says.

"Liar."

He takes a big breath. "I'm as good as I'm going to get."

"That I can believe. Now let's get going before people start wondering where we are."

When we arrive at the high school, the lot is full. I mean, there are cars on the lawn, down the street, around the block, and anywhere else a vehicle can be parked.

"Madeline's mom said there would be reserved parking in the teacher's lot for us," Daniel says when he sees me scanning the rows for a place to park.

"Let's hope so."

Sure enough, there are a few spots open as we pull around the back of the main building.

"You ready?" he asks, turning the key in the ignition.

As I take out the letter from Madeline, my hands begin to tremble. "I can't do this," I say. It's more like I don't want to do this. I don't want to share her with strangers.

"Hey, do I need to repeat the lecture you gave me ten minutes ago?"

"No, but if I do this, if I read this letter, then it means she's really gone. She's not coming back."

"News flash," Daniel says sadly. "Whether you read the letter or not, she's not coming back."

"Not in here," I argue, pointing to my heart.

He takes my hand. "Together? For her?"

Blinking back tears, I nod. "Okay."

Opening the door, the Indiana sun warms my skin. It's unusually warm and for a fleeting moment, I wonder if Madeline sent this weather to tell us she's okay.

"Now?" Daniel asks.

"One foot in front of the other, right?"

"Just like breathing."

"Yeah," I mutter. "Because that's so easy right now."

As we enter the gym, the number of bodies in the stands is overwhelming. "How many of these people actually knew her?" I wonder aloud.

"I don't think there is a person who met her who didn't like her," Daniel says, looking down, probably to avoid the glances of pity people are shooting at us.

"Well, maybe one." As if on cue, Felicity rushes to us, gushing about how sorry she is and what an inspiration Madeline is. I want to punch her. But I don't.

"If there is anything I can do, please don't hesitate to ask," she rambles on.

Daniel's eyes turn black. "You know—" he begins before I cut him off. I really hate having to be the good cop.

"Thanks, Felicity, but I think everything is covered." I grab Daniel by the arm and drag him toward the stage before he can say something offensive.

"I hate her," he mutters.

"Me too. But Madeline would be so ticked at us if we ever said that to her face."

"Yeah, but that girl, she tried to steal from Madeline and—"

"And Madeline forgave her. I think we kinda have to take the moral high ground here."

"Leave it to her to try to teach us a lesson from the other side," Daniel mutters, letting me lead him through the crowd.

Madeline's mother glances up as we approach, her eyes full of grief and something else. It's gratitude. She stands and walks toward us, spreading her arms out just as we near. She embraces Daniel and then wraps me in a tight hug, holding on longer than ever before. "I'm so glad the two of you are here," she says.

She starts to pull away but collapses just as Daniel reaches out to catch her gracefully, then he helps her back to her seat. I see a stack of bottled water to the left of the stage and retrieve one for her.

As I hand her the bottle, I want to tell her how sorry I am and how amazing her daughter was. I want to tell her how I'm a better person because of Madeline and how she made the world a little brighter. But I don't.

"We're ready to begin, Mrs. Quinn," the minister says gently.

She nods and takes a deep breath as he retreats to the stage where my best friend lies, dead, in her casket. Daniel and I take seats behind Madeline's family. In a few minutes, I'll address everyone in the gym. I'll read Madeline's last message to us all. I will get through it without tears because I don't have a choice. But right now, I can feel my heart breaking inside my body. This is real. Death is final.

Most of the time, a voice in my head that sounds strangely like Madeline's says. Great, now I'm imagining I can hear her.

I shake my head to knock reality back in place, but the voice continues. *Don't forget, you have things to do.*

What the heck? Why is my dead friend's voice telling me I have things to do? As I analyze the words and their possible meaning over and over, the ceremony begins. I'm completely lost in thought until Daniel gives me a swift elbow to the ribs. I glance up to find the preacher looking at me expectantly.

"Go," Daniel says in a gritty whisper.

It's time to read Madeline's letter. Slowly, my legs feeling like they're full of lead, I take agonizing steps toward the podium.

I pull out the yellow lined paper and clear my throat. The grating sound echoes off the gym walls. With a quick shallow breath, I begin to speak.

Chapter 33

"A few days before Madeline died," I begin, the last word catching in my throat, "she gave me a letter and told me not to read it until she was gone. Of course, I didn't listen and opened it that night. Her words were inspiring and heartbreaking at the same time. I . . ." The tears are threatening to overtake me as I remember our last conversation. I have to be strong. For Madeline. "I told her the next day that I'd read the letter. She just smiled and said she knew I would. She also said I wouldn't back down when the time came for me fulfill her last request. That I would read it again. Today. At her funeral. To all of you. And since I couldn't keep the first promise to wait to read the letter until she was gone, I will keep this second promise."

I carefully unfold the letter, gently smoothing out each crease. I don't need the paper. The words are a part of me. Every single sentence is etched in my mind. I twist the dolphin ring on my finger and a sense of calm washes over me.

Dear RJ,

I knew you wouldn't be able to resist opening this. You're not very good about waiting for things. You never have been. Sometimes, I think you make life happen by sheer force of will.

I'm sorry I couldn't do the same. I see the frustration and pain in your eyes every time you see me. I tried to fight, I really did. But then I got tired. And as painful as it is to admit, the time has come to let go.

But I want you to know that I have no regrets. I have nothing left to do in my life. I have learned how to love and, more importantly, I have learned how to be loved. I have laughed so hard I thought my insides would burst and I have cried with such passion that I didn't think my heart could take any more. I have known greatness in people even when facing the worst in others.

I pause, trying not to look at Felicity and failing miserably. I watch with satisfaction as she squirms in her seat. Taking a slow, haggard breath, I continue.

I cannot tell you how scared I was to walk up to you and Daniel last year in the cafeteria. I remember thinking how brave you were to hold your head up when you knew everyone was talking about you. But it was your laughter, mixed with his, that made me feel like I was safe. I know that sounds all sappy and corny, but hey, I'm a sick girl. What can I say?

Oh come on. Laugh. It's a much better alternative.

Tears are streaming down my face now as I remember the first time we met. But in my mind, she's the shining star of positive light descending on Daniel and me as we try to stay afloat.

Me, not able to admit I was okay with being alone, and him, not sure how to be around someone without waiting for the other shoe to drop. We were laughing because it was the only thing that made us feel brave. She was what made us feel whole.

Do you remember when I was in the hospital after the transplant? We were talking about legacies and what people leave behind for the next generation. That night, as the monitors continued their never-ending watch over my heart, I knew I wasn't going to live much longer. I can't explain how, but I knew. There was a sort of peace that came over me. And as I lay staring at the ceiling, thinking about whether the world would remember me, I thought about what I wanted my legacy to be.

Which is why I gave you this envelope and told you not to open it. It's also why you are reading this letter at my funeral. (If you aren't then I owe you an apology . . . or you chickened out, but, let's be honest, that would never happen. You are the bravest person I know.)

So here is what I leave behind. It's a list of the things I learned throughout my life:

1. Family is more than the people tied to you by blood. It's also the people tied to you by love.

2. Never, ever give up on family, even when they're begging you to. In fact, that's when you need to hold on to them the most.

3. Learn to cut people out of your life who do nothing but bring you pain. This kinda goes against the hippie love thing I'm feeling because of the pain meds but I learned that having people around you who don't want to be there is a waste of energy.

4. Never turn your back on someone who genuinely needs you. Sometimes this rule trumps number three but it takes a really special person to do so.

She's talking about me. For her, I'm the exception. And somewhere in the back of my mind, I hear her laugh, like she's agreeing with me. It would be amazing if not for the humming that mingles with her sound. I squint my eyes together and when I open them, thankfully, the white noise is gone. But so is the laughter.

5. Love like your life depends on it. Never be afraid to tell someone you love them and never look away when someone says it to you. True love will see through all the masks we wear and will chip away at the walls that we build to protect ourselves. All we have to do is let it.

6. Never underestimate the power of a laugh. It is the music of the soul and has the power to bring joy back into a person's life.

7. Don't discount your importance to the world. Each moment of your life has a purpose, even the ones you think don't matter. And don't forget to make the unexpected choice. You never know how that one moment can transform your life.

8. Also, be aware of the power words have on those around you. They can lift people up but they can bury them, too.

9. Don't be preachy. Yes, I know this seems a little hypocritical, seeing as how I have a captive audience listening, but realize for some things, agreeing to disagree is better than fighting.

10. Find faith in something, even if it's a rock band you would travel across the country to see on a whim. But don't expect to have a seat at the concert if you don't buy tickets.

Behind me I hear Daniel choke back a laugh and I make a mental note to find out what she's talking about.

That's it. My Top Ten Rules of Life. I think I did pretty good at following them. Then again, I did make them up, so I had an advantage.

RJ, I hate this. I hate saying goodbye. To you, my parents, Daniel. To everyone who ever cared about me. I hate going away. And as angry as I am that this is what is happening to me, I can't bring myself to complain about how unfair it is. I mean, there are so many people who have it worse off than me. I could be a Chilean coal miner, after all.

This time it's my turn to choke on unexpected laughter.

My life may have been short in time, but it was long in moments that mattered and in love. In the end, isn't that what life is all about?

Chapter 34

There isn't a dry eye in the place as I gently fold the paper and walk away from the microphone. I'm deaf to the whimpering cries and blowing noses as I take my seat. All I can hear is the thudding of my heart and I swear it skips a beat because of the hole left by Madeline's death.

My eyes cast down to hide the salty tears. I sink against the seat back, looking up to give Mrs. Quinn a limp smile when she turns around and pats my knee. My mother, who's sitting next to me, wraps her arm around my shoulder and tries to pull me close, but I shrug her away. It's not that I mean to hurt her. At first, I think I'll explain later how I can't breathe and how I'm afraid I'm going to run screaming from the room if one more person tries to make me feel better. But then I hear Madeline's voice citing Rule Number One—the one about family. I lean over and whisper, "I love you," in Mom's ear.

The tension in her body eases as relief fills her eyes. I may not like what she's done to our family, and I definitely don't approve of her affair, but she's my mom. I love her and I know nothing will ever change that.

The rest of the service passes in a blur. A couple of girls from the choir sing a series of uplifting and inspiring songs as pictures of Madeline flash before us on a screen. Next to me, Daniel stiffens and then shudders. Even though I'm afraid any physical connection will send me over the emotional edge I'm teetering on, I reach out and take his hand as only someone who shares his grief can do. He hangs onto it like a lifeline and I want to tell him he's hurting me. But I don't because the pain reminds me I'm alive.

When the minister ends his speech, Daniel bravely stands and marches with the other pallbearers to escort the love of his life out of the building, carefully avoiding the red, tear-stained faces that follow him. I wonder if he will ever be able to love someone like he did Madeline.

That's when I hear her voice whispering, "He will. Some-day. It won't be easy, but he will." I can't explain what happens, but I smile at the sound, even if it's only in my head. I get the feeling that she's alright with the idea of him moving on. I watch the procession and try to put aside the fact that I'm hearing the voice of my dead best friend. I allow my thoughts to drift back to the nights spent talking with her in the hospital. I could always tell when Daniel had been in before me by the glow of happiness on her face. I smile as I remember her telling me about their first kiss. She was positively radiant. That hour at the end of the day made the rest of the time bearable.

I look up in surprise as everyone stands to gather their belongings. It's over. All I have to get through is the part where they actually put her in the ground. Mechanically, I stand, fighting the temptation to escape. Only family and a few friends will accompany the body to the grave site. The rest of the crowd will probably go home or head over to the luncheon Madeline's church is hosting. Those of us going to the cemetery will follow the casket out to the waiting hearse.

Daniel moves his car behind the sedan that will carry Madeline's parents to the cemetery. From the driver's seat his eyes plead with me to ride with him. I motion for him to wait and walk over to my parents' car.

"Hey, do you mind if I go with Daniel?" I ask, biting into my lip. It's the first time I've spoken since being on stage and my voice sounds raspy and weak.

"He's not riding with his parents?" my mother asks, looking over my shoulder. "Are you sure he's alright to drive?"

"I don't think he wants to come back here to pick up his car later," I offer, not wanting to give her any reason to say no. "And he's fine to drive. If anything, me being with him will help him focus."

My dad speaks up. "Of course you can. We'll see you there."

"Thanks," I say with a smile and rush back to Daniel's car before my mom can veto his decision.

"Ready?" I ask through the window. I try to sound upbeat but the attempt is an utter failure.

He nods and slumps down in the driver's seat, turning the ignition in one quick motion. I pause, trying to stop the next wave of tears that threatens to flow freely down my face. With renewed resolve to get through this day, I flick the purple magnetic flag the funeral staff put on top of the car to identify us as part of the entourage and climb in. The processional takes us into Indianapolis where Madeline's family has a plot at a cemetery. Did they buy it before their daughter got sick or after? I guess it doesn't matter now.

The drive seems to take forever with neither one of us talking. And when we pull up next to the freshly dug grave, Daniel opens the door and is gone without a word.

Flipping the mirror down, I touch up the flakes of dry mascara sitting on my cheeks. Someone could have told me my face was a mess.

Slowly, I reach out and squeeze the door handle. With a deep breath, I step out into the autumn sunshine and the smell of falling leaves and fresh cut grass fills my lungs.

A gentle squeeze on my shoulder alerts me to my parents' arrival. I resist the urge to move away from them. Instead, I wrap my arm around my mom's waist and fall in step with her. The truth is, I need her to keep me from crumpling to the ground.

She leads me toward the mound of brown dirt with a fake grass topping. Who are they kidding with that cover? We all know underneath it is the earth that will top the remains of an angel. The weight of my grief is staggering and I stumble over my feet. My dad catches me by the elbow and leads me to a seat in the back row. Protectively, he and my mom take the flank positions, each holding one of my hands.

The Indian summer wind rustles my hair, lifting it gently. I stare across the acres of gray tombstones and all I can think of is running away. But I don't. Eventually the murmur of the minister's words stops and around me people begin to move, each person taking a yellow daisy from a pile and tossing it lightly onto the coffin. When did they lower it into the ground? How did I miss it? Oh God, I can't do this. I can't be a part of this. It can't be real. But, of course, I can and it is.

I dutifully stand in line until it's my turn. As my flower descends in slow motion, I see a red rose petal peeking out among the sea of yellow. For a moment, I wonder if Daniel brought it or someone else.

And then my chest tightens and I feel like I'm going to explode. I find Daniel and squeeze his hand, forcing him to look at me. "Let's get out of here," I wheeze.

Like someone waking up from a deep sleep, he nods. The next thing I know, we're racing toward his car and jumping in. I look up to see the shocked expression on everyone's faces. Well, not Madeline's parents. They look envious. I bet they would trade places with us in a heartbeat.

"Where are we going?" Daniel asks, shifting the car into gear before pulling onto the busy road just outside the cemetery gates.

I shake my head. "No clue. Just drive."

He turns toward downtown Indianapolis. "What do you think she would do?"

I notice he doesn't say her name. I understand. It's too soon. Too painful. Too raw. "Something nice," I say, filling the void of silence.

He snorts. "Turning limes into limeades."

That was Madeline. She was always thinking of other people and how to make their lives better. "Maybe we should take lunch up to the nurses on her floor?" I suggest.

Daniel shakes his head. "Her parents did that yesterday. Besides, I don't think it would be good for morale if we showed up with our red eyes and sad faces, do you?"

He's right. "We still need to do something. What about taking coffee and snacks to some random floor at another hospital. You know how Madeline was always going on about how the nursing staff at the Children's Hospital was lucky because so many people would bring treats in for them. What if we pick some other floor?"

Daniel nods thoughtfully. "I think she would like that."

Now we're on a mission. Instead of trying to get through the day, we have purpose. Sure, it's only coffee and pastries, but on days like today, you take what you can get. "Where should we go?"

"There's a coffee shop up ahead. Maybe they could call a floor and get an order for all the nurses. Then we'll grab some food and take it over. Oh wait," he says, the glimmer of life starting to fade. "We need money."

"Never fear," I say, tapping my purse. "I have a credit card. I'm pretty sure I can get Mom and Dad to cover this one without too much hassle."

"You sure?" he asks, knowing how much trouble I've been in before for using the card without permission.

I shrug. "I can always plead insanity. After all, I have the 'my best friend just died' card."

He's silent.

"Too soon?" I ask.

He stares straight ahead, saying nothing.

"Well, then," I say, attempting to get us back on track, "to the coffee shop."

The place is empty when we arrive.

"Good morning," a barista says from behind the counter. Her brown hair with a pink streak down one side of her bob haircut swishes with each movement.

"Hey," I say in return.

"Cute dress. Very bold choice for this time of year."

I instantly cover my chest with my arms as goose bumps pop up on my skin. "Thanks. Um, we were wondering if you could help us out with something."

"Sure," she says, looking at me with intrigue.

I glance at Daniel and he just nods for me to continue. "We're going to take drinks to the nurses at one of the hospitals but we don't know what drinks they might like."

"Okay," she says, waiting for me to continue.

"I was wondering if you could call the nurses' station and see if they can get an order together?"

She glances over at her manager who is listening to everything. After getting the okay from her, she turns back. "No problem. What floor?"

"We don't know."

"Well, then, what hospital?" she asks.

Daniel and I just look at each other. Maybe we should have done a little more planning. "We don't know that either. Any suggestions?" The last part I say as a joke, but she just smiles.

"Actually, my boyfriend is a nurse on the Brain Injury Unit at Community. I bet they would love something like this. I can ask him to organize it if you want."

Wow. This might actually work out. "Sure," I say. "That would be great."

Within twenty minutes we are out the door armed with a specialty drink for the nursing staff and regular coffee and snacks for the family members visiting on the unit.

"You know," Daniel begins, "I feel closer to her now than during almost any part of the funeral."

"Almost?"

His face reddens. "I really liked it when you read her letter. It was classic Madeline. Humbling but not preachy."

As we turn back onto the road, a nagging sensation begins in the back of my mind, like I should be doing something. Have I forgotten something else? And the closer we get to the hospital, the stronger that feeling becomes. I spin the ring on my finger as the humming starts up again.

Chapter 35

The only sounds I hear as we march down the hospital hall are the echo of our footsteps and the steady rhythm of the wheels on Daniel's wooden collapsible wagon. After my ring catches on the metal handle for the third time, I slide it off and slip it into my pocket. I don't want to dent it or knock out one of the stones. I need to ask Mom where she bought it. It's a really cool ring.

"I thought you were going to burn this," I say, casting a glance back to make sure the coffee isn't sloshing all over the place. The wagon was handy for today, but it also carries memories, too.

"Couldn't," was all he says.

I get that. When Madeline was sick, Daniel would cart all the flowers and cards that came to her house up to the hospital. At first, he could do it by hand, but eventually he was making several trips and spending most of his visits riding the elevator. One day, he arrived at the nurse's station and the wagon was sitting there, complete with a bow. Sometimes it's hard to let go of the little things when you lose everything else.

I push the handicap button and wait for the doors to swing open, granting us access to the Brain Injury Unit. Suddenly, the feeling that I'm forgetting something changes. Now, it's more like déjà vu. Grams used to say that's the universe's way of telling you that you're exactly where you are meant to be. Thanks, Grams. My place to be is another hospital ward. Super.

"Well, well, if it isn't the java angels," a voice booms as we near the nurses' station. "When my girlfriend called and told me some random strangers were bringing us coffee, I thought she was joking. But here you are."

"Here we are," I say, smiling and holding up the bags of goodies. "I don't think the customers who were waiting to get their afternoon treats at the coffee shop are going to be happy. We cleaned them out."

He waves his hand through the air. "They should have gotten there sooner." He looks down at the red wagon and his eyes grow wide. "Wow. That is way more than we ordered," he says, looking back at Daniel. "You didn't have to do this, but I can't tell you how much it's appreciated." Daniel's face turns bright red. He still hates it when people single him out, even for praise.

"We thought some of the family members might want a snack, too," he mutters.

The nurse's smile widens. "That's cool, man."

It doesn't take long for the rest of the nurses to claim their drinks and return to their duties.

"You want to take the coffee around?" I ask Daniel.

He shakes his head. "Why don't you? I'll set up what's left of the food."

"Okay." I pick up the metal handle and make my way down the hall, peeking into any open room I find and offering family members what's left of the drinks. By the time I reach the last door, I have a half-melted frappé and a regular coffee.

Except for the patient, the room is empty. He looks like he might be a couple years older than me. His skin is pale, almost gray, and his cheeks sink down below the bones in his face. There are tubes going into his mouth and nose and several wires running out from under his hospital gown.

"Can I help you?" a tired voice asks behind me.

"I'm sorry," I say, turning around. "I was checking to see if anyone wanted coffee."

The woman's features brighten slightly. "That's very kind." She walks past me into the room and sits in the chair near the bed.

"Uh, do you want some?" I ask, trying not to look at the man laying in the bed.

She nods. "That would be lovely."

I tug the almost empty wagon in behind me. "We have a frozen drink, but it's more like a barely frozen drink," I offer.

"Do you have regular?" she asks, her eyes never looking up at me.

"Actually, we do. Do you want cream or sugar?"

"Black."

"That I can do." Not wanting to disturb her, I place the cup down on the side table next to her.

"How old are you?" she asks as I turn to leave.

I turn back slowly. "Me?"

She nods.

"I'm seventeen," I answer.

She smiles. "That was the same age my son was when he left for college."

I look back to the man on the bed. "Is this your son?" I ask awkwardly.

She nods. "Would you mind sitting with me for a few minutes?" The look of surprise on her face makes me wonder if she meant to ask this question.

I want to say no. I should make up some excuse and pull the wagon down the hall and out the front doors, away from this hospital and especially away from this room. Which is what I'm telling myself as I lay the wagon handle against the wall, pick up the melting frappé, and pull up a chair.

We look at each other, neither knowing what to say. Finally, she glances back at her son and says, "This is James."

Okay, now seriously, what do you say when someone introduces you to their coma patient son?

"Um, hi, James," I manage, knowing how stupid I sound. It's taken me this long to almost master small talk with strangers. No one ever told me I might have to do it with a coma patient.

She smiles and I get the feeling she wasn't actually introducing us but looking for a reason to say his name. "He was hit by a drunk driver almost ten months ago. His girlfriend, well, I guess she had just become his fiancée, was killed."

Her story shakes something loose in my memory but it's still foggy and the humming sounds louder than ever. I try to remember but it only gets worse. "I'm sorry," I say, trying to remember my manners and not gasp in pain at the same time. Instinctively, I reach into my pocket for the ring. The humming grows softer and even though it's still there, at least I can hear what the woman is saying.

She smiles at me and for once I think I'm actually fooling someone. "What made you bring in coffee today?" she asks.

I shrug. I don't know how honest to be. I mean, her son doesn't look too far from death's door. How can I possibly tell her it's because my best friend died and we're trying to find the silver lining in it? But that's exactly what I do. Before I can stop myself, the words are tumbling out.

"My best friend, Madeline, died a few days ago. She spent the better part of the last few years in the hospital. Daniel, that's Madeline's boyfriend, and I didn't want to be around everyone after the funeral. We wanted to do something Madeline would like." I stop to take a breath.

"Did she come here for treatment?" the woman asks.

I shake my head. "She went to the children's hospital for treatment. We thought about going to her old unit, but there are kids there still fighting. We didn't want to take even an ounce of their hope away from them with the reminder that Madeline lost her battle."

"That's very thoughtful of you."

I sit back, taking a sip of my drink. "We just needed to do something. And when we went into the coffee shop to order, the barista said her boyfriend was a nurse on this unit, so here we are."

"How very lucky for us," she says. We sit there for a while, each of us lost in thought, when suddenly she asks, "Did your friend fight up until the very end?"

"I'm sorry?" I ask in surprise.

"I didn't mean that the way it sounded. I just meant, did she continue seeking a cure?"

My head is telling me I should take offense. But I don't think the woman is being insensitive. The way she's talking leads me to believe this isn't her real question anyway. "Uh, no. I guess not. She did a bone marrow transplant. It didn't work. She'd tried an experimental treatment, but that didn't work either. So, she stopped. She told everyone she wanted to enjoy the time she had left. She didn't want to waste her life hooked up to machines." I look at her son. I can't believe I just said that. "I'm so sorry," I say, almost falling out of my chair.

She doesn't even flinch. "That takes a lot of bravery." There is admiration in her voice.

"It did," I agree. "She's the bravest person I've ever known. But Madeline wanted to live her life, not just be kept alive. She believed there was something out there that was bigger than this. Something better. I think what made it easier was that she had time to say goodbye. To do everything she could with every second she had. In the end, it was less about being brave and more about being afraid of leading a life that wasn't worth remembering."

The woman nods thoughtfully. "We've been thinking, or rather I've been telling James's father, that it's time to let him go. I wish he was here right now so you could tell him your friend's thoughts about death. More importantly, I wish he could hear how she looked at her life."

"It can't be easy to let go of someone you love."

"He is our only child," she says. "If he's gone, who are we?"

The humming grows intense. I don't know how much longer I can take it. I try to focus on what Madeline would say if she were here. "You're still you. Even if it wasn't as much time as you wanted or thought you should have, you were blessed to know him." I look back at James, "I can't tell you what to do. I don't even know what I would do if I had been in Madeline's shoes, but I can tell you that, once she was gone, in that moment she stopped being here on Earth, she was at peace. And I knew she'd made the right decision. She lived life on her terms."

"Then what do we do?" the woman asks, her eyes pleading with me to deliver some monumental words of wisdom.

Is she crazy? What in the world is she doing asking me for advice? I'm seventeen. I'm not even sure what I'm going to wear tomorrow. So I say the only thing I can think of. "Today, when we were leaving the cemetery, we didn't know what we were going to do either. We thought about what Madeline would do. I'm starting to ask myself that a lot now. Maybe you and your husband should ask yourself the same thing: what would James want you to do?"

She turns away and looks out the window. The blue sky is full of white puffy clouds filtering the sun's rays. A moment later, the clouds part and a stream of sunlight shines on her face. I see her back straighten as she takes a deep breath. "Thank you," she says, still looking up at the sky. "Your words are exactly what I needed to hear today." She turns around and takes my hand. "Thank you so much. You are like an angel."

"No," I say with a sad laugh. "I am the furthest thing from an angel you will ever meet." But I have an overwhelming sense of completion as I stand to leave and the humming fades away. "I didn't do anything but bring in coffee."

Her smile, though still sad, also has a hint of hope. "You did so much more than that. You have the gift of wisdom."

I laugh, in spite of the situation. "Maybe you should tell my parents that."

"I'm sure they already know."

And with that, the sun darts behind the clouds and the room darkens. Our moment is over. Neither one of us knows what to say. I leave the room, wagon in tow, and just as I close the door, I hear her crying softly and telling James how much she loves him.

Is this what Madeline's mom and dad went through every time she went into the hospital? I pull out my phone and dial one of the few numbers I know by heart.

"Mom. What are you and Dad doing for dinner?"

Chapter 36

The twenty miles home drags on forever.

"You sure you don't want to hang out a little longer?" Daniel asks as we pull up to my house. I can hear the sadness in his voice and as much as I want to make him feel better, I know time is the only thing that can do that. Besides, I have my own issues to deal with.

I shake my head. "I really should spend time with my parents," I say. "You know how protective they've been since . . ."

Daniel gets it. His parents are the same way, which is probably why he doesn't want to go home. He hates it when they hover. But after meeting James's mom, I get it. Parents feel as helpless as we do in these situations.

"Look. We'll get coffee in the morning. I doubt anyone's going to care if we ditch school."

"Okay," he says reluctantly. "Coffee in the morning. I'll pick you up."

I lean over and kiss him on the cheek. "See you then." I reach for the handle and am about to step out of the car when he grabs my hand. I look down first at it and then at his face. "Daniel, what's wrong?"

The tears are streaming down his face. "I don't want to go to sleep," he cries. I turn back to embrace him.

"Shhh," I say, trying to comfort him. "How long has it been?"

"Since I slept?" he asks, but his head is pressing against my shoulder and it comes out in a muffle. I nod. "Not since the day she died. I mean, I've taken naps when I can't hold out any longer, but at night . . ." His voice breaks off in a sob. "I'm afraid I'll start to forget her."

I force him to look at me. "That will never happen. No matter how much time passes or how long it takes for your memory to conjure the image of her face, this"—I point to his chest, just above his heart—"this will never forget her. She'll always be there. She's a part of you. She's a part of both of us."

"It's not fair!" he yells, slamming his hand on the steering wheel. "It sucks."

I nod. "No, it's not fair. And you're right. It totally sucks."

"But we'll get over it, right?" he says bitterly.

I think carefully about how to answer him. Finally, with a sigh, I say, "No. I don't think we'll ever get over it. I never got over Grams and she was old. But somehow, in time, we'll learn to get through it."

"I hope so. I don't think I can live with the pain forever." Daniel wipes his eyes with the cuff of his shirt. "You better go. Your parents are already peeking out at us through the curtain."

"Are you going to be okay?"

"Yeah. I'll be alright. Just promise me you won't bail on me tomorrow. I can't face everyone at school without you there to stare them down."

I stick out my hand. Slowly, he takes it in his own. "Deal."

After a quick hug, I get out of the car and walk swiftly up the steep lawn toward the bright porch light of my house.

"I'm home!" I call out as I enter, dropping my purse and jacket on the floor. The smell of my mom's famous sweet and sour chicken makes my mouth water and I head straight to the kitchen where I find my parents, heads bent together, crying. "What's going on?"

"Dinner's ready," my mom says, wiping her eyes before grabbing a heaping bowl of fried rice and heading to the dining room.

"What's up?" I ask again. "We never eat in here."

"We just thought it would be nice," my dad says, sharing a secret look with my mom. Ugh. Do all parents think their children are easily fooled? Something's up and I have a sinking feeling it won't be long before I find out what. My money is on the big news that they're splitting up. Oh man, what if they ask me to pick who I want to live with. How am I supposed to decide that?

The table is set for three. In addition to the chicken and rice, my mom also has crab rangoons and egg rolls from my favorite Chinese restaurant already on a plate.

"Someone's been busy," I note, slipping into my chair and unwrapping a pair of chopsticks. I reach across the table and pour a glass of tea.

"Dad helped," my mom says and I almost drop the pitcher.

"Seriously?" My dad doesn't know his way around one of those plastic kiddie kitchens, let alone one with working drawers and appliances.

Dad feigns offense at my surprise. "I can cut up chicken and open bags of frozen vegetables, thank you very much. Plus, who do you think picked up the carry-out order?"

I grin and for the first time since I can remember, I feel good. I mean, I'm still sad about Madeline, but it's been a long time since home felt safe. I wonder how long it will last. "Maybe I should come home for dinner more often."

My parents sit down and the passing of plates begins. I'm just about to take a bite of my egg roll when my dad clears his throat. "RJ, this may not be the best time, but we need to talk to you about something."

Oh no. Here it is. They're splitting up. Saying this may not be the best time is an understatement. Slowly, I put my food back on the plate and wipe my hands on the cloth napkin. "About what?"

My mother answers. "I need to confess something to you." She's already crying. "Several months ago, I made a mistake. As you know, the real estate market in the area has been slow. Your dad was working a lot of shifts to make up the difference. I was trying to close that deal to settle transfers for the new factory opening up down south. After the meeting, I stopped for a drink and ran in to an old friend. One thing led to another . . ."

She isn't looking at me and I can see the shame on her face. "I already know," I say.

Both of my parents look at me in surprise. "How?" my mom asks.

"Felicity."

My dad puts his fork down. "Is that why you started spending time with her again?"

I nod. "She said she'd tell everyone about Mom and her . . ." I don't want to say the word.

"My what?" she asks.

"Affair," I answer, my chin dropping to my chest in defeat. There. It's out in the open.

Mom pushes back her chair so fast it tips over with a thud. When she reaches my seat, she pulls me in close and I can barely breathe. "You should have told me," she whispers, stroking my hair.

"I didn't want to be the reason you and Dad split up. And now it doesn't matter because you are anyway and I wasted all that time with them when I should have been with Madeline."

"We're not getting a divorce," my father says quietly.

I push myself away from my mom to look at him. "You're not?"

He shakes his head. "Your mother came to me and confessed shortly after it happened. We've been in counseling trying to work through this."

"Wait, you already knew?" I ask. "You told him?"

"Of course." She seems more upset that I thought she would lie to my dad than hook up with someone else.

Dad leans forward. "Judging by the lengths you went to protect your mother and me, I have a feeling you think it's worse than it is."

"Felicity said you were having a long-term affair with some guy. She never told me who, but she said it was scandalous."

"Felicity lied," my mom says. "I did betray your father, but it was one time and it was only a kiss. I wouldn't even call it an affair. It was more of an indiscretion."

"Then why would she—"

"Because it was her father," my mom admits before walking back to pick up her chair. "He and I went to high school together. I told him about the deal I was hoping to close and he mentioned his company was going to bring in new management. He offered me an exclusive contract to represent his new employees when they went to look for a house. With the two accounts, I would be back on top and your dad wouldn't have to pull so many shifts."

"Oh," is all I can think to say. After all these months of thinking the worst of my mother and the wasted time spent with Felicity instead of Madeline and Daniel, the relief is overwhelming. "Then what's with the family meeting?"

"That was it," my mom says. "As your father said, we've been going to counseling so we can work on rebuilding the trust that was lost. The last step was for me to come clean with you so there weren't any more secrets between us."

"Then you're good?" Both my mom and dad nod. "Well, two good things came out of today."

"What was the other?" my dad asks, stabbing his fork into a sauce-covered piece of chicken.

While we eat, I tell them about taking the coffee to the hospital with Daniel. I do not, however, tell them about the woman and her son. I probably will—someday—but for now it feels like a story that isn't mine to tell.

As we're clearing away the dishes, the doorbell rings. We all look at each other in confusion. "I'll get it," I say.

Kicking my purse out of the way, I open the door to see five or six pint-size ghosts and witches and princesses standing in front of me.

"Trick or treat," they say in unison.

Right. It's Halloween, and I forgot to turn off the porch light when I came in. "I, uh, don't know if we have any—"

From behind me, my mother interrupts, her everything-is-fine voice trumpeting, "Of course we have candy, RJ. I stocked up weeks ago."

And that's how, on the day we put my best friend in the ground, I spend the evening passing out candy to hundreds of kids. By the time trick-or-treat hours are over, all we have left are a few plain chocolate bars and a ton of Smarties.

"Why do you even bother buying these?" I ask, picking through the candies and unwrapping the chocolate before popping it into my mouth.

"They come in the mix," my mom says defensively.

I give her a look that implies that's not a good excuse. "They taste like chalk."

My dad picks one up and twists it until the tiny disks fall out in his hand. "I like them."

"Of course you do," I say with a groan.

I can't believe I'm going to admit this, but tonight's been fun. It hasn't been a typical evening, to say the least, but for the first time in I don't know how long, I'm not rushing out the door to a party or to hang out with friends. Unfortunately, thinking about what I used to do only reminds me of Madeline and the walls start closing in. I need air.

"Do you guys mind if I take a short walk?" I ask, twisting the dolphin ring around my finger.

"Are you okay?" my mom asks. "You look pale."

"I'm fine," I assure her. "It's just been a long day. I need to clear my head."

My dad reaches for the remote and turns on the DVD player. "We're going to watch that nightmare movie you like so much."

I grin. "I'll be back before the previews are over. Promise."

Mom looks like she wants to tell me no, but she doesn't. "Make it quick," she says as I lean down to kiss her on the cheek.

"I will. Don't start the movie until I get back."

Chapter 37

Not sure where I'm going, I head toward the park a couple blocks away. There are still a few groups of kids knocking on doors and their excited cries of "Trick or treat" make me smile. Oh, to be a kid again and not to know that bad stuff is going to happen in your life. I miss being naive. Too bad you can't turn back the hands of time and do it all over again. There's that stupid humming again. I take a deep breath of the clean night air. Maybe I should have Mom schedule a checkup with my doctor.

Ahead of me, a trio makes their way up the stairs to another house. The youngest, in a costume that is obviously too large for him, trails behind, yelling for the others to wait. They stop just long enough for him to catch up and then sprint the rest of the way up the walk.

It only takes a few minutes to reach the park, which is completely empty. Looking around to make sure no one is watching, I climb to the top of the jungle gym and let my feet dangle off the end of the bars. I turn my head to the stars.

There's something kind of freeing about being up off the ground and just a few feet closer to the sky.

"Are you out there?" I ask to the vast openness. "Madeline, can you hear me?" My only answer is the distant laughter of children. I wonder if she saw the people who came out for her funeral. I wonder if she saw the impact her words had on those who were listening. I say up to the sky, "Daniel's having a pretty rough time, but I guess you know that. To tell you the truth, we all are." Now silence is the only answer.

"I guess you probably have your answer as to whether Heaven exists, huh?" There's the humming in the back of my mind again. It's like a memory is trying to break free. I push it aside and continue talking to Madeline. "By now I'm sure you've charmed the big guy, haven't you? Is he going to give you a set of wings?" The humming gets louder.

But it doesn't matter. My sudden sobs drown out the din in my head. She's really gone and the only way I can pretend to talk to her is to stare up at the sky and babble to no one. I jump down from the metal contraption and head home. The streets are almost completely empty now and most of the front porches are dark. Coming toward me, on the other side of the street, is the trio of kids I saw earlier

"Come on, Tommy. Keep up. Mom's going to kill us if we aren't home in five minutes," the tallest of the three calls over her shoulder.

"I'm trying," the little boy wails, gripping his pillow case bulging with candy in one hand and hiking up his dragging costume with the other. They cross the road and the two older children zigzag to avoid running into me.

"Guys, wait up!" their brother calls again. Chasing after them like a duckling following its mother, he steps out into the street but his costume gets the better of him. He stumbles forward, the bag of candy falling helplessly to the ground, and skids to a stop in the middle of the road.

Out of the corner of my eye, I see the twin white dots of a car turning the corner. There's no way the driver will see the kid. Without thinking, I dash over to the boy and scoop him up. He weighs more than I expect and I stagger to stand upright while running. There's no way I can get out of the way with both of us. A second later, I launch him toward the grass as hard as I can. He looks back at me, his eyes wide with terror. Off in the distance, I hear screams from his sisters. A moment later, I hear the squeal of tires and feel the impact as the hood ornament slices into my side. I'm thrown through the windshield. My head pierces the glass and the last thing I see as the blood trickles into my vision is the pure whiteness of the air bag blocking the driver from my view.

I close my eyes as porch after porch lights up. Everyone wants to see what's going on. I hear the cries of the little boy as his sister tries to comfort him. I wonder if the other one went to get their mom. I hope they aren't in trouble.

Slowly, just as the wail of the ambulance siren sounds, I begin to feel. First, it's the sharp pain in my head. Next, my leg begins to ache and my wrist does the same not long after that. But it isn't until I breathe that I realize what real pain feels like. Each effort results in a burning sensation. I try to cough, but it sounds more like a wheeze, and I can feel something dripping out of the corner of my mouth.

"RJ," someone is saying to me as they shine a white light in my eyes. "Can you hear me?"

I try to nod, but my neck is stiff and I'm pretty sure it's not working.

"Don't try to talk," the voice commands.

If I'm not supposed to talk, why is he asking me questions?

The next sound I hear is the screech of my mother. "No! RJ, baby, no! Get away from me! That's my daughter!"

I hear my father yelling something, but by now, the world is starting to go quiet. The only thing I can hear clearly is the calm voice of a dispatcher talking to the guy who asked me questions and then told me not to talk.

Red and blue lights begin flashing and in a moment I'm on a stretcher and sliding into what must be an ambulance. "Her parents are en route with one of the officers," the paramedic relays to the operator. "No way am I letting them ride with us when she looks this bad."

Um, hello, I can totally hear you. When I get to evaluate this whole experience, I am definitely going to comment on your poor bedside manner.

"Witnesses say she threw the kid out of the way," the driver calls from the cab. "I'd hate to see what would have happened to him if she hadn't been there."

"Yeah. Little tyke's lucky. Skinned up knee and a fat lip are nothing compared to this."

Okay, how bad is it? I'm guessing I have a broken leg, because that thing hurts like crazy, but other than my head, I hope that's the worst of it.

"I'm going to give you something to help with the pain, RJ. But stay with me, okay?"

The cool sensation starts to move through my body, covering every ache and pain until I feel like I'm floating on a cloud.

The next time I try to open my eyes I have to shut them against the harsh light. I can hear my mom crying from the other side of the door. My lids are too heavy and I give in to the strong urge to sleep.

I have no idea how much time passes until I feel like I want to wake up. But this time, I can't. I can't lift my eyelids open. I can't flex my fingers. I can't move at all. The constant beep of my heart on the monitor is the only thing that reassures me I am not dead, and I sink back into the warm abyss of not caring.

While I sleep, I start seeing flashes of Madeline and Grams. They keep telling me that everything is going to be okay and that I should just relax. Apparently neither of them ever had the drugs I'm taking because that is not a problem.

I wake up briefly. This time, there's something covering my eyes. I can't see anything, but I can hear my mother crying softly. I must be in my hospital room or something. I want to tell her that I'm okay, but I can't. My throat is sore and the thought of talking makes me want to gag. I hear my father come in.

"Drink this," he commands, but his voice is broken and weary.

Without warning, I feel a pull, like I'm supposed to go somewhere else. Which is crazy, right? I mean, I have a broken leg for sure, so it's not like I can walk out of here.

But the nagging feeling doesn't go away. Finally, I turn my attention away from my mother and the beeping machines and wait for something else. But the only thing I feel is the occasional zap of static electricity. It's kinda like that zap I get when I shuffle my slippers across the carpet and then go behind someone and touch them so that they get a shock. But it doesn't hurt. In fact, it kind of tickles.

"RJ," a soft voice says behind me.

I know that voice. And I don't want to turn around to see the too-familiar face.

"RJ," the voice says with more authority. "It's time."

"No," I say, this time without any problem finding my voice. "It's not. Not again."

Not again? Wait. What do I mean not again? There's that fuzzy static sound in my brain, but this time, when I try to push it aside, it pushes back and I am flooded with memories I couldn't possibly have.

Or could I?

"RJ."

The pain in my leg is gone and my head feels fine. I gingerly reach up to touch my face, vaguely aware that my wrist doesn't hurt. The scratches on my face are gone. "You have got to be kidding me," I say, whirling around to see who's talking to me.

Standing before me, complete with his black robe and sickle, is Gideon, my personal, repeat Grim Reaper.

Chapter 38

"You've got to be kidding me!" I roar. "I didn't even get a full day."

"Technically, you got a little more," Gideon claims.

My jaw drops and I stare at him. "How much of that time was spent in a drug-induced state?" I ask.

He shrugs.

"And what happened to my seventy years, anyway? I thought I had decades left before I was supposed to see you."

Gideon shrugs again.

Stupid Reaper. But this time, I'm not letting him hustle me onto the train before I get some answers. Sitting down cross-legged, I look up him with my most defiant face. "I'm not going until you tell me what's happening. Why am I here? Why did I die?"

Gideon rubs his eyes with the tips of his fingers and then, to my surprise, plops down next to me. "We have to do this now?" he asks.

"You know as well as I do, once I'm on that train, it's a short hop to the Lobby where you dump me off and leave me until they call me for processing."

He looks at me quizzically.

"What?"

"Once again, you defy what's supposed to happen."

"How so?" I ask, careful to pay attention for any tactic that might distract me from getting the answers I need.

"No one thought you would remember being here before. Not yet, anyway, but you do."

I know what he's doing. He's trying to distract me with something odd and fascinating about myself. Not gonna work. "Whatever. Tell me why I didn't live to be a hundred or something like that," I demand.

"You changed your past and those changes showed up in your present. They also changed your future."

"Wait, are you telling me that by jumping through the hoops the Tribunal set out for me, I ended up trading in a long life for one more day?"

"I suppose you could look at it like that," he says with annoyance.

"What other way is there?" I ask with equal annoyance.

He stands and extends his hand to help me up. I don't take it. With a sigh he says, "You could look at it like this: while your old timeline offered you many years, it was a wasted life void of true friendships, compassion, and accomplishment, whereas your new life, though shorter, was full of putting the needs of others before yourself and thus leaving the world a better place. You literally changed people's lives."

"I don't see how," I mutter.

He stretches his hand a little farther. "Just walk with me. I won't make you get on the train until you're ready."

"Why would I believe you? If memory serves me correctly, the last time you didn't exactly give me a choice."

He holds his other hand up like he's taking an oath. "On my honor."

"You're not going to wait until the last possible moment and then shove me through the doors?"

"Just get up."

This time I do, but not with his help.

"Some things will never change. You're still as stubborn as always."

"So how did I change lives in just a couple of hours?"

"A day," Gideon reminds me.

"Whatever," I spit out.

"Well, you saved that little boy."

Okay, it's hard to argue with a Grim Reaper when it comes to death. "That's just one person."

"What, that's not good enough for you? Seriously, you don't have to worry about me pushing you through the door of the train. What you should be worried about is me pushing you in front of it."

"I'm already dead, remember," I mutter.

"True, but the ride to the Lobby is pretty bumpy. Better to be inside than out."

We must be nearing the station, because I see more and more souls and Reapers filling in all around us.

"This is my real time, huh? This is what I fought against the angels for? One more day?"

"And a life well spent," he adds.

I can see the train pulling in ahead of us. I know he's right, about this being my time to die. I don't like it, but in my gut, I know he's right. I wonder if this is why everyone else is so catatonic. It's their soul's way of stopping them from totally freaking out about being dead until they are able to see their life in review. Except for the really old. They still seem almost joyful.

"Hey, Gideon," I say.

"Yes?"

"How come I'm more like the geriatrics than the walking zombies?"

"Hard to say. Unlike the young or those who quickly departed, older souls have spent an entire lifetime preparing for this moment. It's not a surprise. In fact, in most cases it's a relief. Maybe since you've already been through this your soul isn't as, oh, what's the word?"

"Freaked out? Hysterical? Going full-out mental?"

"Something like that."

His answer gets me thinking. "What about those who have been sick, like with cancer?"

"Depends on whether they were prepared when their time came or not. But I will tell you, no matter how much someone is prepared on Earth, the younger the body, the harder it is on the soul. When death interrupts the perceived circle of life, preparation is meaningless."

"So we're really just born to die?" I ask.

Gideon shakes his head.

"What's the reason, then?"

"Everyone has something to learn and something to teach. Once you have done those two things, you have accomplished your life mission and it's time to come home."

"Then why the big deal about Heaven and Hell? If you are on Earth to do a mission, why have all the hoopla about whether you go up or down?"

"Because not everyone learns or teaches. And if they cannot come to terms with what they were sent to do and their failure, eternal peace is out of their reach."

"So they get sent to the place of fire and brimstone?"

He shakes his head. "Hell isn't like that. Think of it as rehab. Most people who enter the Gates of Hell do so with the intent of being reborn. Of being given a second chance to get it right."

"You're kidding? Hell is a revolving door back to Earth?"

He nods. "Sorta."

I'm about to ask another question when one of the Reapers pushes past me. "Hey watch—"

Gideon grabs my arms and starts to pull me in the other direction. "Come on, RJ. Let's get in the other car."

"Why? What's going on?" I look over my shoulder, and that's when I see James. I spin back to face my Reaper. "You knew," I hiss. "You knew he was going to be on the train and you were trying to hide him from me."

"You can't talk to him, RJ. You can't break through to him. We have no idea what he will do."

I yank my arm away and run through the almost full station toward the next car. Scanning each window only to find nothing, I'm about to give up when I see James sitting slumped in one of the chairs.

The ding of a bell warns that the doors are closing and I leap in between them, trying to push them open. To my horror, the train begins to move while I'm still stuck. Suddenly, two hands reach in over my head to create just enough space for me to slide through and sprawl on the floor. I look up to see Gideon grinning down at me.

"Just don't tell anyone I pushed you on the train. You've caused enough trouble for me lately."

"Funny," I say, as I stand to dust myself off. I look around to the spot where I saw James, but he's gone.

"Leave him alone," Gideon pleads.

"Why? He should know Sandy is waiting for him."

"It's against protocol."

"Right," I laugh. "Since when have I followed protocol? No one will blame you, if that's what you're worried about."

He steps back in surprise. "I'm not worried about me, or you, for that matter, but James has been in a vegetative state for almost a year. His soul has been trapped inside his body. He needs time to process."

"He needs to know she's waiting."

Gideon doesn't say anything as I start to move through the train car, looking for James. In the far back corner, a Reaper stands with his cloak-clad back to me. I try to peek around him, but he shifts his weight.

"It's alright, Elijah," Gideon says from behind me. "We all know you can't stop her once she's made up her mind."

That doesn't sound like a compliment. The Reaper turns to face us. "She'll get us all in trouble with her meddling," he says, glaring down at me.

"I'll take the blame if it ends badly," Gideon assures him.

Elijah steps back, muttering something about childish whims and in his day, but I ignore him and focus on the crumple of a man sitting in front of me.

I kneel down, careful not to touch him. "James," I say softly. "James, can you hear me?"

He gives a slight nod, and whether it was him or the train, it's enough encouragement for me to keep going. "James, my name is RJ. Do you remember hearing my voice in your hospital room? I was talking with your mother." Again he gives a faint nod. This time it was definitely James and not the train.

"Good. Now, James, I need to tell you something, and we don't have much time." I take a deep breath before continuing. "James, Sandy will be waiting for you when we get off the train. She's been waiting for you since the night she died."

Slowly, as if fighting against invisible chains, James raises his head. His eyes, cloudy with confusion, try to focus on me.

"She didn't want you to come here and be alone. So she waited," I continue.

James opens his mouth, but no sound comes out. Not at first. Finally, after several attempts, he says, "Sandy." His voice is hoarse, but there is no denying what he's saying.

His right arm twitches and then raises only to plop down at his side. He tries to stand but his legs don't cooperate.

"I knew this was a bad idea," I hear Elijah say to Gideon.

"Just give her some time," my Reaper says. "She's got a way with the souls."

I'm not sure if it's confidence or not wanting a colleague to prove him wrong, but Gideon's faith in me bolsters my own. "Hold still, at least for now."

"Where is she?" James asks, his words coming out slowly.

"She's not here. We're going to see her. You have a little time, but James, I need for you to look at me."

And he does. "Okay, I know you feel like something is holding you down, like you're in a fog, but you aren't. You can control what's happening to you. You just have to concentrate."

He begins rocking back and forth, repeating, "Sandy. Sandy. Where is she?" over and over again.

I look up at Gideon, pleading for help. But his face is stone and unreadable, unlike Elijah's, whose I-told-you-so grin makes me sick. I turn back to James and lay my hand on his knee. Without warning his eyes clear and he reaches out and grabs my wrist, yanking my fingers close to his face.

The ring. I forgot I was wearing the ring I found under my bed. But it's not mine. It's Sandy's.

"Where did you get this?" he growls with such fierceness that I'm glad I'm already dead. Otherwise, I'm pretty sure he might kill me.

"She gave it to me," I say, trying to pull my arm away. "She gave it to me so you would know I was telling the truth."

Slowly, he slides it off my finger and holds it up. Gone is the initial anger. Instead, his eyes fill with a mixture of love and sadness.

"The car," he says. "It pinned her under the water."

I nod. "Yes."

"But it didn't kill me. Not right away."

"No."

"My parents didn't want to let me go and then . . ." He looks at me. "And then you came to my room. You told my mom that being hooked up to machines forever wasn't a way for someone to live."

I glance back at the Reapers. "Well, that's not exactly what I—"

My words are cut off as he lunges forward and pulls me into a bear hug. "Thank you," he whispers. "Thank you for giving them permission to let me go." He pulls back. "You told them about your friend, right? The one who died of cancer."

I nod. "Madeline."

"Right. That's what made them change their mind."

Gideon clears his throat. "We're almost there."

I turn back to James, who is looking around at the rest of the passengers on the train. "Why are they so quiet?" he asks.

"Because," Elijah says, "that's what they do. This way, Romeo, let's go find your Juliet."

"Sandy," James corrects, and Elijah smiles gently.

"Of course. Sandy." Elijah turns to Gideon and says, "I would get rid of that one as fast as you can. She's nothing but trouble."

"Hello," I say, waving my hand. "I'm right here."

Gideon just smiles. "Something tells me getting rid of her is going to be easier said than done."

Chapter 39

James doesn't waste any time racing to the Lobby doors. I follow behind, not wanting to miss the happy reunion. Which is why, when we get there and Sandy is nowhere to be seen, a sense of dread fills my stomach.

"Where is she?" James asks, scanning the room.

"I don't know. She was waiting near the doors when I arrived last time. She should be here."

Overhead, a voice rattles off a list of names. Sandy's name is not one of them.

"Oh no!" I cry, heading to the line for the front desk. "This is not happening. We can't be too late."

"What is it?" James asks when he catches up. "Do you know where she is?"

We reach the line a moment later. "Look for her. If we don't find her here, it's too late."

"How do you know?" he asks.

I wave his question off. "Just trust me." I jump, trying to see the faces in the middle of the line, but I don't see Sandy anywhere.

Everyone takes two steps forward and that's when I see a high ponytail bob at the front of the line. She steps toward the front desk and the smiling processing angel.

"It's about time," I hear the angel say in a sing-song voice. "We've been wondering if you would ever give up and move on."

"James!" I yell. "At the desk. Stop her!"

I hear a commotion behind me and turn just in time to see Lillith and her band of determined angels descend upon me, pulling me away from the line.

But James is faster than they expect and he dodges their grabbing hands and pushing the other souls aside, leaping over the red velvet ropes. I watch in silence as he reaches Sandy, yanking her hand away just as she's about to accept her life disc.

"Sandy," he says. But even from this distance I can see that her bright sparkling eyes are devoid of emotion. She's become one of them.

The ring. It has to be because she gave me the ring. She had nothing left to hold on to.

"Give her the ring!" I yell as Lillith tries to pull me away toward the small room she reserves for the hopeless souls. "Give her the ring."

And, in one swift move, James drops to his knees and presents Sandy with her engagement ring. Even Lillith stops to see what happens. I guess they don't get a lot of proposals in the Afterlife.

As he slips the ring on her finger, her eyes clear but the reality of the moment takes a little longer for her to process.

"It's you," she says, kneeling down in front of him and touching his face so gently I wonder if she thinks it's a dream. "You're really here."

"I am," he says before kissing her sweetly on the lips.

She shakes her head in disbelief. "But how?"

"Your little bird," he says before pulling her close again.

She looks around until her eyes meet mine. I shake Lillith off and walk slowly toward them.

"You did it," Sandy says, bringing me into their huddle. "I tried to hold on as long as I could, but without the ring to remind me, I kept forgetting why I didn't want to go when they called me. I guess eventually I gave up." She looks at James and me. "But you made this happen."

Her eyes widen and she looks back at me. "Oh no. You're back. Why are you back so soon?"

"Change your past . . ." I begin.

"Change your future," Sandy finishes. "I'm so sorry."

I nod. "Me too."

"Well," Lillith says, walking toward us, "now that this little reunion is over, perhaps we can move along and let the rest of these souls find peace."

"No arguments here," Sandy says, taking James's hand and striding back to the front desk. She takes her life disc and waits for James to collect his. Before they exit the Lobby she looks back at me. "You coming?"

"Yes, RJ," Lillith says in my ear. "Are you going or are you waiting for someone, too?"

The truth is I have no one to wait for. I have nothing left to fight for. I'm exactly where I should be. But why don't I want to go on?

"You don't want to do it, do you?" Lillith says. I shake my head and she continues. "This is why the soul protects the mind, shielding it from what all humans fear."

"And what's that?" I whisper.

She laughs. "Why, the unknown, of course."

"How come I didn't have this problem last time?"

"If you remember, you did, but you were more concerned about being right. That arrogance pushed you to overcome your fear. Now, there is nothing for you to do but move on and receive your Judgment." She motions to the angel behind the counter who slides my life disc across to me. "But first, you must review your life. Who knows, maybe you'll like it better than your last one."

Time slows to a crawl as I reach out and gingerly pick up the ordinary object. Once it's in hand, she propels me to the opening of the hallway full of rooms. I can hear Sandy and James arguing about not wanting to be split up. A moment later, I hear her squeals of laughter and clapping of hands.

"It's time," Lillith says and with a deep breath, I step over the threshold.

The sounds of the Lobby fade away and I walk forward, searching for the nearest open room.

"Need a little help?" a familiar voice says.

I look up to see Yeats standing before me. A smile spreads across my face and I run to him, almost tackling him.

"You're here."

"Of course," he says, "I'm still your Guardian, after all."

"Yeah, about that," I say, pulling back. "You could have given me a heads up."

"I didn't know it was going to turn out like this, not exactly."

I sigh. "I know, but you could have sent me a dream or a fortune cookie or something like that."

He laughs. "And what would the fortune say? Fail to save a little boy from a speeding car and you will live a long and prosperous life?"

"Well, when you put it like that," I mutter before glancing into the room. "Guess I better get this over with."

"I know your life didn't last as long as you wanted it to, but I think you will be happy with the outcome."

"I better be," I say, only half joking. "I'm not sure if the Tribunal is ready for another appeal."

"Right," Yeats says, giving me a nudge into the room.

After he closes the door, I carefully remove the disc from its case. It's hard to believe that somewhere in the clouds an angel is looking at my life and deciding what to put on my highlight reel. I wonder how someone gets that job.

The lights dim and my birth flashes up on the invisible screen, just like last time. But everything else has changed. Instead of petty fighting and backstabbing, each scene is full of laughter and silly moments with my friends. There is a dark period where I start hanging out with Felicity, but even then, I find time to spend with other friends. I watch as I read Madeline's letter and see the faces in the crowd. Her words touch them and I can't help but wonder how many of them will change because of her.

The last night of my life flickers in front of me. The screeching of the tires and my mom crying when they tell her I'm gone. I haven't given much thought to what she and my dad are going through and I'm so glad the last night of my life was spent with them.

I expect the recording to end, but unlike the first time, it continues with my funeral. It's held in the same gym as

Madeline's, but this time, rather than a sea of yellow, the bleachers are full of every shade of purple imaginable.

I see Daniel, his face stricken with grief. I'm not sure how he manages another funeral for one of his best friends. But he does, though he staggers to his feet as he escorts my casket out of the building and to the waiting hearse. His sadness is unbearable and I wish I could tell him that I'm okay, that I'm sorry he's hurting. But I can't. All I can do is sit and watch him carry his pain.

I wonder how my life, and more importantly my death, will impact his future. Is he still going to be a brilliant doctor and find a cure for cancer? Or does my sacrifice for a little boy change that?

Luckily, I don't have to wait long to find an answer. After my funeral scene ends, another set of clips begins. I'm not in a single one of them. You know at the end of some movies, when the director is kind enough to give you a glimpse at what the future has in store for the main characters? Like, marriage, kids, working in some magical office or something like that? That's what this is like. Instead of focusing on my life, the images are of those I love and what is in store for them.

My parents manage to stay together, holding tight to the strategies they began during their marriage counseling. In fact, they eventually adopt a little boy. I feel like I should be angry at seeing my replacement, but I'm not. I'm happy that they are able to find a way to come to terms with my death and to take a chance on being parents again.

Next, I see Daniel, his face smiling as his blushing bride walks down the aisle. He's the same old Daniel, except for one thing. The twinkle in his eyes has lost some of its brightness, and, for a minute, there's even a flicker of sadness there and I wonder if he's thinking about Madeline. But as quickly as it flashes, the look is gone when a vision in white appears at the end of the aisle.

Turns out his bride, Jackie, is also his lab partner in medical school. Together, they break the sequencing code that opens up cures for several different types of cancer. They have three children. Two daughters they name Madeline and Rowena, for which I could kill him, and a son, Casey, who bears the name of Jackie's brother, another victim of cancer and the reason she went into medicine.

And the little boy whose stupid costume cost me my life, well, he's a priest. I really hope I get some extra points for saving a man of the cloth. He helps run a support group for grieving parents that my mom and dad started after I died.

Several other faces flash on the screen, but I don't know any of them. And then, the images stop. The whirl of the disc player slows and everything goes quiet. I didn't realize it before, but tears are streaming down my face. Not because I'm sad. I mean, I am, but that's not why I'm crying. It's because my life means something. Even in the future, my choices make a difference.

"Are you going to sit there all day?" a voice booms from the doorway.

Standing, larger than life, is Death Himself in his typical Hawaiian shirt and Bermuda shorts.

"You could have told me," I say, standing up to face him. "You knew it would turn out like this, didn't you?"

"No, not at first, but I saw the changes taking place in the Records."

"So *that's* why they were sealed?"

He nods. "I was afraid if you knew what would come to pass you would change your mind. Just didn't seem fair."

"To me or to you?" I scoff.

"To you, mostly. And the world. You were intended to be a supernova. To burn brightly and powerfully and then to suddenly burst, leaving a legacy behind."

Great. Death Himself compares me to a dying star and I have nothing to come back at him with. "What happens next?" I finally ask.

"Well, you still have to go to Judgment, but since I know how that ends, you should be in and out in a blink of an eye."

"And then?"

Death Himself swings an arm over my shoulder. "Have you given any thought as to what you want to do with your Afterlife?"

I ponder his question for a moment. "Not sure. What kind of opportunities does this place have for a reformed mean girl?"

His smile widens and takes on an almost gleeful twist. "Oh, I have a couple of ideas. How do you feel about counseling?"

I shake my head. "Who could I possibly help? It's not like I killed myself. What could I possibly do to help a suicide? "

His eyes twinkle. "What? You think you're the only soul who arrives believing they should get a second chance?"

"Yeah, actually, I thought I was."

Death Himself throws back his head and laughs, the booming sound echoing throughout the hall. "Sorry, sweetheart. You were only the first who actually had a case. No, we get all kinds and their assimilation needs to be handled delicately. On a case by case basis."

"Who are you talking about?"

He begins to tick his answer off on his hand. "Celebrities, politicians, self-entitled offspring of the rich and powerful who crash their mom's car going one hundred and thirty miles an hour. And lawyers. We get a lot of lawyers trying to talk their way out of death like it's a speeding ticket." His laughs again and the air around us becomes charged with energy. "We need souls who are willing to help them assimilate."

"Wait, how come I didn't see anyone like that in the Lobby?" I ask, crossing my arms over my chest.

"The Reapers funnel them onto a separate car that unloads away from everyone else."

"Why didn't Gideon take me with that group the first time?"

"What can I say, kid? You're one in one hundred and nine billion. So, you in?"

"What if I say no?"

He shrugs. "It's your choice, but this gig comes with an automatic bid through the Holy Gates and the power to pass back through them whenever you like."

"So this is like a job."

"Yep. One you are perfectly suited for."

"What about my memories? Will I keep them?"

He nods. "You'll need the experiences from both of your timelines to help the souls adjust."

"What's the catch?"

"None."

"Can I quit whenever I want?"

"Sure."

"Can I get that in writing?"

Death Himself tries to look like he's offended. "My word isn't good enough for you?"

I just stare at him.

"Fine," he says with a theatrical bow in my direction. "I will have the scribes write something up and deliver it to you posthaste. Is that alright with you?"

I nod.

"Then you'll do it."

"What the heck. It's not like I have anything better to do. Hey, what do you call this program or whatever it is?"

"Diva Boot Camp."

Oh, no. What have I gotten myself into?

Acknowledgments

As an extrovert, writing a novel was sometimes an affront to my nature. It wasn't until I started working on these acknowledgments that I realized just how many people were involved in *It's a Wonderful Death* making the transition from an idea to "save a cheerleader" to a real-life book.

There is no alternative reality that *IAWD* gets published that doesn't include Liza Fleissig and everyone involved with Liza Royce Agency. Within a few minutes of talking to her, I knew she was the agent for me. Even when things seemed bleak, you never stopped believing this day would come. Thank you for seeing the "diamond in the rough" and having faith in me. You have transcended the role of agent and become my friend.

To my fantastically talented editor, Julie Matysik, thank you so much for fighting to give this book a second chance. I truly believe everything that happened in the course of getting *IAWD* out was to make sure it landed at Sky Pony Press, or as I like to call it: home. Thank you for taking a chance on a debut novel about a cheerleader, a Hawaiian shirt–wearing Death, and a power hungry angel. You're brilliant, and I am a better writer because of you!

I had a much longer intro to the Fall Fourteeners & Fifteeners and the Fearless Fifteeners, but if I wrote about how amazing you all are, I would probably exceed my total word count for this book. I do want to single out Josh, JRo, Kitty, Stephen, Kristen, Kris, Amy, Joy, Kendall, Austin, Lisa, Kate, and Shallee. I have thanked the stars every day since we joined forces. From Social to Business, Squee to OMG, you have been my never-ending link to sanity and I am in awe of the collection of talent that has been assembled! We're like nerdy superheroes!

And then there is my agency and pub sis Amalie. Girl, we have really gone through some ups and downs in the last two years. You are an amazing talent and have always been there when I needed advice on what to do next.

I don't think I could write YA lit if I didn't have day jobs where I get to hang out with teens and talk books. Thank you Jack, Emma, Alex, Kyle, Zoe, Erin, and the rest of the New Pal teens who stop by just to say hi or to marvel that I haven't yet finished the latest new release: You keep me on my toes and I adore you all! And to my coworkers at HCPL: thank you for your ongoing support, especially Deborah and Cathy who are more than flexible with my schedule. To the other Sarah, I look forward to seeing what kinds of chaos we can create. Don't worry, we'll keep telling Dave we're "programming." Team Sarah rules!

To the staff and students at SMCS! I am so blessed to be a part of our amazing community. Your enthusiasm is contagious, and I love getting to work with so many students who have a great passion for reading! I would be remiss not to say a special thank you to Terri, Jessica, Storm, and Jane who have endured my constant disorganization over the last two years, all the while instilling a deep love of learning in my kidlets! Sorry for all the permission slips that were turned in under the wire. We're working in it!

Whenever the negativity gets to be too much, I know I can always turn to you, Shannon. Unless of course you're having trouble with the battlefield of the mind, in which case you are always welcome to share my mud puddle. Thank you for always being there when I need you and reminding me that I'm not the only blue in town.

To Chris Maples who left this world far too soon. Thank you for reminding me that the prize is our life journey, not the things we leave behind when we're gone. I really hope there is a Denny's in Heaven. I'll be the one with the twitching shoulder.

Carrie, Shari, Kristin, and Chris (note I didn't call you Cheasley), thank you for your support and encouragement. With cheerleaders like you, how could I doubt this day would ever come?

Oh, Jessica Z. Where do I start? We bonded over diapers and cake decorating, not at the same time, of course, and even though time and distance have challenged us, I still count you among my closest friends. You hold the rare distinction of being the one person who has seen almost every page I've written during my adult life. Thank you for your brutal honesty and unwavering support. I would not be here without you!

A huge thank you to the friends and family who willingly answered my plea for a safe place to farm out the kidlets so I could meet a deadline or take a mommy timeout to avoid utter meltdown mode! Emily, Vicky, Julie, Monica, Becky S., my outstanding in-laws, and "pseudo" in-laws, without you I would still be staring at a blank screen.

To my beautiful niece Grace. You remind me the best beat to march to is the one that leads you to follow your passion. I am so inspired by the amazing woman you are becoming. I only have one question for you: What's your favorite "real" book now?

Many years ago, I attended the Midwest Writer's Workshop (shout out to Jama!) and it changed my writing life in ways I never dreamed possible. I'm not talking about the exceptional faculty and staff, although they truly are! I'm referring to my favorite Cool Kids. Kelly, Joe, Dan, Kelsey, Irene, Lisa, Julie, and Terri, my soul sista; I don't know what I would do if not for our annual retreats! Every writer should be blessed to have a writing family like mine. You are so imPRESSive! Can't wait to see who gets the "Fancy Pants" next!

It's a little-known fact that the chances of finding your bestie for life increase dramatically when you dance in the rain together. Becky, we have been friends since voting was the only "adult" thing we were allowed to do, and while the road hasn't always been easy, and we sometimes get lost, drive the car into the ditch, and then get "attacked" by a hot-dog dog, you have always been my person. Thank you for growing up with me, although I could have done without the tennis ball wake-up calls.

To Mom and Nickle-nae, there are no words to capture just how much I love you both. Mom, you have encouraged me to follow my passion even when I rolled my eyes and ignored you. Thank you for never giving up. And, I really am sorry for ever being whatever age the kidlets are now. To my beautiful sister, I may not tell you this enough, but you are one of the strongest women I know. Stay true to yourself always and forever! To the rest of my family who number too many to count . . . literally . . . thank you for being exactly who you are. I am blessed to be loved by all of you.

Keegan and Cooper (a.k.a. Kidlet #1 and #2, or the two halves of my heart), being your mom is the greatest privilege I have ever been granted. You are both so full of life and love that my heart overflows with joy every moment I'm around you. Except when I step on a LEGO. That is an entirely different emotion. Still, no matter what, I hope you always follow your dreams and when things get in your way, make your own path and push on. I love you!

Finally, to Louis, the light of my life. You are the greatest person I have ever known. Between your patience, sense of humor, and unwavering love and devotion, I have all I could ever need. Thank you for supporting me and encouraging my dreams. I look forward to the time when we sit on the swing, telling the same stories over and over again as the sun sets over the Western sky. Until the mosquitos come out. You're on your own then! Never forget olive juice!